THE WARRIOR KINGS

KEITH MILES was born and brought up in Wales. He read History at Oxford and lectured in the subject for some years before becoming a full-time freelance writer. He has written several plays for radio, television and the stage and has contributed to many series and serials. He has published a novel, some short stories, and a critical study of the German author, Günter Grass.

Keith Miles is married and has two children.

KEITH MILES

The Warrior Kings

based on the BBC Television series

The Devil's Crown

FONTANA/Collins

First published in Fontana Books 1978

© Ken Taylor Scripts Ltd and Hic Jacet Ltd 1977, 1978
This novelization © Keith Miles 1978

Made and printed in Great Britain by
William Collins Sons & Co Ltd Glasgow

'The spirit of medieval Europe was not static but dynamic. The best and worst of the Middle Ages was that they were full of wolfish life and energy. Their sins were the vices not of decrepitude but of violent and wanton youth . . .'

G.M.Trevelyan: *HISTORY OF ENGLAND*

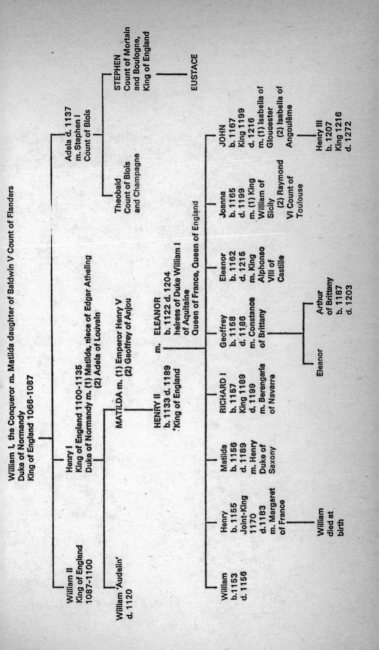

William I, the Conqueror m. Matilda daughter of Baldwin V Count of Flanders
Duke of Normandy
King of England 1066-1087

William II
King of England
1087-1100

Henry I
King of England 1100-1135
Duke of Normandy m. (1) Matilda, niece of Edgar Atheling
(2) Adela of Louvain

Adela d. 1137
m. Stephen I
Count of Blois

STEPHEN
Count of Mortain
and Boulogne,
King of England

William 'Audelin'
d. 1120

MATILDA m. (1) Emperor Henry V
(2) Geoffrey of Anjou

Theobald
Count of Blois
and Champagne

EUSTACE

HENRY II
b. 1133 d. 1189
'King of England

m.

ELEANOR
b. 1122 d. 1204
heiress of Duke William I
of Aquitaine
Queen of France, Queen of England

William
b. 1153
d. 1156

Henry
b. 1155
Joint-King
1170
d. 1183
m. Margaret
of France

Matilda
b. 1156
d. 1189
m. Henry
Duke of
Saxony

RICHARD I
b. 1157
King 1189
d. 1199
m. Berengaria
of Navarra

Geoffrey
b. 1158
d. 1186
m. Constance
of Brittany

Eleanor
b. 1162
d. 1215
m. King
Alphonso
VIII of
Castile

Joanna
b. 1165
d. 1199
m. (1) King
William of
Sicily
(2) Raymond
VI Count of
Toulouse

JOHN
b. 1167
King 1199
m. (1) Isabella of
Gloucester
d. 1216
(2) Isabella of
Angoulême

William died at
birth

Arthur
of Brittany
b. 1187
d. 1203

Eleanor

Henry III
b. 1207
King 1216
d. 1272

CHAPTER ONE

It was the perfect place for an ambush. The hill commanded a clear view of the road for several miles. There was good cover on its wooded summit, where the ash and beech and durmast oak were in full leaf, to muffle the sounds from the small encampment. The steep, grassy slope to the road below would lend speed and impetus to a heavy war-horse. Descent would be swift and sudden.

Eustace sat among the shadows on a fallen tree, looking around his men in search of an excuse for anger. Even at his age, he had learned to enjoy the relief of a violent quarrel. It would make the long wait less irksome. He took another large, impatient bite out of the roast mutton, chewed vigorously, then swilled it down with a gulp of wine.

A jerk of the hand brought a man to his side.

'Double the guard!'

'At once, my lord.'

The command was passed on and guards immediately went off to take up their positions on the hilltop. They had been taught to respect this strong-willed boy, who was now biting into the mutton again with the appetite of a young wolf. Eustace drained the wine in his cup and grew complacent.

'He will not expect us here,' he said, speaking in rough Norman French.

'No, my lord,' replied the soldier, with a pronounced Flemish accent. 'He will think he is safe here.'

'We shall take him by surprise.'

Eustace allowed himself a smirk of pride as he recalled how far into enemy territory his bold thrust had carried him. Gloucestershire was still fiercely loyal to the Angevin cause, yet he had found his way to the very heart of the

9

county. It would be a fitting place to affirm his claim to the throne.

'Noon tomorrow,' he grunted, tossing the leg of mutton aside. 'He will not be this far south before noon tomorrow – unless he rides like the devil!'

The sergeant moved in closer.

'Dead or alive, my lord?'

Even in the gathering gloom he could read the answer in his commander's eyes. Unlike his father, King Stephen, Eustace was not troubled by any notions of generosity and mercy.

A nod dismissed the sergeant, who went off about his business. Eustace poured himself more wine and thought about the morrow. One successful ambush might bring years of strife and indecision to an end: one quick death would put his hand firmly upon the crown. The wine tasted sweet as he put the cup to his lips.

His men ate or rested or talked quietly in groups. Horses had been unsaddled, rubbed down, fed, then saddled again. Weapons had been tested, sharpened, made ready. Ignoring discomfort, the soldiers wore their hauberks and coifs in the chafing warmth of a summer's evening, their helmets and mailed gloves within easy reach.

These men were professionals, hardened by experience in the field, at once relaxed and alert for action. Their loyalty had been bought and they were eager to earn their pay. Eustace might see some great significance in the ambush: all that the mercenaries saw was one more skirmish in a long and profitable war.

Evening became night and the darkness encouraged a light sleep. Under a pale and featureless moon, the guards found themselves peering into a great black void that was full of strange noises. They could not be at all certain what they were hearing.

'Listen!'

The other man strained his ears for a moment then shrugged.

'Nothing.'

'But *listen!*'

The two sentries at the northern edge of the hilltop crept forward a few paces and craned their necks. It was the heftier of the men who thought he could identify the sound.

'Horses.'

'They could be our own,' suggested his companion, catching the faintest jingle of harness. 'They could be our horses.'

'Warn the others.'

But the smaller of the guards was more cautious. He wanted to be quite sure before rousing the whole camp unnecessarily. He had no wish to expose himself to the keen blade of his commander's temper.

'Warn the others!'

For the second time he delayed and the wait was fatal. There was a loud neighing from the road below and the faint jingle of harness became the unmistakable sound of horses – two, three, at most, four – at full gallop. Metal hoofs clacked on the hard track and every man on the hilltop was awake and struggling to his feet. Helmets and gloves were pulled on, swords and lances were grabbed, horses were mounted and spurred.

Eustace was first in the saddle, cursing the guards, yelling orders, leading the charge through the trees, scenting blood. His destrier reached the top of the slope, checked slightly, felt his fury, then lunged forward down the hill. Behind their leader came an avalanche of Flemish warhorses, hurtling down the sharp incline at a pace that was bound to claim victims. One man was thrown as his mount lost its footing, and he was trampled, then another horse fell sideways, crushing its rider under its own weight.

Nobody stopped to see to the casualties: they had someone to follow and money to earn. A carefully-planned ambush had become a desperate chase across hostile terrain.

Thundering along the road, Eustace and his men rounded a bend and caught their first glimpse of their quarry, silhouetted against the moon. Three figures sat bolt upright in their saddles as they tried to out-run their pursuers.

Eustace knew instinctively who one of the riders would be. Gripping the wide reins in one hand, he seized his sword and waved it above his head.

'Spread out!'

The horses ahead had left the road and chosen to gallop across a wide field towards a distant wood.

'Spread out! Spread out!'

Eustace led his men on to the short cropped grass and called for more speed from his destrier. Ahead of him the three horses were slowing a little, their advantage of a few hundred yards being cut back with each minute. A herd of sheep protested at the approach of riders, and scattered in a frenzy to make way for them. Eustace hacked at some of these luckless animals as he passed.

The ground began to rise unevenly and the gradient punished the already tired horses out in front. It seemed lighter here on open ground and the chasing pack could make out the three figures more closely. Eustace saw one of them veer off to the right in a solo bid for escape.

'Sergeant!'

Six men followed the sergeant as he swung off in pursuit of the lone rider. More sheep complained about their disturbed night.

Hunter and hunted had covered well over a mile now and the fresher horses continued to make ground. As the two figures finally reached the expanse of woodland, they were barely twenty yards ahead. It was dark under the trees and there were many hidden dangers, but the horses did not slacken their pace. They surged on, oblivious to stings, bruises, cuts, pain.

Still leading the chase, Eustace was just able to pick out the two shapes ahead of him as they tore across a clearing and into some more trees. He saw them race beneath a huge overhanging bough and heard the terrible clang as metal hit wood. The force of the impact knocked the helmet clean off and it embedded itself deep in the soft ground. The rider's neck must surely have been broken, yet he was still erect on his horse as it charged on.

A lance thrown from close range seemed to pass right through the man, yet he remained in the saddle. A second lance struck home and his crippled mount came down with a crash.

Eustace rode on past the stricken beast, interested only in the surviving rider. He had seen the man's short cloak when it had been lifted by the speed of his passage across open land. This was the person who had to be killed that night.

The cloak was less than a yard away from him now: Eustace was within a sword's length of his inheritance. With a fearsome swing of his arm, he let his blade fall. The blow almost bent the rider double and it seemed to knock the spirit out of the horse. As the panting animal slowed to a halt, Eustace reined in his own horse and came round to face his adversary.

Lowering his shoulder, he drove the point of the weapon straight at the heart. He was surprised when the sword bit through the hauberk and went in up to the hilt.

'Light! Bring light!' he screamed.

Two men from the rear of his troop brought blazing torches. He grabbed one and thrust it near the face of the sagging rider, only to find himself staring at a rival of straw. They had come all this way after three effigies, strapped into their saddles and kept upright by backbones of timber.

Eustace jabbed the torch at the straw and it caught fire at once, sending the horse careering off into the undergrowth in total panic. There were questions to be asked of the two guards from the northern edge of the hilltop.

While Eustace was asserting his discipline, Henry Plantagenet, still riding like the devil, was heading south-west in the direction of Bristol.

'I think it wise, my lord.'

The old man was saying no more than Henry had thought

himself, yet he resisted the idea. They had driven out his mother, the Empress Matilda, and they would not drive out him.

'It is the best course.'

Though he was only sixteen years old, the soldier in Henry was more than fully-grown. He stuck out his massive chest and strutted about the room, his great, leonine head lifted high in defiance.

'We could gather all our forces and strike back hard.'

'That is exactly what Stephen wishes us to do, my lord,' reminded the old man. 'He wants to tempt us to one final battle.'

'It *would* be final!' boasted the young man, still on the move. 'Did I not beat Eustace at Devizes? Did I not capture Bridport? Did I not smoke hundreds of Stephen's supporters out of their holes?'

'You did, my lord.'

'Then why advise me to turn tail and run?'

There was fire in Henry's blue-grey eyes and Roger waited until its flames had died a little. He looked admiringly at his extraordinary companion, who had the physique of a wrestler and the stamp of real authority in his features. Henry might have his mother's arrogance, but he was not deaf to reason as the Empress had been. Roger spoke quietly and slowly.

'There is a time for a pitched battle and a time for harbouring one's strength. Stephen's main forces outnumber us – it is as simple as that. As long as you are in England, he and that son of his will try to drive you into a corner.'

'They will never succeed, Roger.'

'Then they will make someone pay for that fact.'

Roger paused as Henry moved restlessly away from him. He joined the young man at the arched window and kept his voice low.

'They have destroyed houses, castles, churches, even an abbey that was thought to favour our cause. They have killed and plundered and fired all the crops in some areas.

14

People face the winter with no home, no food and no hope of—'

A gesture from Henry stopped the old man and they stood in silence for several minutes. Through the window they could see more snow falling on the courtyard below. Christmas, 1149, would be white, cold and cheerless for the Angevin party in England.

Henry considered the six months he had spent in the country and weighed his judgement of that time against Roger's counsel. He turned to face the old man.

'It would be good to see my father again.'

Roger nodded his agreement with a wry smile.

'I will travel to Normandy quite soon,' announced Henry, pacing restlessly once more. 'But I shall return, Roger. Nobody is hounding me out of England. I am merely choosing to withdraw.'

'That withdrawal will be timely, my lord.'

Roger was relieved. Henry's departure would mean yet another admission of failure in the Angevin camp, but it would ease the suffering that had become so widespread and acute. King Stephen and his despised Flemish mercenaries would no longer have a target for continuous attack.

'You have my promise, Roger. I shall return.'

'I know, my lord.'

Ten days after their conversation in Bristol Castle, Henry Plantagenet crossed the Channel to Normandy.

Louis VII, King of France, sat in his bed with an expression of sheer petulance on his face. His wife, Eleanor, who lay beside him on papal advice, was amused by his pursed lips and puffed, reddened cheeks. She laughed.

'Go to sleep, Eleanor,' he advised, tetchily.

'Have you forgotten the words of His Holiness so soon?' she asked, nestling under the brocades and furs.

There was a mockery in her voice which offended him to the core. Devout and ascetic himself, Louis had tried throughout the twelve years of his marriage to bring his wife to a clearer recognition of her spiritual needs and to a more ready acceptance of the will of God. It was an impossible task.

'The Pope says that we must live together as man and wife,' she taunted. 'In Tusculum he helped to prepare our bed with his own hands. We went to him to talk about divorce, and we came away as lovers.'

'Go to sleep!'

'Lovers do not sleep, Louis.'

He tore at the hangings around the bed, then got up quickly and went to kneel before the crucifix on the far wall. Eleanor sighed as she watched him in this all too familiar position. In profile, Louis looked almost saintly and she had no need at all of a saint in her bedchamber.

She had met Louis when she was a dark, vivacious girl of fifteen, celebrated for her wit and beauty, presiding over the Courts of Love in her native Aquitaine with a grace and charm that was well beyond her years. She had become Queen of France and mistress of a great nation. Yet here she was, shivering through a Paris winter, pining for the warmth of her homeland, tied to a dull, peevish, boring husband.

'Louis!' she called, resignation settling on her face.

He remained deep in prayer and out of reach.

'You should have been a monk,' she decided, with asperity. 'Celibacy becomes you.'

It was a long time before he rejoined her and his irritation was still evident. Eleanor snuggled up to him as a last resort and tried to sound sympathetic.

'I know what is troubling you, Louis,' she whispered. 'Put it out of your mind for this night. Let me help.'

Not even hearing, the King of France continued to brood upon the events of an unhappy day.

News had arrived from Normandy that Henry Plantagenet had been invested with the ducal title by his father, Geoffrey of Anjou. After proving his courage and resourcefulness in England, Henry had sailed back to a magnificent welcome, crowds flocking to acclaim the resolute young man who had survived so many attempts upon his life.

By installing his son as Duke of Normandy, Geoffrey was not merely acknowledging his prowess as a soldier, he was signalling the end of Henry's formal training as a leader.

The significance of all this had burned its way at once into Louis' mind. When he and his queen had left for the Crusade over two years ago, there had seemed little chance of a reunion between Normandy and England. He had come home to find the situation transformed, and his security threatened because a sixteen-year-old boy had attained manhood.

To anyone with foresight – and pious, ineffective Louis had considerable foresight – the new Duke of Normandy was also a potential King of England.

'Forget him,' suggested Eleanor, reading her husband's thoughts.

Fear made Louis tremble violently for an instant and he pulled his wife close to him, grateful for the warm re-assurance of her supple body.

'France needs an heir, Louis,' she urged in the darkness. 'We need a son. Make me bear a son.'

Without hope or expectation of any pleasure, Eleanor of Aquitaine paid the marriage debt once more.

In the summer of 1151, Geoffrey Plantagenet, Count of Anjou, rode to Paris with his favourite son to pay homage to a king with whom they had been fighting for the last eighteen months. On their way they stopped to rest their horses and to take refreshment.

'When I was in England, I rode forty – sometimes fifty miles in a day.'

'That was when Stephen was chasing you,' recalled his father, stretching his legs. 'He is not at your heels now. He is too busy hounding the church.'

'We must ride faster,' insisted Henry, striding up and down, ignoring the offer of food.

'Let Louis wait a little longer,' chuckled Geoffrey. 'When you get to my age, you learn to take your time – on a horse, and on a woman.'

The knights and squires in their entourage laughed appreciatively. They knew how the Count had earned his nickname of Geoffrey the Fair, and how gloriously he had exploited his good looks.

Henry grinned knowingly, having shared the same whore with his father on more than one occasion. Geoffrey had been eager to neglect no aspect of his son's education.

'Tomorrow you will see Paris,' he declared, slapping Henry's thigh playfully. 'Such a city as you have never known! I envy you. To be young, strong, lusty and in Paris for the first time – God, how I envy you!'

'One city is much like another to me,' shrugged Henry. 'I am more interested to meet the King.'

'Louis is no king!' sneered Geoffrey. 'Where is his kingdom? It's a battleground of warring houses – Normandy, Blois, Anjou and Aquitaine. Every man is a king in his own territory. His job is to look after that territory, and to make it bigger. Can you look after Normandy and make it bigger, Henry?'

'Yes, father,' he said with casual assurance. 'But first I must be confirmed as Duke.'

'It is the kind of chore which Louis can just about manage,' retorted Geoffrey. 'We swear an oath of fealty to him and he recognises you as Duke of Normandy. He has no choice. Even with his brother-in-law, Eustace, he was unable to pierce our defences. You protected Normandy well.'

'Yes, father.'

The same casual assurance, accompanied by a smile as Henry remembered the number of times that Eustace had been rebuffed along his frontiers. With each defeat, Eustace's hold on the crown of England was weakened.

'And then there is the Queen.' Geoffrey's eyes twinkled.

'Is she as beautiful as they say?' asked Henry.

'A man could die for someone like that,' replied his father in a whisper. 'She is a remarkable woman.'

'And brave, too,' observed Henry. 'Riding to Jerusalem with the crusaders at the head of her own troop. They say that she wore golden boots. They say that she had a royal crest on her arm and a great plume in her hat. They say that, even dressed like a knight, she looked like a lady.'

'Eleanor would make a fine queen for the right man,' mused Geoffrey, staring into the distance.

'She *is* a queen, father.'

'Louis is a milksop!' snarled the other. 'Pope Eugenius sent him back to bed with his wife and all that he could give her was another daughter. For the right man, Eleanor would produce a host of sons – and there would be real sport in their making!'

Henry grew pensive and stood aside for a few minutes. When they mounted their horses to ride on, he set a faster pace than before.

Queen Eleanor of France sat in her high room in the old tower while her ladies dressed her. She was wearing a linen underskirt and an inner robe of white silk bound from wrist to elbow with thin gold cord. One of the ladies held the outer robe, its wide sleeves hanging loose, its embroidered hem measuring ten and more yards, its olive-green colour as rich as it was striking.

'Quick, Eleanor! They are coming!'

Her sister, Petronilla, was poised at the window, keeping watch as intently as any guard. Eleanor brushed aside her ladies and crossed to her sister.

The sight which greeted her down below filled the Queen with an excitement she had not felt since those first, thrilling days of the Crusade. Where she expected to see two vassals coming to the Frankish court to kneel before her husband, she found instead two kings on a royal progress through the streets of Paris, drawing every eye towards them as they rode along, attended by knights and squires whose bonnets were sprigged with bright yellow broom. Amid all this flashing pageantry, Petronilla singled out the man who was now stirring up memories of her headstrong and passionate past.

'Look at him, Eleanor! The Count of Anjou. Have you ever seen such a sight on a horse?'

'Yes,' answered her sister. 'Beside him.'

While Petronilla responded to the seasoned charms of Geoffrey the Fair, it was his eighteen-year-old son who aroused the Queen of France. Henry Plantagenet, son of a count and an empress, had a presence and regal bearing which set him apart from his father. Eleanor was impressed at once with the young Duke of Normandy, whose powerful frame was upright and unafraid in his saddle, whose clear, open face spoke of honesty and courtesy, whose sharp eyes were alive with curiosity to take in all that was around him.

When Eleanor finally turned and submitted herself to the attentions of her ladies, she knew that she had seen a man who was destined for greatness.

King Louis of France sat in state while a huge parchment map was rolled out. The bitter negotiations began under the cool gaze of Abbot Bernard of Clairvaux, a wise, wily old man of sixty, who exemplified the Cistercian disregard of worldly pleasures yet had an astonishing hold on the political realities of the day. There were outbursts of temper from Geoffrey, some forthright speaking from Henry and displays of sheer exasperation from Louis, but Abbot Bernard was there at all times to exert a stern, calming influence and to plead the cause of peace.

At length the two sides came to agreement: in return for his confirmation of the investiture of Henry as Duke of Normandy, Louis gained the castles of the Norman Vexin, key strongholds which commanded the north-western approach to his capital.

Eleanor had followed all this with immense interest, full of admiration for the way that Henry bore his part. Here was no rash soldier, bent on achieving his ends by a threat of force: Henry was evidently a man who valued peaceful negotiation, who enjoyed the diplomatic wrangling for its own sake, who was ready to concede territory now which he knew he would regain some time in the future.

Struck by the maturity of his vision, as well as by his physical attributes, the Queen of France ventured to speak with him alone. They found themselves in a garden, sharing a marble bench beneath the heat of the afternoon sun, listening to the song of a troubadour. When the song was over, Eleanor dismissed the man with a grateful nod.

'Louis fills my ears with plainsong from morning till night,' she complained. 'My troubadour keeps me sane.'

Henry said nothing, meeting her eye boldly.

'One day you will be King of England.'

'England already has a king,' he reminded her.

'Stephen is too weak!' she said, scornfully. 'England has been racked by war ever since he seized the crown from under the nose of your mother. Fifteen years of fighting and misery – that is all King Stephen has given his country. God preserve us from a weak king!'

She spoke with such feeling and conviction that Henry was quite dumbstruck for a moment, marvelling at the way her handsome face shone when she was angry. He forgot that she was nearly twelve years older than him, he forgot that her reputation had been called in question by events at Antioch during the Crusade, he forgot that she was married to another man.

'I shall not be a weak king,' he vowed. 'Sometimes I dream that I hold the world in my hands. Here.'

'Your hands are rough and hard,' she noticed, taking them in hers. 'Why do you wear no gloves?'

'I see things – with my hands.'

He tightened his grip and she felt the strength of purpose which this strange young man had. Ideas began to revolve in her mind but she did not need to put them into words. Henry more than understood.

'What do you think of Paris?' she asked, as he relaxed his hold on her and moved his calloused hands away.

'It is a fine city,' he conceded.

'It is a boring city, ruled by a silly, boring man. Aquitaine is a garden of delight, and I am stuck in Paris.'

'We are in a garden ourselves, my lady.'

'No, Henry. We are in a prison. Will you help me to escape?'

He did not pause to make a decision. There was a blend of determination and tenderness about her which won him over in an instant.

'I will help you. My hand on that.'

'Is it a pledge?' she tested.

'It is, my lady.'

She was content and rose to go, leaving him a smile that contained the whole pathos of her situation.

'I shall remember, Henry Plantagenet.'

Eleanor disappeared into the castle and Henry was left to consider the enormity of his commitment to her. He did not hear his father, a skilled eavesdropper, chuckling to himself in the safety of his hiding place. Henry may have surrendered the castles of the Vexin, but he had gained far more than the King of France, or even the astute Abbot Bernard, could possibly imagine.

In the month of September, 1151, Geoffrey and his son left Paris and took the road to Angers, the Count's capital. They were in excellent spirits, pleased with the results of their visit, joking about their conquests among the maids of the fair city behind them. But Death walked between them and looked Geoffrey full in the face. On the banks of the Loire, he was suddenly seized by a fever and lay ill for three days before taking his leave of the world.

From his father's bonnet, Henry took the sprig of broom – the *Planta genesta* – which had given the family its name, and hurled it into the river. Then he strapped Geoffrey's body across a horse and headed due west towards Le Mans. When he arrived with a dead man in the city of his birth, he was both Duke of Normandy and Count of Anjou-Maine.

There was a will. Henry saw it for the first time in the crypt where he was paying his respects to his father. Over the corpse of one Geoffrey, he had an argument with another – his younger brother.

'How did you come by the will?' he demanded.

'The elders found it for me,' explained Geoffrey, a sly expression stealing into his face.

Henry snatched the parchment and unfolded it in one swift movement. Geoffrey spoke with the complacence of one who had already seen the document.

'There are special provisions, it seems. Father left orders that he should not be buried until you have given your oath to abide by the terms.'

'Chinon, Loudun, Mirebeau ... you're to have those,' noted Henry, glancing up. 'I accept that.'

'Read on, Henry.'

Geoffrey watched with amusement as his elder brother came to the critical section in the will, paused, read it again with great care, stared at the cold, grey face of his father, then paced up and down to control his annoyance. The younger son relished his moment of advantage.

'If you are recognised as King of England, then Anjou and Maine must come to me.'

'He did not mean it!' exploded Henry.

'Nevertheless, it is in the will.'

'He *could* not mean it, Geoffrey! I am the first-born. Anjou and Maine should be mine. I must be Count – and Duke – and King!'

'You will have to swear the oath or we shall never get him buried. He stinks already.... What do you say?'

Henry inhaled the noisome air deeply through his nostrils, then muttered his reply.

'I shall swear the oath.'

'And forget it afterwards,' challenged Geoffrey.

'I shall ... swear the oath.'

'England will keep you more than busy, Henry. It was too much of a handful for mother, and far too much of a handful for Stephen. England is enough. It you leave Anjou to me—'

'If I leave Anjou to you, I should be mad – as *he* was.'

Henry took his brother by the shoulders and tried to reason with him.

'Think what will happen, Geoffrey. Anjou and Maine to you – England and Normandy to me. That makes us rivals not brothers. We should be at each other's throats in no time.' He pulled him towards the tomb so that they stood either side of the corpse. 'Agree it now – over his body. You shall have your castles – I give them freely. But I must have Anjou and Maine.'

'You will have them – until you become King of England.'

'It's a legacy of hatred. You know the story of our family as well as I do. Let's end it now. Let's put a stop to the curse before it kills us both.'

Geoffrey sniffed at the body and turned away in disgust.

'Swear the oath, Henry, and let our father sleep in peace.'

He left his elder brother in the crypt, still staring at the will in disbelief.

After much deliberation, Henry Plantagenet took an oath that he would accept the terms of the will, and his father's body was finally laid to rest in its tomb. As he joined the solemn procession out of the crypt, he felt the dead hand of Geoffrey the Fair on his shoulder, holding him back from the prizes that had beckoned him.

While Henry was attending to the burial of his father, Queen Eleanor of France was preoccupied with the burial of her marriage. Worn down by years of regret and disillusion with his wife, Louis proved surprisingly amenable. Abbot Bernard, set against the match from the start, gave his approval from the privacy of his cell. Since there was no male child, the question of succession did not arise and so the Pope raised no objection to the divorce. The synod was held at Beaugency on March 21, 1152, with the noble Archbishop of Sens presiding.

King Louis of France set aside his wife on the grounds of consanguinity: the couple were within the prohibited cousinship of fourth degree. The two princesses were declared legitimate and awarded to their father. Eleanor was given all her domains on condition that she remained a loyal vassal. With her little entourage, she withdrew south to Poitiers. Louis, tears in his eyes when the decree of separation was read out aloud, returned a lonely man to Paris.

'It will ruin your eyes, mother,' warned Henry.

'My eyes are no bother,' she snapped, working with difficulty at her tapestry frame. 'They will be all right.'

They were in Matilda's solar at Rouen where the light was not good enough for detailed work with coloured thread, yet she stuck to her task with the grim persistence of a woman who has found her mission in life.

'Will you ever finish that map of England, mother?'

'Some day. With your help.'

'There are other things ...' he mumbled.

'England must come first,' she insisted. 'Have you not heard the reports? Stephen has lost control of everything, and the barons do as they please. England needs a strong man and all he can do is to bicker with the church. England, Henry! It is time to mount a fresh campaign.'

'I took that stupid oath,' he said. 'If I become King of England then I lose—'

'Forget Anjou!' she snarled. 'What does Anjou matter? England is the place for us.' She fixed him with an imperial stare. 'My father, your namesake, gave me England and the barons paid homage to me – Stephen amongst them. Then he broke his oath and stole my crown. I fought him, Henry. I went to England and fought Stephen and beat him. They even crowned me Queen.'

Henry knew the story only too well. His mother's arrogant and high-handed behaviour had offended the citizens of London, who had put their new Queen to flight. When Stephen had been released from captivity, he was welcomed back as King.

'Stephen is getting old now. And there is no-one to come after him, unless you want Eustace to reign in your place.'

'Never!' he snorted, stung by the very mention of the name.

'Then go to England again, Henry. Raise my standard and they will rush to support you.'

'I swore that oath, mother. I will forfeit Anjou.'

'Then let it go.'

'But I want England and Normandy and—'

'Let it go!'

The explosive force of this compelled his silence. There was cold steel in her voice as she continued.

'I hated your father, Henry. I hated him when I married him, and I hated him when he died. What has Anjou ever done for me? I was the widow of an Emperor when I became betrothed to your father. Do you imagine I wanted to leave the German court for *that*? But my own father sent for me because he wanted an alliance with the Angevins. So I was sacrificed to Geoffrey Plantagenet, a foolish, wilful boy of fourteen, son of a mere count.'

'I was once the son of a mere count, mother.'

'No – you are *my* son, Henry, with royal blood in your veins. Your grandfather, Henry Beauclerk, was a great King of England. You will be the same. If your father's will takes Anjou away from you – let it go. Because your mother's lineage gives you England and a crown!'

Henry pondered, studied the tapestry map, then paced around the solar with his usual restlessness.

'It is not enough, mother. King, Duke and Count – that is what I will be. And besides Normandy and Anjou-Maine, there may even be ... Aquitaine.'

Matilda's eyes widened with alarm as she realised the implications of her son's ambitions.

'Henry, what are you thinking?'

'It has been decided.'

'But Aquitaine ... No, Henry. Why look for trouble in France? Louis may have set his wife aside, but she is not for you.'

'Set her aside?' The news exhilarated him. 'Then the rumours are true?'

'The Church did its duty at Beaugency. The Queen of France is now the Duchess of Aquitaine once more.'

Henry was in the saddle within minutes.

In the seven weeks since the divorce, the Duchess Eleanor, happily returned to her homeland, had become a new woman. Freedom from a tiresome husband, and the prospects which invited her, gave her step the spring it had lacked for so long. To the fine, old castle of Poitiers, she brought life and colour and an air of celebration. Vassals came from all parts of her domain to pay homage to her, counsellors and churchmen stood by to offer advice, and poets and troubadours made her court blossom.

Surrounded by an atmosphere of chivalry, her heart was light again, her soul yearned for romance, and her thoughts turned to a knight who would come and honour his pledge.

She was in her sumptuous room in the lofty keep when he finally arrived, tempering his ardour with politeness as he bent to kiss her hand. His bonnet, with its sprig of broom, had been removed with a sweep.

'You came too late,' she chided, gently.

'I had business in Normandy.'

'I needed a knight at my command. On the road from Orléans my train was ambushed by an impudent boy. They said he was your brother.'

'Geoffrey,' he murmured. 'I will kill him one day.'

'Your brother is a rough suitor. However, I managed to escape him and to reach Poitiers unharmed. There have been many other suitors since then. Far too many.'

Henry had been courteous and formal until now. It was time to be more direct. If the Duchess was under pressure from a host of suitors, all anxious to seize the rich domains of which she was mistress, any delay was foolhardy.

'In Normandy I had to see my barons. I needed their approval before I came to redeem my pledge.'

'Your Norman barons may have approved,' she said, skittishly. 'But I am not sure that I approve.'

'You promised!' he yelled.

'Did I? Lovers' promises are as light as thistledown. The

faintest wind of change can blow them away.'

He was glowering at her now and it softened her manner. She came close to him and tested his resolve.

'You're young, Henry. Have you considered it? We are related in the fourth and fifth degrees, which some would argue is a bar to our marriage. You are Louis's vassal. He would never dream of giving me to you. It would make you lord of Normandy, Maine, Anjou, Poitou and Aquitaine.'

'You left out England,' he said, stubbornly.

'You would be the greatest man in Europe and you expect the King of France to give his blessing.'

'We do not need his blessing. You shall be my queen, as I pledged. The loveliest, most powerful and sweetest lady in all the world. My hand on that.'

The rugged certainty of his manner banished all her doubts. She made him kneel before her to give another pledge.

'Listen to the words, Henry Plantagenet ... I give to you my pledge of love. For ever.'

'I give to you my pledge of love forever.'

'And if I break my oath ... may the god of love torment me until the day I die.'

Henry repeated the sentences in clear, ringing tones then rose to enfold her in his thick arms. The bargain which had been struck in a Paris garden was now sealed with a fond and lingering kiss.

Five days later they were married.

The news struck France like a thunderbolt. Terror entered many a heart as people saw the map of Europe altered with such dramatic speed. King Louis of France, shocked, enraged, wounded by Eleanor's betrayal, hurled his armies against the Norman frontier. But Henry came out of nowhere to defend his land and the ailing Louis, now stricken with fever, was forced to leave the field and accept a truce. Marriage had made Henry Plantagenet lord of a vast domain. It was the one contingency which the wise and well-intentioned churchmen at Beaugency had not foreseen.

Six months passed and Henry's position became more secure. When Geoffrey rebelled against him, he put down the insurrection with speed and ruthlessness. Henry was determined that his brother would never become Count of Anjou, and a later challenge by Geoffrey was suppressed with firmness as well.

Troublesome vassals had now been subdued, the King of France had been kept at bay, and the whole world had been made aware of Henry's strength of purpose. On all sides, his enemies began to pay him a greater respect.

As Christmas approached, he paid a snatched visit to the southern regions of Aquitaine. His wife sensed his impatience.

'When do you go?'

'There is time yet,' he reassured her, spreading his palms before the crackling log fire. 'There is a little time yet.'

'Then let us *enjoy* it, Henry. I bring you to my beautiful Aquitaine to show you its fields, its forests, its vineyards. But you see nothing – your thoughts are all of England.'

'I am needed there,' he said, simply.

'You are needed *here*,' she argued. 'The truce will not bind Louis. He can be like a serpent and will strike back at any moment. You know that he plans to recognise Eustace as Duke of Normandy. Insult first, battle second. You are needed here.'

'That is why I must go to England. Because nobody expects me to. Wallingford must be relieved. Stephen is set on taking Wallingford.'

'Stephen is no threat to you, Henry. Since the Queen died, he is only half a man. The Pope refused to crown Eustace as his successor and openly prefers you. Stephen is a failed man and he knows it.'

Henry looked across at her as she sat in her high-backed chair, wearing a saffron-coloured gown and with her long

29

hair brushed back and surmounted by a golden circlet. Eleanor of Aquitaine was his wife and she was carrying his child. Marriage to her had been both love-match and political gamble. There would be moments when the lover in him would clash with the political adventurer. Such a moment was at hand.

'We need you here, Henry. *I* need you.'

'Then I will stay, my love. Until tomorrow.'

A few weeks later Henry braved a violent storm and sailed to England with an army of mercenaries.

King Stephen was dismayed by this turn of events, having brought Wallingford – last symbol of Angevin resistance in the Upper Thames area – to the brink of surrender. Eustace raced home to his father from France and they awaited together the sight of the Empress's standard.

But Henry was a tactician. Instead of a long march to Wallingford through barren, rain-swept countryside, he opted for a surprise attack on Malmesbury, the Royalist stronghold in the west. The town fell, the castle was besieged, and it was Stephen who had to drag a tired army into the winter wind. Across a River Avon swollen with floods, the two commanders agreed upon a six-month truce.

At the end of that time, the seige of Wallingford was resumed and Henry brought his now sizeable army to face Stephen across another river, the Thames. A pitched battle seemed inevitable and both sides were busy with their preparations. Common sense saved the day, however, both commanders seeing the folly of fighting for something which could be achieved by peaceful negotiation.

Henry rode out to meet Stephen at Crowmarch. Two horses were waiting for him.

'Alone, Stephen. It must be done alone.'

'My son, Eustace, is here because he—'

'I shall parley with the *King* alone,' insisted Henry.

Eustace glared at his rival with unconcealed loathing before turning his horse. It was four years since he had failed to kill the Angevin pretender and he had paid a terrible price for his blunder. He set off at a gallop and did not stop when he reached the Royalist battle-lines drawn up in readiness under their fluttering banners.

'Eustace wanted us to fight,' explained Stephen. 'He is much too fond of the sight of blood.'

'He can never be king!' asserted Henry, coming at once to the crux of the argument. '*Never.*'

Stephen looked deeply hurt, then sad, then almost relieved. His voice took on a world-weary note.

'Why do you want England, Henry?'

'It is my inheritance. England and Normandy.'

'Can a man rule them both – and control his other lands?'

'I think so.' Henry plotted his course with confidence. 'What England needs is justice and order. That was my grandfather's way – justice in law, and order. I believe that England can live in peace under one king and not go on tearing out its own guts.'

'I wanted peace, too,' confessed Stephen. 'But I have given England almost eighteen years of ...' He looked from one army across the river to the other.

'It will be different, Stephen.'

The King looked into Henry Plantagenet and saw qualities he had despaired of finding in Eustace. In fighting the Angevin party, he had plunged his kingdom into anarchy. It was time for the fighting to be stopped for good.

'We must talk terms, Henry.'

The agreement that was made in principle at Wallingford was ratified at Winchester in November of the same year. King Stephen and Duke Henry came together once more and reached a formal settlement. Before the assembled barons, earls and other magnates, the king acknowledged Henry's hereditary right to the throne of England. Until his death Stephen would remain king. Henry Plantagenet was assured of an undisputed succession.

What reconciled Stephen to the finality of this treaty

was the fact that he no longer had to consider the position of his elder son. Enraged by the truce at Wallingford, Eustace had ridden off into East Anglia with a troop of men and earned himself notoriety for his cruelty and wanton destruction. After plundering an abbey and abusing its inhabitants, he met his end without warning, strangled by a dish of eels.

When Henry heard of this, he laughed long and loud.

Less than a year after the Treaty of Winchester, Stephen himself took his leave of the world. He died on October 25, 1154, at Dover Castle and bequeathed an unsettled, ill-tempered country to his young successor.

Early in December, Henry and his wife made a difficult crossing from Barfleur, the small fleet taking a day and a half to reach the new kingdom. Characteristically, Henry was the first to sight land.

On December 19 Henry II and his Queen were crowned together in Westminster Abbey by Archbishop Theobald of Canterbury. King, Duke and Count. Henry was twenty-one and he had fulfilled his dream. He felt that he had the luck of the devil.

CHAPTER TWO

Thomas Becket strode briskly through the narrow streets of Cheapside, smiling benignly at every familiar face and warmly returning every greeting. It was his first visit to London since the death of his father, Gilbert, some six years earlier. He was delighted to be back under happier circumstances and found time, in each full day, to seek out old haunts, to meet old friends, and to enjoy the simple pleasure of being home again.

At one time or another, he had seen most of the great cities of Europe, but he had always been proud to be called Thomas of London. With its swarming life, its amiable clutter, its colour, its excitement and its sense of well-being, London was truly without compare. It was a cheerful, noisy, busy place with a character of strong independence and a mind of its own, a large, sprawling, cosmopolitan city lit by its own ebullience.

Thomas turned a corner and felt a pang as he saw Gilbert Becket's old house, its gaily-painted board still creaking on its iron rail, the sign of the snipe still reminding passers-by that Gilbert had once been a citizen of some prominence. The board had earned his son the nickname of Thomas the Snipe, and that son now remembered with fondness those golden days of his boyhood.

'Thomas!'

His sister, Agnes, was the first to welcome him in the small forecourt of the Cheapside house, crying with joy to see her brother once again.

'You will squeeze me to death, Agnes,' he laughed, detaching himself to shake hands with her beaming husband. 'I hope that Agnes looks after you properly,' he said, with a wink.

'Everything is fine, Thomas,' assured the young Fitztheobald. 'Everything is fine now – thanks to you. We have never forgotten how much you—'

Thomas disposed of the subject with a raised palm. He had been only too glad to help the couple over the money worries in the early days of their marriage. His was a generosity that did not need to be made aware of itself all the time.

'You have grown even taller,' suggested his brother-in-law, gazing up into his clear, handsome face.

'I am a steeple of the church.'

The joke caused the young Fitztheobald to burst into such hysterical laughter that his wife had to apologise for him. She led the way into the house, then turned to appraise Thomas once more, pride bringing more tears.

'You are the tallest man in London. And one of the most important.'

'I would not say that, Agnes,' he replied, modestly.

'Archdeacon of Canterbury and provost of Beverley. Is that not importance? You came to London to plan the celebrations for the King and Queen. You stood close to the Archibishop at the Coronation. You have met the highest in the land and discussed affairs of state with them. You have—'

'I have come back home to my father's house to be Thomas, your brother, and nothing more.'

But there was no holding Agnes now that she had embarked. The questions came thick and fast and made his head reel.

'What is the Queen like, Thomas? Why does the King wear that short cloak? Were they pleased with their welcome in London? How long will they be staying in Bermondsey? Did the King really fidget and yawn all through the Coronation? Does the Queen always wear her hair brushed back like that – is it the fashion in Aquitaine? When is her next child due? Has the King chosen his ministers yet? Who is to attend his Christmas court?'

Thomas answered the last question involuntarily.

'I am.'

'As was agreed at Winchester, my lands shall be delivered from the tyranny of unlawful barons and from the instruments of their tyranny. Thus are these measures taken.'

It was Christmas Day and Henry was wearing his crown for the first time before his people. His strong, rough, outdoor voice penetrated to every corner of the long, packed hall at Bermondsey. He spoke quickly, in faultless Latin, dispatching the business of the court with firmness.

He announced that he would expel all foreign mercenaries, those hated vultures who had fed off the rotting carcass of England during Stephen's reign. He warned that he would destroy all unlicensed castles, over a thousand of which had been built by irresponsible barons. He declared that he would reclaim all the Crown lands that had been bartered off by Stephen.

'It is our intention to have one authority, the Crown, as

guarantor of peace and justice in our land.'

The business was concluded and the King rose to leave the crowded hall. On his way through to the porch, he caught sight of a face he recognised and paused.

'Thomas . . .'

The man stepped forward, a blush darkening his fair skin.

'Sire . . .'

Henry had spoken to many about Archdeacon Thomas and none could be found to deny his intelligence, application, diplomacy and absolute discretion. In the man's honest, willing countenance Henry discerned something else and was satisfied.

'Hunt with us tomorrow.'

Without waiting to hear the stuttered thanks, the King swept out into the porch with eager courtiers at his elbow.

Thomas was awake next morning before anyone else in the priory at Bermondsey. His imagination was fired by this example of royal favour and he managed, before prime, to have a few words alone with the Archbishop. Soft-tongued and silver-haired, the venerable Theobald of Bec would give little away.

'You have served me well for eleven years, Thomas,' he said with affection. 'But I think you are not for the Church.'

'Father, I would be happy to stay in your household for—'

'God will decide, my son.'

The tolling of the bell ended the interview and Thomas puzzled over it while he knelt, ostensibly in prayer, in the chapel. It was true that he had not felt impelled to be ordained as a priest, but he could still serve the Church in his present capacity. What did Theobald know that he would not tell?

Time limped slowly until the hour when Thomas had to present himself at the royal residence. His falconer was in attendance and Thomas took something from him before meeting the King.

'Sire . . .'

Henry acknowledged the bow with a nod then grinned broadly.

'For me?' he asked, indicating the hawk which sat on Thomas's gloved wrist.

'If my lord accepts the gift.'

Henry appraised the bird with an expert eye and was pleased.

'She's a gerfalcon. Norwegian.'

'Yes, my lord. Of her first moulting.'

'I had one before. Lost her at mew.'

'You should feed unwashed meat at that time, my lord. The meat of cats and dogs is best.'

'I never heard that,' said Henry with surprise.

'I trust my lord forgives me,' apologised Thomas, bowing again. 'I would not seem to instruct my lord.'

'Kings need instruction sometimes.'

Henry motioned to the falconer who took the bird from his master's wrist then stepped back into the shadow of the gateway. It was now Thomas's turn to be appraised and he felt his worth, his manner, his clothing and his reputation being weighed by the stocky, unkempt King.

'How old are you, Thomas?'

'Thirty-five, my lord.'

'Young enough to be ambitious and old enough to have experience. Would you serve me well?'

Again the bow, the blush, the stutter. Henry had his answer.

'I need a Chancellor, Thomas. One that can tell the difference between a gerfalcon and a peregrine, between a merlin and a sparrow-hawk.' He put a hand on the other's shoulder. 'What do you say, Thomas?'

There was no trace of nervousness or hesitation this time.

'If my lord wants my service . . .'

Henry came close and took Thomas's hands between his own horny palms, bestowing the kiss of peace to confirm the appointment.

'Thomas Becket – I name you Chancellor.'

It was over as quickly as that and both men relaxed.

Henry slapped his towering companion good-naturedly across the back.

'The Archbishop told me that you always get what you want. So do I, Thomas. We should be great friends.'

'Yes, my lord.'

England soon learned that she had a new King. Henry began to impose law and order upon a country which had seen little of either for nineteen desperate years. Moving about his realm with bewildering speed, he put down baronial revolts, razed illegal castles, and repossessed Crown property with merciless determination. Some resisted, some refused to pay homage, some fled abroad, but the greater part of the kingdom welcomed the new monarch. England was weary of war and grateful for peace.

Yet it never took its new King to its heart. Indifferent to the world's opinion of him, Henry was in no way perturbed. Unlike lesser men – Stephen, Louis VII, Thomas Becket – he was was not handicapped by the desire to be liked and loved.

Strong government requires able ministers and Henry had chosen well. In the year between the Treaty of Winchester and his accession, he had kept himself well-informed of events in England, singling out and studying certain people, trusting his judgement of what they would do for him in the future rather than what they had done for others in the past.

Accordingly Henry had picked Richard de Lucy to head the royal administration even though that noble lord had once fought against him at Oxford. To prevent de Lucy's power from becoming paramount, the King appointed as co-justiciar Robert de Beaumont, Earl of Leicester, the most influential baron in the realm. It was a partnership which did all that Henry had expected of it, consolidating his power and putting the rule of England on an efficient basis.

Richard de Lucy, the Earl of Leicester, Thomas Becket – he had no reservations about the men he had selected. Thomas, especially, was proving to be an inspired choice.

Not everyone agreed.

'He is pompous, self-satisfied, grasping ...'

'Be quiet, Eleanor!'

'He is a dangerous, upstart—'

His hand covered her mouth and his body provided the only conversation. They were in her bedchamber at Bermondsey and Henry was taking his wife with his usual frenetic energy. Eleanor dug her long fingernails into his back and her teeth into his hand, letting her desire mount until it screamed and shook together with his. For several minutes he lay panting on top of her.

'I certainly did not marry a monk this time,' she said.

He rolled over and looked at her body, still slender and clear-skinned despite her years and the effects of child-bearing. The sweat ran down his chest and he wiped it off with his arm.

'I do not like the man, Henry.'

'Mm?'

'Thomas. Your Chancellor. Thomas Becket.'

'Take care what you say. Thomas is a friend.'

'Thomas is a friend to Thomas,' she persisted. 'He gets richer and richer.' She reached for her white shift. 'He dresses better than you – but, then, who does not? – he eats better than you, he lives better than you. As for that house of his—'

'Bermondsey is not to your taste, I know,' he said, affably, 'but do not be jealous of Thomas's house. They work in Westminster every day on our palace. Thomas does not have a palace.'

She slipped on her shift, picked up her mirror and was displeased with what she saw in the shining metal speculum. It put more acid into her next remark.

'He is as cold as any stone.'

'That gerfalcon he gave me ... The best I ever had.'

'When he is with me or any other woman, he is as cold as any stone. Does he like boys?'

'Ask him.'

Henry got up with a grunt and began to dress. Eleanor

watched him and her lip curled in derision.

'You dress as if you are leaving one of your whores, Henry. Is that all I am to you? What of your pledge to love me?'

'What of your pledge to love me?' he countered, swinging around to confront her. 'Well?'

'I have been faithful to you, Henry. I have remembered my vows and been faithful to my husband. But you....'

'Ignore the rumours.'

'When one of my own women is involved?' She had surprised him. 'Yes, that is right. The night I was suffering the birth pangs with Young Henry, you took her in the next room. Like an animal.'

'It was some time ago,' he shrugged. 'I do not remember.'

'She remembers. She has something to remember you by.' Her voice deepened and took on extra scorn. 'Common whores and one of my own servants! Where is my gallant knight now?'

He pulled on his boots without ceremony, collected his cloak from the floor and made to leave.

'Please, Henry!' she implored, her tone altering completely. 'Love me. I am your queen and I need to be loved.'

A pity mingled with contempt swelled up inside him and he spared a thought – at once wistful and mocking – for that glorious day in the castle-city of Poitiers when he had come to claim his lady and honour his pledge.

'I must visit a friend,' he told her, and was gone.

The house of Thomas Becket was a monument to his prosperity and his hall was wide and clean and welcoming. Men of all ranks came to sit at his table, dining in style and receiving his own courteous, personal attention. In the Chancellor's house, the Chancellor wanted everyone to be entertained royally and his generosity knew no bounds.

As he sat at the head of his table, eating off gilded platters and drinking from a bone and silver tankard, he might have been mistaken for a king himself but for one thing. Thomas could not wear his new eminence lightly. Behind the kind, enquiring manner and the open hand was the ghost of what he had been and whence he had risen. The Chancellor of England had qualities of character which made him the equal of any in the kingdom, but he was bedevilled by the ostentation of the self-made man.

'Make way! Make way!'

Through the huge iron-studded doors at the end of the hall came a prancing horse, its hoofs scattering the golden-green rushes which covered the floor, its sudden arrival causing many of the assembled company to reach for their swords.

'Gentlemen ... Put up your swords,' called Thomas, un-ruffled by the incident. 'The King would speak with me alone.'

As the hall was cleared, Henry dismounted on to the table and dropped down beside his Chancellor. He helped himself to a plate of goose and sampled the wine.

'Eleanor is right. You do eat better than I do.'

Thomas smiled indulgently, used to these sudden appearances of his majesty. He saw the King examine some silver plate.

'A gift from the Abbot of Battle, my lord. Etched with the scene of Lazarus the Beggar, as you see.'

Henry began to roam around, picking up and putting down, admiring, appraising, assessing. Thomas had clearly become a man of great wealth in the time – almost three years now – that he had been Chancellor. He had trans-formed the office by dint of unflagging work and made it a position of immense importance. The King found no envy in himself.

'You have earned all this, Thomas.'

'I value your friendship more,' said the other, and there was a bluff sincerity in his voice. 'If I have earned that, I am indeed a fortunate man.'

Henry laughed and embraced him with rough affection.

'I can be at ease with you, Thomas. That is the greatest compliment I can pay a man. To be at ease in his company.'

'My door is always open, my lord.' He poured wine into

the king's goblet. 'And my heart.'

'Do you love me?' asked Henry, with a chuckle.

'Of course.'

'Yet you never love women! What sort of man are you, Thomas?'

'A chaste one, my lord. Are not you?' Henry's laughter filled the hall. 'Men cannot all be chaste. The church forgives them. Peter Lombard teaches that for a man to desire his wife with passion is to commit adultery.'

Henry's face clouded as he recalled his wife in her bedchamber.

'I call it passion : she calls it love.'

'True love is Christian love and passion is a sin.'

'I love nobody, Thomas,' admitted the King. 'It is the same with all my family. We love no-one. Not even one another. We're the devil's kind, you see. That is why I had to slap down my brother, Geoffrey, when he tried to claim Anjou. We are a family that thrives on hatred.'

'I shall be sorry if that is true,' said Thomas, earnestly.

Henry embraced him again, struck once more by the man's incredible straightforwardness. Thomas had his faults but his friendship was a source of pleasure and strength to his King.

Henry remembered something.

'The Queen was asking me . . . Do you like boys?'

'I hate all children. Boys and girls.' The Empress was blunt. 'There are two, then.'

'Our first-born died, mother. That was William. Now – this is young Henry, and this is our daughter, named after—'

'Take them away!' she snapped at the nurse. 'I hate brats.'

The nurse quit the solar and Henry was left alone with his mother. It was the spring of 1158 and the afternoon light in Rouen was excellent, but the Empress could work at her tapestry map no longer. She remained as haughty and alert as ever. Though her eyes were failing fast, her perception of events was still crystal clear.

'Why do you talk of Ireland, Henry? It is a land of rain

41

and bogs and barbarians.' She sat rigid in her great leather chair. 'Where is your policy? You campaign against the Welsh and lose half your army. Now you babble about Ireland!'

'It is ripe for conquest, mother.'

'And what about Normandy, Anjou, Aquitaine – do you think they are not ripe for conquest? My God, you have enough troubles here! Look to Louis. He must come before Ireland!'

Henry wondered if he had ever loved this martinet.

'Louis has been busy,' she warned. 'Those daughters of his. The ones that should have been yours.'

'It was the price of my divorce,' he said, defensively.

'A high price – and stop fidgeting! Louis has betrothed them to the houses of Blois and Champagne – your rivals to the throne of England. Look to the future, Henry.'

'If you have any advice, mother ...' Did this carved marble statue of a woman have any real emotions?

'Take a leaf out of Louis' book. Trap him with marriage.'

'Young Henry and ... ? The name escaped him. 'My son and the daughter of Louis' second wife. Their son – my grandson – would be King of France *and* England.'

'And for her dowry?' The Empress had worked it all out.

'The castles of the Vexin!' he exclaimed.

'Yes – the castles between you and Paris. That is your security. Ask for the Vexin back.'

Doubts began to steal into Henry's mind and he became restless, fiddling with his bonnet.

'Louis would never agree. How could I persuade him to part with the Vexin? He is not such a complete fool. He has not forgotten Poitou and Aquitaine. Louis is too wary of me.'

'Then you must not go, my son. Send your best counsellor. Send someone who can dazzle France. Send someone to parade the wealth of England so that Louis' mouth hangs open. Send the most able and cunning man you have.'

The embassy which Thomas Becket led through the streets

of gaping Paris in June, 1154, was a study in flamboyance and magnificence. Guards and trumpeters led the mighty procession, each dressed in the scarlet livery of the King. Eight massive wagons followed, drawn by five dappled horses apiece, and bearing the Chancellor's personal effects. Behind them came the carts, loaded with English food and beer to be presented to the French. Then came twelve sumpter horses, then the array of the huntsmen, then the astonishing sight of two hundred and fifty men-at-arms in march formation, singing lustily and waking all Paris with their cheer and bravado.

The mounted cortège was equally stunning, the knights resplendent in their coloured surcoats, their destriers sleek and well-groomed. In the person of the Chancellor, riding last on a superb black stallion, the parade reached its summit. He wore jewelled gloves, golden spurs, and a vast, silver-threaded cloak that shimmered in the sunshine. Surrounded by the gaudy, multi-coloured robes of his courtiers, this imposing man, with the Great Seal of England dangling around his neck and with an air of supreme authority in his brow, seemed to represent the very pinnacle of elegance and power and fabulous wealth. If this was but the Chancellor of England then the King must be truly awe-inspiring.

France was duly dazzled and Thomas brought his negotiating skills into play. In the fullness of time the young Prince Henry, aged five, was betrothed to Princess Marguerite, aged three, daughter of Louis VII and his Spanish wife. The castles of the Vexin were to change hands again and the Empress was given some balm for her ailing eyes.

Three and more years passed. Battles, treaties, alliances and diplomatic wrangling kept Henry at full stretch. His Angevin Empire, extending from the border of Scotland to the Pyrenees, survived threats from without and opposition from within. More sons put deeper lines in Eleanor's face and brought more frost into her marriage. Thomas Becket continued to astound, whether as soldier, ambassador, collector and dispenser of revenues, or genial host.

Death signed its autograph across these years with vivid clarity. In 1161 it added the name of the great and good Theobald of Bec, Archbishop of Canterbury, to its long scroll.

'My lord . . .' It was genuine hesitation.

'What *now*, Thomas?'

'Well, is it wise?'

'It is what I choose!' roared the King, slamming his fist down on the oak table. He mastered his ire. 'It is what I *choose*.'

They were in a room in the main keep of the castle of Falaise. It was March, 1162, and England had been without a Primate for a long time.

'I understand your anxiety . . .' began Thomas.

'You have never crossed me before,' accused Henry, his freckles becoming bright specks of anger.

'But to name *me*, my lord . . . I am so unworthy. You have seen into me and must know what a worldly person I am. Archbishop Theobald – God rest his soul – told me that I was not for the Church. He said to me that—'

'God's wounds!' yelled Henry, hurling a chair against a wall with enough force to shatter it. 'Will you listen to what *I* say?'

Thomas glanced down at his clothes which were as splendid as ever. He gave an amused, self-deprecating shrug.

'They would never accept me, my lord.'

'They will do as they are told. If the German Emperor can give the office of Chancellor to the Archbishop of Mainz, then I can make my Chancellor an Archbishop.'

The lawyer in Thomas began to quibble about the nature of the precedent, and then he finally came to the truth.

'I would hate to lose your friendship, my lord.'

'You never shall. You know me, Thomas.'

In that instant Thomas understood the perils and the conflicts that must lie ahead for him. The friendship between the King and himself – meaning so much to both – could never be the same again. The real tragedy was that

44

Thomas perceived this while the King most certainly did not.

'You will be my man and my Archbishop,' continued Henry. 'That is the unity I mean to have in England — between the Church and Crown.'

'If my lord wishes it to be so ...'

'Your lord and *friend* wishes it to be so.'

The magnitude of what was happening began to be borne upon Thomas. He was the son of a merchant and he was to be the Primate of all England. His ambition was stirred, his vanity was flattered, and his soul was profoundly moved. As he met the King's eye, he felt something else being roused deep down inside him, something that might not show itself yet but which would not be denied. Thomas Becket kept his combative instinct hidden behind a smile of thanks.

'I will be Archbishop, my lord.'

'You will be *my* Archbishop, Thomas ...'

But Thomas had already chosen which side he was to be on.

'I will be Archbishop,' he repeated.

The King's wishes carried all before them. Henry charged his justiciar, Richard de Lucy, with the solemn task of effecting his purpose. The justiciar crossed the Channel with Thomas and the young prince Henry, left them at Winchester, and went on to Canterbury in the company of three men of impressive rank. The monks of Christchurch were acquainted with the royal will and the implications of resistance to it were not concealed from the holy men.

As prior and monks conferred behind the locked doors of the chapter-house, there were fear and concern expressed by many. But the King had spoken and his dark shadow stalked them even here in their private sanctum. When the monks filed out of the chapter-house with tonsured heads owed, the prior announced their decision and Richard de Lucy congratulated them. It remained only for a convocation of suffragan bishops to pronounce its blessing at Westminster Hall and the preliminaries were complete.

On June 2, 1164, Thomas Becket was ordained. The following day he was consecrated Archibishop of Canterbury by Henry of Winchester.

There was great joy and thanksgiving in Gilbert Becket's old Cheapside house. Agnes was suffused with pride at the honour and distinction which her brother had brought to the family. A simple, uncomplicated, God-fearing woman, she had no insight into the meaning of what had happened.

CHAPTER THREE

It was a hazardous crossing. Treacherous winds blew the flotilla off course, a choppy sea made the small craft heave and roll, and the intense cold confined the men of the King's escort below decks where they groaned on their canvas beds. Queen Eleanor kept to her quarters as well, huddled in furs as she comforted her frightened children and cursed the need to embark on this voyage in the depths of December. To her the hostile weather was an omen.

King Henry remained on the castle deck, chiding or encouraging the mariners, seemingly impervious to the elements. In a tempestuous reign which had now lasted eight years he had never fled before a storm. Wrapped in furs that were soaked by the icy spray, he was kept warm by the heat of his wrath. When they eventually sailed into the harbour at Southampton, the wind had dropped, the sea was calmer and the air was almost mild. But Henry's wrath still smouldered.

Approaching him over the quayside was the object of that wrath.

'Welcome, my lord! Welcome to England!'

Thomas's greeting had all the old enthusiasm in it. He released the hand of the young prince and the boy ran to his father's arms. Henry ruffled his son's hair, listened to his chatter for a minute, then sent him across to his mother. He was alone with Thomas, his anger burning slowly.

'You will no longer be young Henry's tutor,' he said.

Thomas bowed, accepting the implied reproach with dignity. The King sounded at once annoyed and confused.

'*Why?*' he demanded.

'No man can serve two masters, my lord.'

'I charged you to remain Chancellor – yet you resign!' He was incredulous. 'Without my permission, you resign!'

Thomas spoke quickly, hoping to stem the King's rage before it took a real hold on him.

'Let there be no enmity between us. I am still your loyal subject. There is no cause for us to quarrel.'

Everyone on the quayside was watching and the presence of an audience soothed Henry slightly. It brought out the actor in Thomas, giving more pitch to his voice and enlarging his gestures.

'I served you faithfully and well, my lord,' he continued, arms outstretched. 'Now I must serve the Church. It will take all my time to do that properly, which is why I have moved to Canterbury. I am not able to be a good Chancellor as well, you must understand that.'

Henry was beginning to see reason in Thomas's action. The latter reinforced his point.

'Rather than be a bad Chancellor who is not able to discharge his functions as he should, I resigned my office. But I still serve my lord and King.' He spoke louder and slower so that all might hear. 'In everything I shall submit myself to you – excepting only my obligations to the church of Christ.'

Henry looked his Archbishop up and down, then walked around him.

'You do not sound like my Chancellor any more, Thomas.' He touched the canonical robe which the other was wearing. 'And you certainly do not dress like my Chancellor.'

Laughter from the onlookers seemed to take the tension out of the situation and Henry laughed, too.

'One of my monks rightly complained about my rich apparel,' said Thomas, beaming. 'I now wear the canonical garb from my student days at Merton.'

'A Chancellor who dressed like a King – and now an Archbishop who dresses like a student!' Henry's laughter stopped abruptly. 'Do you still love me, Thomas?'

'Yes, my lord.' Thomas was suspicious of the ease with which he spoke. 'Yes, I do.'

Henry's wrath had vanished now. A week of bitter, vengeful brooding had been obliterated by the frank smile of a friend. The King was eager to preserve that friendship.

'You must trust me. I shall not betray you, Thomas. If you are true to me – nothing shall come between us. Show me that trust and I shall never harm you.'

'We must each trust the other,' cautioned Thomas. 'Else we are lost. Quite lost, my lord.'

'Give me your hands!'

Before the waiting crowd Henry took the thin, pale, white hands between his own palms then gave the kiss of peace. The two men were at one again and Thomas's sudden resignation was forgiven and understood. He was to remain tutor to the King's eldest son.

As they walked across the quayside together, talking in the old relaxed, amicable way, Queen Eleanor thought about the vow she had just heard her husband make. Poitiers flashed into her mind and cynicism hardened her heart.

If she had had the slightest affection for the Archbishop, she might have feared for him.

The impression of harmony between the two men continued into the New Year. On Palm Sunday, 1163, Henry went to Canterbury to walk in procession with Thomas. The man who had once led the glittering parade through Paris now wore his rich vestments with grim humility.

Henry had noted the physical changes in his Archbishop when they had met at Southampton but they now alarmed him. Obsessive fasting was turning Thomas into a stooping, emaciated creature whose skeletal fingers were forever clutched around his breviary. It transpired that Thomas had forsaken the lavish comforts of the Archbishop's palace for a tiny, cold room with thirl cloth at the window. On the bare pallet in the corner, Henry saw a knotted cord. Self-denial was matched with self-scourging.

The King tried to recapture earlier days.

'Hunt with us tomorrow, Thomas.'

'No, my lord.'

'Then we will play chess. You were the only man in England who was a match for me at chess.'

'I play no games now, my lord. Recreation is unbecoming.'

After observing Thomas's austere life at first hand, Henry was not surprised to learn that his Archbishop invited thirteen beggars into the cathedral each day, washed their feet himself, then fed them and sent them off with a penny. It was of a piece with the new, self-denigrating Thomas. Henry could not help thinking about the silver plate, so treasured by his friend in earlier days, etched with a scene of Lazarus the Beggar.

A change of appearance and a change of heart in Thomas was bound to lead to changes of another kind. They were not long in coming.

'Enough!' bellowed the King.

'My lord King. I have not finished,' protested Roger of York. 'I put it to you that—'

'Enough!'

The sheer venom made the Archbishop of York slump to his seat. Nobody in the packed Westminster Hall dared move a muscle as Henry descended and began to prowl around.

'I summoned this council to ask a question. Are men in holy orders to be subject to the laws of England as are other men?'

'With respect, my lord . . .'

It was the haggard Thomas, acting as spokesman on the delicate issue of criminous clerks. He and the King had already clashed over this, but he showed no caution. There was in fact a note of condescension in his voice.

'We do not see it as you perhaps do. The clergy are tried

in our courts and – if found guilty – deprived of holy orders. In our view that is sufficient punishment.'

'Sufficient punishment for rape and murder!' growled Henry. 'Such criminals should be deprived of holy orders then handed over to the secular courts for justice.'

'That would mean they are punished twice.'

'I will not have dangerous criminals protected by the church and given lenient punishments! It was not the custom when my grandfather was king – and I shall not endure it now!' His voice became a menacing hiss. 'Either you swear obedience to our royal customs or you refuse me. Which?'

The bishops looked to Thomas for guidance and he stared at his sovereign unafraid. He felt that the power of the church, as vested in him, was greater than any temporal power. Henry had to be taught this lesson in public.

'My lord ... we promise to observe the royal custom, as you have called it. Saving our order.'

'Saving your order!'

It was a cold snarl. Henry saw no trusted friend and counsellor before him. He was looking at open defiance and betrayal.

'We can swear to nothing that would transgress our sacred vows.'

Henry looked accusingly at each of his bishops in turn but all, except one, emboldened by Thomas's stand against royal authority, returned his answer. They would obey the king in all things – saving their order. Henry was livid with rage and stormed up and down shouting and waving his arms.

'You think that you are above my law, but you shall not find it so!' He opened the massive door to the hall. 'And who will help you then?'

As the door slammed behind the King, Thomas Becket permitted himself a faint smile of victory.

The victory was short-lived. Henry struck back at once, demanding that Thomas give back castles and honours he

held as Chancellor. When the Archbishop used legal loop-
holes to evade him, the King applied other pressures, setting
spies to watch his enemy, harassing him, working upon the
other bishops – Roger of York, Gilbert Foliot of London,
Hilary of Chichester – to turn them against Thomas.

Three months after the Council of Westminster, Henry
convened another at Clarendon, in January 1164, attended
by peers of the realm as well as bishops. The result was the
Constitutions of Clarendon, sixteen articles which bound
the Church hand and foot and which attested the supremacy
of secular law. Cowed and beaten, the bishops gave verbal
oaths of assent, Thomas among them. Less willing to affix
his seal to the documents, he had to be cajoled and bullied
into doing so. Immediate repentance followed, Thomas
believing that he had perjured himself. He suspended himself from officiating at mass and wore sackcloth and ashes.
Unimpressed by his antics, Pope Alexander III told him to
resume his duties.

Friction between King and Archbishop intensified to the
point where Henry vowed to cut his enemy down. The place
chosen was Northampton, the weapon selected was the
English law.

'I came yesterday, my lord King, in answer to your writ. I
hoped to greet you then, but you did not appear.'

'I was hunting,' said Henry, off-handedly.

'I pray then you will greet me now ...'

But the King was in no mood to give his Archbishop the
kiss of peace. Humiliation and destruction awaited Thomas
Becket in the Hall at Northampton and Henry showed no
mercy. Taking his seat on the dais at the end of the hall,
the King looked down the line of barons on one side, then
up the line of bishops who faced them. Thomas felt the
indignity of being kept waiting again.

'I am here to answer a complaint by John the Marshal.'

'He is busy at the Exchequer,' said Henry. 'I shall hear
the case myself. This court is now in session.'

Thomas glanced around the men who were sitting in

judgement upon him and quailed a little. Animosity showed in the faces of many bishops, a distant pity in the faces of his known friends.

'Thomas Becket ...' began Richard de Lucy, 'you have been summoned to appear at this council at the palace of Northampton to answer the charge that on the fourteenth of September, 1164, you failed to make appearance in the King's court in answer to a complaint by John the Marshal under Article Nine of the Constitutions of Clarendon. How do you answer?'

'I answer, my lord, that John swore falsely against me, using a prayer book and not a Bible. This answer was sent to the Sheriff of Kent before I was summoned. It was conveyed to him in person by four of my knights.'

'But you did not attend yourself,' emphasised Robert of Leicester.

'No, my lord Robert. I considered that—'

'My lord King,' interrupted Robert. 'I hold that Thomas be declared guilty of contempt of court and at the King's mercy. I call on the lord bishops here assembled to pass judgement upon him.'

There was a buzz of murmured protest, Henry of Winchester rising to argue that fellow priests could not pronounce sentence on an archbishop. He was quashed by the King who ordered the bishops to give a judgement.

'This is the first fruits of Clarendon!' said Thomas, wounded to the quick. 'So much for secular justice!'

The bishops had no alternative but to find him guilty. It was an embarrassing moment for Henry of Winchester.

'It means that all your lands are forfeit.' He saw a way to soften the blow. 'However a fine is sometimes accepted ...'

The King, Robert of Leicester and Richard de Lucy conferred with their eyes. A sum of five hundred pounds was agreed upon as the fine, the bishops – Bishop Foliot dissenting – standing surety for the Archbishop for this amount.

Thomas was relieved that his ordeal was over, but he had reckoned without the vindictiveness of Henry Plantagenet.

'We will go on,' said the King. 'Since all his lands are

forfeit, we must take account of other debts. As Chancellor he has the manors of Eye and Berkhampstead with £300 for their maintaining. As also—'

'It was spent, my lord,' bleated Thomas, 'on this and on repairs to the Tower of London.'

'I have no account of it.'

'My lord, I never knew—'

'As also! One thousand marks he borrowed from me at Toulouse. Five hundred marks from my own purse, and five hundred on my security from a Jew.'

'It was a gift and no debt!' insisted Thomas. 'Those sums were spent on your campaigning. I took Cahors and besieged Toulouse in your service. I led a company of seven hundred knights and—'

'As also!'

This was no trial for contempt of court. It was a death-grapple between two sworn enemies. Thomas could feel the hands at his throat and the King thundered on.

'As also! All the sums that he obtained as Archdeacon of Canterbury – an office he retained, against the custom, when he became Archbishop. As also – all the revenues of all the abbeys and bishoprics that fell to him during his time as Chancellor. As also ...'

'These sums are past assessing!' wailed Thomas. 'Nobody could say how much it all—'

'I'll take thirty thousand marks,' offered the King, levelly.

Panic made its way into Thomas's cool mind.

The figure knelt on hard stone in the chapel, its head bowed, its body in pain, its soul in distress. Words of prayer ascended to the altar and far beyond. Pride wrestled with humility.

'Oh my father, if it be possible, let this cup pass from me. But if it may not pass except I drink it, thy will be done. I sinned. And I was proud. Now you have humbled me. The world has turned away. Princes also sit and speak against me – as once they sat and spoke against your martyr, Stephen. Here we have no abiding city, but we seek one to come. Wherefore let us take upon us the whole armour of God – that we may be steadfast in the evil day. And at the end – having done all – stand!'

Thomas felt renewed, refreshed, almost transfigured.

'Have I told you the story, Thomas ... ?'

It was Henry's voice, haunting him, tormenting him, telling him a story he had heard so many time before.

'My great-great-grandparents, Thomas. He was a Devil. Robert the Devil, Count of Anjou. His wife was a witch. And very beautiful. When they went to mass, she always slipped away before the holy sacrament. One day the Count gave orders. Four soldiers held her and as the priest approached with the holy sacrament – she flew away out of the church. A witch, Thomas. Wife to a Devil. That is why we are the Devil's children.'

Thomas Becket against Henry Plantagenet, the Archbishop of Canterbury against the King of England, the Church against the Crown – and God against the Devil!

Henry and the barons reassembled in the hall to hear judgement passed. There had been a delay, Thomas claiming to be sick, but he had been commanded to appear that morning.

'My lord Archbishop ... wait!'

'You must not carry it yourself ...'

Brushing aside those who sought to stop him, Thomas Becket, a soldier in the service of God, swept into the hall with the great cross held aloft and scattered all before him.

'If the King's sword can kill the body – my sword smites the spirit! And it can send the soul to hell!'

Above the commotion, Henry's voice rose firmly.

'Well, Thomas, how do you answer?'

Inspiration made the words pour out of him in a torrent, and the King was forced to listen.

'My lords and my lord King. In honour and fealty I am bound to offer you obedience in all things – save what I owe to God. I decline this suit – nor shall I render account for any other case except for that of John the Marshal. I served my lord and King faithfully, both here and overseas, and gladly spent my revenues on his behalf. And when by divine permission and the grace of the lord King I was elected Archbishop ...'

Rapt attention on all sides, Thomas relishing his moment.

'I was released by the King and given free to the church of Canterbury – no longer subject to secular claims.' He continued quickly as the King bristled. 'Though in his anger he may deny this now, many of you know it – as do all the clergy of the realm. I pray, beseech and abjure those who know the truth to remind our lord King of it. I appeal and place my person and the church of Canterbury under the protection of God. And I appeal to the Pope!'

Pandemonium ensued. Henry yelled for judgement, the barons accused Thomas of treason, and a swirling mob took over the body of the hall.

'Stand back – at your soul's peril!'

Thomas swung the cross in an arc like a battleaxe, felling two assailants before making his escape through the door. Some of the barons chased off after him, others crowded around the King for his command. As the tumult died down, Henry seemed unperturbed by what had happened.

'Let him go,' he shrugged. 'Why should it trouble me? If he flees the country, it only proves his shame. Ranulf!'

'Sire ... ?' Ranulf de Glanville was at his shoulder.

'We shall go hunting in the morning.'

That night Thomas Becket left his hiding place in the Abbey of St. Andrews and journeyed through East Anglia to Kent. He left England, secretly, by boat and sailed into exile.

Henry spent Christmas of that year at Marlborough with his family. He spared a thought for the family of his late Archbishop.

'How many kinsmen?' he asked Bishop Foliot.

'Thousands. His family has been in England for many years.'

'Turn them out, Gilbert. All of them. Wives, husbands, children. Babies at the breast. Drag them from their homes and ship them out as naked as they were born!'

'His one sister is a nun, my lord. Mary of Barking.'

'She goes, too. I will have nothing of Thomas Becket's in my kingdom. I'll take the revenues of Canterbury and everything he owns!'

'Yes, my lord,' said Gilbert Foliot.

'Let him run to Louis! Let him squeal to the Pope! He shall not come back. Never!'

'Then who will sit upon the throne of Canterbury, my lord?'

A monument to his own self-esteem, Gilbert Foliot advanced his claim with a righteous smirk. Henry ignored it.

'Drive his family out! The kin of Becket have the mark of the leper upon them. Drive them out with the sword!'

Now in her early forties, Queen Eleanor remained a stately and imposing figure, but the passage of time obliged her to be more artful in the choice of clothing, hairstyle and perfumes. Her fading charms could still arouse her husband but his desire was always sullied with dynastic ambition.

'Come to bed.' He was an unsubtle lover. 'Christmas is the time for another child.'

'That would make it six in all. Seven, if poor William had lived.' She looked weary. 'I am too old to have more children.'

He lay on the bed, naked, unworried by the chill in the air.

'Do my children love me, Eleanor?'

'They hardly ever see you to find out. You race here, there and everywhere. England, Normandy, Maine, Anjou, Brittany, Poitou ... you ride like a man on fire, Henry.' She studied him, almost touched by his need for reassurance. 'They should love you. It is no more than a father expects.'

'Richard hates me. You have done that to him.'

'My Richard hates nobody,' she said, defensively. 'He is a dear, kind, sweet boy. A true knight in miniature to his mother.' Sadness softened her. 'I must have *one* knight at my command.'

'Young Henry, Matilda, Richard, Joanna, Geoffrey,' he mused. 'They will make my dominions secure with their betrothals. What does their love matter?'

'The people of England loathe you, Henry,' she sneered. 'They have loathed you from the first, long before you disgraced their beloved Archbishop. They think that all Angevins are barbarians. Ignorant, uncouth, unfeeling barbarians.' There was a vicious satisfaction in her tone. 'I know what they mean!'

Henry shook with mirth at this outburst, then pulled her to the bed and tore off her long, emerald-green gown.

'Let me plant another devil-child in your belly!'

The following summer Henry was ready to invade Wales with a large army. Soldiers had been gathered from all his continental dominions, mercenaries had been hired from Flanders, vessels had been brought from the Norse colony of Dublin. The King intended to march from Woodstock to set up his supply base at Shrewsbury. Before leaving he received a request for a safe escort.

'You are Walter de Clifford's child.'

'Yes, my lord. I return to Hereford to see my father.'

She was seventeen, schooled by the nuns at Godstow, unawakened, a vision of loveliness, a gift of fate. Henry concealed from her the fact that his army did not march near Hereford and she accepted the protection of his strong arm.

Foul weather saved the Welsh from certain defeat and turned the mountain passes into rivers of mud. His supply system in a state of collapse, the King was forced to retreat in disarray. He found compensations.

'Wales has given me you, Rosamund.' He was tender. 'I have lost two armies there, but I have gained you. Do you love me?'

'Yes, my lord.' Her tears confirmed it.

'Rosa Mundi. Rose of the world.'
Henry had at last found someone to love.

A rose, a thorn. As a new friendship grew, an old one declined into sourness. Thomas Becket nursed his rancour in the Cistercian abbey at Pontigny. He wore the white habit of the strict monastic order, lived on bran, lentils and water, and did his share of the gruelling daily tasks.

Study, fasting and prayer made him feel closer to God and it was in God that he placed all his hopes for revenge. Still Archbishop of Canterbury in spite of Henry's demands for his resignation, Thomas held out stubbornly for a complete vindication. The Pope, needing the support of England against the Anti-Pope, was less ready to insist on all that the exiled primate felt his due.

On a baking afternoon at the end of August, 1165, Thomas was working hard in the fields with the other monks when a messenger brought the news which had set every bell in Paris ringing with jubilation. Adela of Blois, third wife to Louis, King of France, had given birth to a son. The infant Philip Augustus Dieu-Donné was truly a gift from God, a saviour who would deliver his nation from its enemies.

A rose, another thorn.

Thomas was pleased with the news and added his prayer of thanks.

The four years that followed brought little comfort to Henry. With the Capetian succession now assured, France became more of a threat. Rebellion raised its head in Brittany, Aquitaine, England even, and the King was kept forever on the move.

Queen Eleanor saw even less of him and became even more embittered, her romantic yearnings crushed beneath the heel of his indifference. She gave him another daughter, her namesake, whom she loved; and another son, the dark-haired John, whom she disliked. The curly, fair-skinned, affectionate Richard was still her favourite child, a bold young knight who was already wedded to her chivalric ideals.

Relations with France worsened until warfare broke out. While throwing his armies against the borders of Normandy, Louis – along with the Pope – continued to petition for a reconciliation between King and Archbishop, but the rift remained deep and wide. Sympathy for Thomas was widespread among the common people of England, and Henry was constantly made aware of this.

Rosamund de Clifford was a rose among many thorns.

At Montmirail in January, 1169, France and England settled their political differences. The pious Louis finally brought Thomas and Henry together, and a semblance of friendship was seen.

'Come with me to England, Thomas,' urged the King. 'Return and consecrate Young Henry as heir to the throne.'

'Grant me the kiss of peace.'

'I need you, Thomas. Trust me. Trust me.'

'Grant me the kiss of peace first.'

But Henry would not and the reconciliation was only partial. Thomas stayed in France to brood and mutter and stand upon his dignity.

The dignity was sorely ruffled on June 14, 1170, when the young Henry was crowned in Westminster Abbey by the Archbishop of York. Thomas was incensed that a function which belonged exclusively to him should be discharged by his rival. Louis was incensed because his daughter, Marguerite, wife to young Henry, had not been crowned with her husband. The Pope was incensed at the high-handedness of the English Church.

His Holiness drew up sentences suspending the Archbishop of York and excommunicating Gilbert Foliot, Bishop of London, and the Bishop of Salisbury. These were sent to Thomas Becket who was authorised to publish them at his own discretion.

When Thomas met his King again a month later at Fréteval, he made no mention of the Papal action. He listened impassively while Henry swore to restore his lands, his wealth and his eminence.

'And my kinsmen?'

'They shall be welcome in my kingdom, Thomas.'

'Who is to make amends for the injuries you have done them?'

'They shall be welcome,' repeated the King.

Thomas looked searchingly into Henry's face. The man who was now protesting his friendship had once shamed him, abused him, hounded him and driven him out of England. He was the devil's child and had spat in the face of God.

'Give me the kiss of peace, my lord,' asked Thomas, concealing his thoughts. 'The kiss of peace which you denied me at Montmirail.'

But again the King refused. Thomas knew his way.

In November, 1170, Thomas Becket crossed the Channel in a small bark. Ahead of him went the letters of suspension and excommunication to be pressed into the hands of those involved. Thomas landed at Sandwich where he was met by a huge crowd of townspeople ready to defend him against the armed forces of Ranulf de Broc, sheriff and keeper of Saltwood Castle. In hurling his Papal thunderbolts, Thomas knew the clamour he would provoke.

A shock lay in store for him at Canterbury. Poverty and neglect had transformed his once splendid palace into a sorry ruin. It was a symbol of all that he had endured and it steeled his purpose. He was the instrument of God and he was up against the work of the Devil.

He set out for London to see the young Henry.

'He rode into the city with a company of armed knights! The whole of London flocked to see him!'

Gilbert Foliot, still breathless from the ride to Bayeux, let Roger of York take up the story.

'Thomas has been welcomed like a messiah, my lord King,' he warned, shaking a finger. 'They fight to be near him.'

'He is a dangerous man now,' added the panting Gilbert.

'While he lives, my lord King, I do not think there will be peace and quiet for you—'

'Hell and its angels! Tell me no more – I've heard enough!'

Henry was on his feet, struggling to control his anger. He had been spending a quiet Christmas with his family at the castle of Bur and this had happened. Suspension, excommunication, open provocation. Thomas was spurning his offer of friendship in the most final way. Henry felt his gorge rising and years of hatred and enmity give his words a mordant sting.

'I gave him *everything*. I took him from the gutter and I gave him everything.' He looked around the hall in desperation. 'Will no-one rid me of this low-born priest!'

Four knights left at speed.

Henry flopped into a chair and stared ahead of him. Why had it happened? Why had his closest, most trusted friend become his worst enemy? He had made a supreme effort to be reconciled with Thomas. This was cruel repayment.

On December, 29, 1170, Thomas Becket, Archbishop of Canterbury, walked slowly through the dark of his cathedral around the hour of vespers. Armed intrusion was at hand and the men about him begged him to find a safe hiding place. He showed no fear and went about his business calmly.

As he turned into the north transept four knights burst in and accosted him. They accused him of being a traitor and he answered them with resolution. Four swords swung and he raised no arm to protect himself. He died in a pool of blood beside a great stone pillar.

Denied the kiss of peace, Thomas had sought the hand of death. It gave him the ultimate victory over the king. While Thomas embraced immortality, Henry stood condemned for the rest of his life.

CHAPTER FOUR

Richard Barre was a serious man with no aptitude for laughter, and with a lurking fear of being the object of amusement himself. He was deeply hurt by the loud snigger.

'Do you find it so funny?' reprimanded Henry.

'I am sorry, father.' Young Henry swallowed another grape and nodded an apology. 'I am sorry, Master Barre. It could not have been amusing for you. To have crossed the Alps alone in such perilous conditions, and then to be refused an audience by the Pope.' He offered Richard a grape, which the latter refused. 'You were even snubbed by the cardinals.'

'What happened in the end?' asked his father.

'We eventually overcame these scruples, my lord king. We saw His Holiness. But at the very mention of your name ...'

It was well over a year since the murder of Thomas Becket and the name of Henry Plantagenet was still anathema to the Church.

'We could do nothing to any purpose,' continued the sombre counsellor. 'His Holiness was determined to place an interdict upon you and your lands. And he would have done so ...'

'But he took the bribes,' grinned Young Henry, with irreverence.

'They were very large sums.' Richard relaxed slightly. 'But you are out of danger, for the time at least.'

The King was offended and spoke with intense feeling.

'I lost a *friend* in Thomas. For forty days and nights, when they told me at Argentan, I could not eat, or speak. God grant you never know the torment of an action you are not able to call back. "If only I had not, if only I had not, if only ..."' He turned to his son. 'Thomas loved you, too.'

'I know,' agreed his son, solemn for a moment. 'He was like another father to me. When he returned to England and came to London, I refused to see him. Was that wrong?'

The King walked Richard Barre to the door.

'When the papal legates arrive here in Normandy, I shall have gone to Ireland. I will bring my authority and the authority of the church to that unholy land. It may make the Pope think more kindly of me.'

Richard Barre bowed and left him alone with his son. Young Henry was seventeen now, burly, handsome, energetic and with a true Angevin temper. Like his father, he had been educated by the best of tutors but he lacked Henry's abiding interest in books and learning. He was more ready to enjoy pleasure for its own sake.

'Why do you never come to mother's court at Poitiers?'

'We never agree.'

'Poitiers is fun. Your court is always full of scholars and soldiers and dull dogs like Richard Barre. I prefer some fun.'

'There is no fun in being a king,' emphasised Henry. 'Only blood and sweat and disillusion.'

'Power is fun,' argued his son. 'That is what I want. Give me England now. Or Normandy.' His father shook his head. 'Richard has Aquitaine. Geoffrey has Brittany. I should have something!'

'You will have it all – when I am gone.'

There was an awkwardness for an instant then Young Henry attacked the grapes again.

'So you go to Ireland, father. And I go to Poitiers.'

'To see what your mother is plotting against me.' Again, an awkwardness, dispelled by Young Henry's flashing smile. 'Give her my love.'

'Is there a message?'

'Make one up. You know what pleases your mother.'

Queen Eleanor was pleased to be at home again, presiding once more at her Court of Love in Poitiers. The sun-kissed days, the gorgeous foods and rich wines, the romantic setting of the castle itself enabled her to feel light of heart again and to surrender to a more beautiful world.

Poets, musicians and troubadours brought the spells of their art and she was subdued by their magic. What delighted her more was that her sons, too, were captivated by it all and nothing gave her more pleasure than to watch them – Young Henry with Marguerite, Richard with her sister, Alys, and Geoffrey with Constance – yielding to the soft, sly music of the dance.

She had the warm pagan spirit of the south and this was her element. It helped her to forget tiresome journeys to cold English castles and a husband who neither danced nor understood romance. It helped her to forget him altogether and to think of them as *her* sons and the creatures of her purpose.

The Archbishop of Sens stood on the steps of the cathedral, flanked by two cardinals. Henry came forward and knelt at their feet, one hand on the Bible and the other on the relic of the saint. Young Henry and his wife watched and listened, brought to Avranches to witness the repentance.

For the murder of Thomas Becket, which had shocked the whole of Europe, there could never be adequate atonement. But Henry had discussed the matter at great length with the papal legates. They had agreed on something which at least proved Henry's contrition.

'Here by the holy scriptures and by the sacred relics of St Andrew and in the presence of these witnesses, I do declare that I, Henry, King of England, neither ordered nor desired the death of Thomas, Archbishop of Canterbury, which was as grievous to me as the death of my own father....'

He paused, remembering Geoffrey of Anjou shivering with the fever on the banks of the Loire. His sadness then did not compare with what he had felt for Thomas.

'Still was I deeply troubled and shall continue in this anguish that some words I spoke in anger and vexation against the Archbishop, the flashing of my eyes and my distempered features may have prompted his assassins to avenge my wrath ...'

Reginald Fitz Urse, Hugh de Morville, Richard Brito and William de Tracy. Four knights who sought to do his bidding and who pulled the full force of the Christian world down upon his head.

'Because of this I now present myself for due correction. Trusting in your mercy and in the redemption promised by our saviour, Jesus Christ, I here acknowledge this my full and true confession of my sins against Thomas, martyr, of Canterbury.'

The Archbishop of Sens looked down his nose and spoke so that all might hear.

'My son, the sin you have acknowledged to us is very grievous. Will you submit yourself to mortification of the flesh?'

'I will,' answered Henry.

The Archbishop motioned two monks to prepare the penitent. They stripped off all his clothing above the waist.

'For the absolution of your sins,' intoned the prelate, 'it is decreed as follows. One, that you make oath of loyalty hereafter to our father, the Pope ...'

His Holiness had already instructed Henry to provide and equip two hundred knights to fight in the Holy Land for a year.

'Two, that the customs introduced by you to the prejudice of the churches of your kingdom you shall utterly abolish ...'

The Constitutions of Clarendon to be revoked – another victory for Thomas from beyond the grave.

'Three, that the possessions of the church of Canterbury you shall restore in full ...'

It would be costly. Thomas's flight had sent Henry into a paroxysm of confiscation.

'These things by the authority of our lord, the Pope, we do for the remission of your sins enjoin you to observe without fraud or ill intent. Which in the presence of these witnesses and in due reverence of the divine majesty you do now swear faithfully and honestly to observe hereafter.'

'I swear,' promised Henry. 'I swear it.'

Young Henry was called forward to swear to observe the terms of the charter of absolution. With his hand on the book, Young Henry swore the oath. The punishment began and the first of the monks brought the scourge down savagely across the King's back.

'Harder!' screamed the penitent. 'Never in rage again! Never in anger! Harder!'

As the monks took it in turn to flay the skin from his back and to make him twist and stiffen in agony, Henry tried to think of Thomas and the love there had been between them. The memories streamed through his mind in no particular order, rapidly shifting scenes that were linked by each stroke of pain – the embassy to Paris, a game of chess, the kiss of peace at Southampton, the gift of the gerfalcon, a lavish banquet on gold and silver plate, a ruthless attack on Cahors, a visit to Gilbert Becket's old house in Cheapside to please his friend, a hunt for deer through the royal forests, a progress through crowds down the Thames, a race on horseback, a good-humoured argument in Latin, a siege at Toulouse, the first Christmas court in England, a playful wrestle in the mud of a London street.

Henry heard Thomas's laughter again, enjoyed his wit, respected his counsel, marvelled at his honesty, smiled at his chastity, understood his ambition, relished his company.

'Harder! ... Harder!'

Thomas Becket had not lived like other men, nor did he choose to die like them.

'Harder! ... Harder!'

But the King's voice was a gasp now and went unheard.

As blood made rivulets through the scorched flesh of his back, Marguerite, his daughter-in-law averted her eyes, unable to watch the terrible punishment. Her husband had no such revulsion and noted each downward swish of the scourge with keen satisfaction.

'And was it painful?'

It was Christmas at Chinon and Eleanor was at table with her husband once more.

'Torment,' Henry sunk his teeth into a chicken.

'Father was very brave.'

'Eat your food, John!' snapped his mother.

Her dislike of the dark-haired boy had deepened over the six years of his life. John was selfish, cunning, quarrelsome, sulky.

'Father is *always* brave,' boasted the boy.

A glance from Henry made him carry on with his meal. The King stood up and stretched before wandering around the dining hall.

'It is all over. I am absolved. Free from it. Free from Thomas at last. I shall lead a new life from now on. I shall be a new man, Eleanor.' She seemed about to speak. 'Well?'

'I do not wish to argue at Christmas, Henry. Besides, it is the only time I see you.'

'You wanted it that way. We agreed to live apart. I gave you Poitou and Aquitaine.'

'No, *I* gave them to *you* when we married.' She was icy and dignified. 'They have simply been returned to me. I can now hold my court at Poitiers – with my angel, Richard, to watch over me.'

John sneered at this mention of one of his elder brothers.

'I took my Richard,' she repeated, 'and you had young Henry and . . . this one. The eldest and youngest.'

'What have you done to young Henry?' pressed the King, suddenly annoyed. 'He and Marguerite are spending Christmas with Louis. They would not come to me.'

'Louis is his father-in-law,' reminded Eleanor.

'You have got at that boy. Lured him down to that Court of Love or whatever it is called. You have been working on young Henry as you worked on Richard. I know what you have been teaching him in that academy of yours and it is not *Ars Amatoria*!'

'I teach a new code of conduct, Henry, and you could never understand it. Chivalry. The rule of women. The dedication of the knight to the service of his lady.'

'The same old nonsense!' he sighed.

'You have no romance in your soul, Henry. I am sorry for you.'

He caught her wrist as she raised a goblet of wine to her lips and spoke with seriousness.

'I want to live at peace, Eleanor. You said that you wanted it as well.' He released her wrist. 'Do you?'

'I think I have what I want.' Her expression gave nothing away. 'And you, my dear husband ... well, you always have Rosamund.'

Rosamund de Clifford, his rose among thorns, mistress of the House Beyond the Gate at Woodstock, where she looked after the two children she had borne him. There had been some romance in his soul. Rosa Mundi, his rose of the world.

Animation seized him and he was on the move again, grabbing a chicken leg, pouring more wine, kneading John's shoulder.

'I want to see all my family again!' he announced. 'We shall arrange a reunion now that we have something to celebrate.' She looked blank. 'I am negotiating another marriage. For John.'

The boy began to giggle.

'I am meeting the Count of Maurienne in the New Year. It will be a chance for us all to get together again. One happy family – a king and queen with their sons and daughters.'

John's giggling became hysterical and he was sick over the floor. It was not the best way for a potential bridegroom to behave.

Limoges, the ancient captial of Limousin, was an impressive city built of stone and sited on the banks of the meandering River Vienne. It combined a quaint charm with a sense of solidity and this seemed to make it an ideal place for the business in hand. Prince John was to be betrothed to Aalays, the infant daughter of Umberto, Count of Maurienne. It would be at once a union of hearts and a strengthening of the Angevin empire.

Henry was in buoyant mood, therefore, as he rode

through the twisting streets of Limoges towards the castle in the old part of the city. He was at the zenith of his power, and on his way to finalise an astute diplomatic manoeuvre. He had done his penance for the death of Thomas and was free of the burden of guilt. He was about to see his family again.

'It is not fair!' stamped young Henry.

The family gathering in the Great Hall was neither as happy nor peaceful as Henry had hoped. The terms of the marriage settlement had annoyed his eldest son, who was interrupting the banquet.

'John is designated heir to the throne of Ireland and that is enough!' insisted young Henry, still on his feet.

'Sit down!' ordered his father.

'Everything you have given John has come from me!' wailed the other, strutting up and down behind his chair. 'Ireland. His estates in England. And now you give him three castles on the borders between Richard and me – Chinon, Loudun and Mirebeau!'

'How did you know about that?' asked Henry, who had not published the details of the settlement to his family. 'Oh. I see.' His eye had fallen on Eleanor. 'Your mother told you.'

'Sit down again, please,' suggested Eleanor with a graceful gesture of the hand. 'We are here to celebrate, after all.'

Young Henry glowered before taking his place beside his father. He glanced across at John, who had taken a malicious pleasure in the proceedings. Young Henry's wound continued to fester.

The feasting continued and the musicians brought their soothing touch to the evening. Henry began to relax again, even to enjoy the occasion. He looked around the table with the satisfaction of a man surveying his domains. They were all there – young Henry and his wife, Marguerite; Matilda with her own Henry, Duke of Saxony; elegant Richard with his betrothed, Alys of France; Joanna, with her betrothed, the heir to the Sicilian throne; Geoffrey, Duke of Brittany, with his betrothed, Constance; young, pale Eleanor with her mother's flashing eyes; and John, the youngest and most wilful of them all.

There was someone else whose presence brought joy to the King of England. Raimund of Toulouse had come to pay homage, recognising the suzerainty of Henry instead of that of the King of France. It was a moment of real triumph for Henry, whose empire now extended from the northernmost tip of Britain to the southernmost border of France.

'I hear that you must pay Umberto five thousand marks.'

Eleanor, queen of the Court of Love, liked to know the financial implications of a marriage. She was able to move from romance to reality with chilling ease.

'In instalments,' explained Henry, watching someone further down the table. 'Small price to pay for fiefs between Aquitaine and the Italian border. When John marries, we shall control the Alpine passes.'

'You are still anxious to please His Holiness, then?' she said with wry amusement. 'I loathe John. He will make Aalays a dreadful husband.' Her manner was hard now. 'I suppose we shall have to toast him, though.'

Henry was on his feet in an instant, jumping on to the table athletically to attract attention.

'Are your wine cups all filled?'

Servants scurried with jugs of choicest wines.

'I want to ask you all to drink a health.' His buoyant mood had returned. 'To the youngest of the Plantagenets, John, Lord of Ireland ... and to his small wife ... still sleeping in her cot, but we shall think of her ...'

Everyone in the room had risen with two exceptions. John was entitled to remain seated but the sulking young Henry was not.

'We are going to drink a toast!' The king was roused.

His eldest son was sullen, ignoring even the whispered chiding of his wife. He would not drink to his brother's health.

'I *order* you to drink a toast!' Henry dropped to the ground to confront the offender. 'We are here to honour John and his bride—'

'Then I will leave, father!'

'Stay!'

The atmosphere was suddenly charged, father facing son in a contest of wills. Richard decided to declare his allegiance.

'I will leave as well, father,' he said with a mock bow.

'Stop where you are!'

Young Henry, Richard, who else would defy him? He looked across at Geoffrey and found no comfort there. Three disaffected sons – two risking an open challenge to his authority. He knew where to look for the cause of it all.

'Do not look at me like that, Henry,' laughed Eleanor. 'It is not my fault. You have forgotten what the Empress, your mother, said about your sons before she died. They are hungry falcons.'

'Hungry and ungrateful falcons,' growled Henry.

'To tame a falcon you must keep it hungry. But you have fed them on scraps of land, on lumps of power.'

Henry tested his authority one more time.

'We are going to drink at toast . . .'

Young Henry, then Richard, then Geoffrey poured the contents of their goblets over the floor.

Henry II, King of England, was renowned for his sudden departures and unpredictable dashes across his territories. But he had never left anywhere with such unceremonial speed as he quit Limoges. Well before dawn the next morning, after frenzied packing, his train followed him at a canter through the great arched gateway of the castle. Alert to the danger that was all around him, the King wanted to be in a less vulnerable spot.

He rode north up the Vienne and reached Chinon, most beautiful of all his castles, and a fortress of reassuring solidity. Chinon was one of the castles willed to Henry's brother, Geoffrey, and it had come to the King on the death of his brother. Set in the very heart of his continental dominions, it seemed an appropriate place in which to seek safety.

The danger now revealed itself in its true guise. Young Henry fled the court as it came within sight of Chinon and headed for Paris to ally himself with Louis. It was the first move in a planned rebellion.

'You are my prisoner.'

Eleanor, disguised as a man, had been caught trying to flee from Chinon. She was bitter.

'I have always been your prisoner, Henry. You rescued me only to lock me in a dungeon yourself.'

'Where are the girls – Alys, Joanna, Constance...?'

'At Poitiers.' She was quietly triumphant. 'But that is all you will find ...'

The hungry falcons showed their claws. Richard and Geoffrey joined their elder brother's revolt against parental authority, and the King of France supported them. Rebellion broke out in the west, then in England, then in the south. Henry faced the severest crisis of his reign.

He was equal to it, confounding his enemies by speed of movement and unexpected attacks. The coalition formed against him was shattered and the mild-mannered, dithering Louis decided that it was time to leave the field, disgraced by Henry yet again. At the end of the year, the renegade sons came to discuss peace terms at Gisors.

Young Henry was still boastful and arrogant, Richard was still unwilling to concede defeat, Geoffrey demanded the release of the female prisoners. No peace was made and the hostilities resumed in the New Year.

Henry sailed to England where the rebellion had been given fresh impetus by the support of King William of Scotland. He took his prisoners with him, confining Eleanor in Salisbury Tower, Marguerite in Devizes, and Alys and Constance in Winchester.

At the height of the revolt in England, he found time for a visit to the shrine of Thomas Becket in Canterbury.

'I did not mean to kill you, Thomas. You know that. I have done my penance. I have paid that debt....'

Dressed only in a shirt, he crawled forward over cold stone to prostrate himself between flickering candles.

'Teach me how I should pray, Thomas. God has never answered me. Only the Devil grants my wishes and his gifts are hollow ...'

His voice took on an almost piteous whine.

'Eleanor is cold, she does not love me. Rosamund is dying – she can no longer love me. She has gone back to Godstow and taken her vows. My sons raise their weapons against me because they do not love me. They only love power. I want them to love me for my own sake. I want them to love their father as sons should. Teach them to love me as you loved me. ...'

Henry looked up and tried to find faith. When Thomas had been murdered in his own cathedral the common people came to dip their hands in his blood. The miracles began, the shrine was erected, the pilgrims came in their thousands. Henry tried to be one of those pilgrims, believing in the miracles, trusting to a power that was greater than anything he could know.

'If you still love me – If I can be forgiven, Thomas – then give me a sign. I came to you barefoot through the streets. I was flogged, I fasted, now I pray. Let there be peace between me and my sons. Give me a sign. If there is any love for a lonely man there in heaven – show me a sign. ...'

That night Ranulf de Glanville awakened the fatigued Henry with the news that the King of Scotland and his army had been captured in one fell swoop.

The sign had been given. Another miracle had come from the shrine of Thomas Becket.

Within a month, the invigorated Henry brought the English rebels to their knees. One by one they were humbled and came to swear their loyalty – mighty Bigod, Ferrars, the haughty Clare, Mowbray, the Bishop of Durham. It was a signal victory for royal authority over baronial independence and Henry emphasised this point at once. Castles were confiscated and feudal powers reduced so that barons would henceforth remember that they were mere subjects of a king.

The war ended in Normandy. Louis was marching on its capital, Rouen, with a large army when the ubiquitous Henry dropped out of the skies and set up his standard. Feeble, indecisive, conscious of his personal safety, the King of France turned tail and ran home to Paris and prayed.

Three sons met a father once again at Gisors and this time their submission was final. Henry was magnanimous in victory. His treasurer pronounced his verdict on the revolt – 'So the mighty have learned that to wrest a club from the hand of Hercules was no easy task.'

'Why have you brought me here, papa Henry?'

Alys was shy, beautiful, apprehensive, irresistibly young.

'I want to show you something.' Torch in one hand, he led her along. 'It is my little secret.'

They were in the cloisters at Winchester Cathedral, near an arch that was covered by a sheet suspended from scaffolding. It was cold and unwelcoming and their voices echoed in the darkness.

'Let us go back to the others. *Please*, papa Henry.'

Her fear only made her more appealing. She was frailer than her sister, Marguerite, more delicate, more refined, more exquisite.

'You must see my fresco first.' He grabbed the sheet. 'It is almost finished.'

With a sharp tug he pulled the sheet away from the scaffolding and exposed the large, vivid fresco. He held up his torch so that Alys could get a better view. She seemed puzzled by it and even more eager to leave the place.

'I had it done when Marguerite was crowned with Henry. Do you understand it?'

The fresco showed an eagle being attacked by four eaglets – two at it pinions, one at its breast, one at its eyes.

'An eagle – devoured by its young. Four eaglets, Alys. Not hungry falcons. Four eaglets who will tear my heart out.'

He grabbed her arm and thrust her close to the mural.

'No, papa Henry! Please! Let me go!'

He had noticed her when she first came to his court as a child. He had watched her grow into a bewitching loveliness. Alys was wasted on Richard with his ideals of chivalry and his ignorance of passion. Alys must be his. He took her face in his hands.

'You're the Devil's creature, Alys. Beautiful, beautiful.' His face was contorted in pain for a second. 'Give me some comfort, Alys! Please, *please*, give me some comfort!'

She knew it was wrong and guessed at the terrors that would follow but she did not resist him. His pain was met by her pity and she forgot her vows to Richard.

'Alys, little maid of France. God will forgive us. They want to eat my guts ...' He was in her hair, her clothes. 'The eaglets who devour the eagle ...'

It was over quickly and their nakedness was a mark of their guilt. As Alys wept and the King soothed her, the hungry eaglets watched.

CHAPTER FIVE

Taillebourg was impregnable. The castle itself, massive and forbidding, stood on a huge rock which made it inaccessible on three sides. On the fourth side was the township, itself protected by triple walls, triple ditches, and the unassailable confidence of its inhabitants in their own security. Geoffrey de Rancon, who commanded the great fortress, feared the approach of no man. He had a garrison of a thousand men and unlimited supplies of food. Taillebourg was quite impregnable.

Richard, Duke of Aquitaine, had other ideas.

'Destroy them! Burn them to the ground!'

He watched his men set fire to every house in the village. The small church was still smoking as Richard led his forces to the next venue for destruction.

Every village, farm and dwelling in the vicinity of Taillebourg was obliterated. From the battlements of the great fortress, the furious Geoffrey de Rancon could see mile after mile of scorched earth and desolation. When the arrogant Richard pitched his tents under the very ramparts of the town, Geoffrey organised a sally to disrupt the siege operations. But Richard was prepared for the attack and proved himself the finer general, repulsing the enemy and seizing control of the town gates.

With ferocity and daring, he made himself master of the town. Two days later the castle itself surrendered and its walls were levelled to the ground. Taillebourg was no longer impregnable. The Duke of Aquitaine had subdued yet another rebellious baron in his territories, and earned himself fame. No place was safe against the skill and determination of this man.

Richard left a firm imprint upon the memory of the people of Taillebourg. When the first batch of prisoners was taken, he decided their fate with a peremptory nod.

'Cut off their hands!'

In that same year of 1179 two kings met at the shrine of St. Thomas in Canterbury. Louis VII, frail, anxious, already failing, had come to pray for the recovery of his dying son, Philip Augustus. Henry II, still carrying the painful leg wound which had troubled him for so long, watched as the old man struggled to his feet.

'I have prayed for another miracle, Henry. God will not let my only son die.'

'What have the doctors told you?'

'Nothing. It happened when Philip was hunting – he got lost. A charcoal burner brought him home next morning. My son seemed so strange. So weak and listless.' Louis looked around for a moment. 'It is a fine cathedral. Thomas talked about it a lot.' He was sad. 'My first visit to England. Only this would have brought me.'

He staggered slightly and Henry steadied him with an arm.

'You need rest, Louis.'

'It is all over now!' promised the other with sudden conviction. 'We have struggled too long, Henry. It is all past.' He brightened. 'When Philip is well and has been crowned, we shall go on our crusade. The two most powerful kings in Christendom. Together! That would scare the infidel. Saladin would tremble when you and I rode into Jerusalem.'

'Yes, he would.' Henry leaned on his stronger leg.

'But you will not come.' There was pathos in Louis's voice. 'You have promised but you will not come.'

'There is never time. So much to do. Never time . . .'

Louis was silent for some minutes as if gathering his strength. There was a tentative note in his voice.

'My daughter, Alys. She is betrothed to Richard.'

'So?' Henry's manner was brusque.

'People wonder why you have kept her in England so long. She is twenty years of age. Richard should marry her now.'

'Richard would not be much use to any wife!' He had heard many rumours about the hero of Taillebourg. 'Thank God you only have one son, Louis.'

'Have a son . . . if he lives,' murmured Louis. 'But Alys . . .'

'Do not worry about her. Think of Philip.'

'Philip, my son, my gift from God. He will live now. I shall see him crowned, Henry. I shall.'

Another miracle came from the shrine of St. Thomas the Martyr. Philip confounded his doctors and made a complete recovery. Plans were made for his coronation, but his father was unable to be present. After an exhausting and thankless reign of forty-three years, the fragile old man passed away in his sleep. In 1180, his only son, not yet fifteen, became King Philip II of France.

'You're hurting me,' she complained.

'Give me your mouth again, Alys. Your kiss.'

She let him writhe on top of her again and felt the rough

77

hands squeezing her breasts once more. He was coarse, sweating, inconsiderate. He stank of horses.

'No, Henry. Please ...' She pushed him away. 'You are too heavy.'

'Most women would be proud to bear the weight of a king.'

'You are getting fat. You do not take enough exercise. That leg of yours. It is making you fat and heavy.'

'But I am still alive, Alys! My blood still races for you! I am still young and strong when I am in your arms! I make you happy, Alys.' He grabbed her and forced her to lie beneath him again. 'I make you happier than any other man could.'

'Henry ...'

'Tell me. Tell me how good I am. Tell me how much I please you, my sweet.' His hands were everywhere, his sweat running off her thighs. 'I need you to tell me, Alys. Tell me now.'

'You are *hurting* me.'

'The very first time – some servant-girl in Anjou – I was good. My father laughed – he had watched it all. He said that I did it royally.' He was ready for her now. 'Let me take you, royally.'

'Do you love me, Henry?'

'Afterwards ...' he grunted.

'You do *not* love me. You only love *this*.'

Henry's mouth stopped hers and he took her savagely as a punishment, driving like a demon, biting, scratching, bruising. It was over in minutes and he felt contrite.

'I will marry you one day, Alys.' He could feel her scorn in the half-dark. 'You *shall* be my queen.'

'You do not love me, Henry. You do not know *how* to love.'

'They always talk about love!' he sighed, rolling on to his stomach. 'Always the same.'

'Did Rosamund ask you for love?'

His wound began to throb and his mind was cloudy for a moment. Rosamund de Clifford, his rose among thorns, had died some four years before at Godstow and he had found cause for many tears. Since that time Henry had been generous in his gifts to the nunnery and had visited the tomb of his Rosa Mundi on more than one occasion. He would let nothing besmirch her memory.

'Did you tell Rosamund that you loved—'

'No more!' His howl was more anguish than rage. 'No more!'

Alys had only been a child when Henry had called on Rosamund de Clifford at Woodstock. She had known nothing of the friendship, still less would she have been able to understand its importance to him. Yet now the name of his one true love was on her lips. Only one person could have told Alys the story.

Even here in the intimacy of their bed, Eleanor lay between them. She had struck at him herself, she had fought him through her sons, and now she was using another weapon.

'I shall marry you, Alys!' he shouted. 'I shall divorce that bitch of a queen and marry you!'

He held her close again and she did not mind his weight.

But Queen Eleanor remained a prisoner in Salisbury Tower, well-treated and living in comfort. She had ample time to reflect on the vices of her husband – on his cruelties, his infidelities, his intrigues. She was determined not to consent to a divorce. Richard had been invested with her Duchy of Aquitaine and a divorce would leave her without land or real status. Queen Eleanor clung grimly to a man she hated and hoped that her sons would one day strike him again.

'It will be painful, my lord king,' warned the surgeon.

'It already is painful, you fool! Go on – cut it clean!'

Henry was back in Anjou again, still plagued by the leg wound. They were in his old room in the castle at Angers but he had no time to dwell on childhood memories. Leg propped up on a chair, he steeled himself against the torture that was to come. Pain was so much easier to bear when penance was involved.

Young Henry, Richard and Geoffrey watched tensely as the surgeon, a short, stooping man, laid out a selection of crude instruments on the table. Their father's leg injury looked worse than ever – purple, swollen, angry. The surgeon chose a long, thin-bladed knife and warmed it in the flame of a candle. His incision was quick and deep and he was not perturbed by Henry's scream of agony. He carried on quietly with the task in hand.

'More wine!' gasped the King, holding out his goblet.

Richard filled it at once and stood by to refill it as his father gulped down the strong, welcome liquid.

'It was healed,' insisted Henry, mastering the pain. 'First it heals, then it swells.' He smiled grimly. 'But at least you can enjoy the sight of my blood.'

'I see enough blood,' said young Henry, looking away.

'Yes, at those tournaments of yours.' His father was critical. 'You spend all your time at tournaments. There are other things in life.'

'I know, father.' A rueful glance at Richard, before the eldest son continued. 'But I am not able to take advantage of them.'

'Tournaments are not a waste of time,' argued Geoffrey. 'William Marshall collects large forfeits for us. It is not just a sport. It gives us an income.'

Richard was almost supercilious.

'The tournament is an important part of a knight's training but it is not an end in itself.' He turned to Geoffrey. 'Nor should it simply be a way of making money.'

'Some of us have to get money wherever we can!' Geoffrey blurted out. 'Father does not give us—'

'Be quiet, Geoffrey,' ordered Henry, annoyed by the reference to the financial aid he had given to Richard. 'Your brother has done what I want in Aquitaine. He has put down the barons and that has been costly.'

Young Henry was unimpressed by the hero of Taillebourg.

'Let him stay in Aquitaine and continue his good work, then. I do not want him in *my* lands. He built a castle in Clairvaux.'

'It is on the border,' shrugged Richard.

'It should be mine!' The eldest son returned to his favourite song of complaint. 'I am supposed to have England and Normandy and Maine and Anjou – and I have nothing! Richard has Aquitaine and Poitou and yet he steals Clairvaux!'

'Don't bicker!' Henry looked down. 'Is it done?'

'It must bleed, my lord King,' explained the surgeon. 'To drain the wound.'

Henry sat back in his chair again and looked up at his three sons. The eaglets had grown and wished to be eagles in their own right. Young Henry was now twenty-eight, brash, disgruntled, impatient for his inheritance. Richard, two years younger, was the epitome of knightly virtues – courageous, honourable, self-sacrificing. By repute he was the best soldier, the finest poet and the most loved troubadour in the whole of Europe. Geoffrey, at twenty-five, was a veteran of tournaments and an able administrator in his dukedom of Brittany, but he had neither young Henry's thrusting personality nor Richard's romantic glamour.

'If you are not fighting your father, you are fighting each other. *Why?* You are brothers – you should love one another.'

All three were sullen and unconvinced. Geoffrey spoke for them.

'It would destroy the family tradition, handed on by you, father. Brother against brother – a legacy of hate.'

'God's teeth, do you want to bleed me dry!' yelled Henry at the surgeon. 'Bind the wound! And do it tightly!'

The man busied himself with a bandage and Henry rounded on his three sons. For almost a decade now they had been his surgeons, too, making incisions, draining his life-blood, enjoying a privileged position of causing him pain. He had taken enough of it.

'I did not build an empire to see you tear it up. And I will not throw you pieces to stop you snapping at my heels. When I am dead – and it will not be soon – you will have to learn to live at peace without me. So learn to do it now *through* me. You will swear allegiance to me. Each of you. On your knees!'

The three of them hesitated, slightly abashed. At length young Henry took the lead, kneeling before his father.

'I *want* to love and serve you, father. I have always wanted that. If only you would trust me.'

The King looked sternly at his next son, who knelt at once.

'I swear allegiance,' said Richard. 'And you can take possession of Clairvaux.'

Geoffrey knelt beside his two brothers and swore his allegiance. Henry dipped his hand in the blood which had oozed from his leg.

'We will trust each other. If you want blood to seal the compact – here's mine! I am your liege-lord now. Louis is dead and you owe your lands to me. You will not do homage to his son, Philip. Only to me. Do you understand that?'

The surgeon had finished binding the wound. The pain had suddenly ebbed away.

The unity which an angry father imposed upon three sons at Angers did not survive long. Young Henry and Geoffrey, jealous of the success and fame of Richard, formed a league with those barons who were chafing under the Duke of Aquitaine's iron rule. Fearing a general rising in the southern half of the Angevin empire, the King tried to reason with the hot-blooded rebels but their hearts were set on defiance.

In the spring of that year, 1183, the order which had been brought to Aquitaine was threatened by yet another family brawl. King Henry of England and Richard joined forces to subdue young Henry, Geoffrey and those barons in league with them. Campaigns were short, frequent, fierce. There was much side-changing, betrayal of allies, wanton cruelty. The house of Plantagenet maintained its traditions.

Henry was finding difficulty in the field. He could not ride or fight with anything like his old spirit, and it was

Richard who emerged as the superior commander. When he saw his son astride his destrier, leading his men in a charge, Henry admired him as a soldier. But he saw in the dashing knight no husband for the lovely Alys.

'You swore an oath.' The King jabbed a finger at him. 'You swore an oath to me at Angers!'

'I know, I *know*, father,' conceded young Henry. 'That is why I came to see you with William Marshal here. There have been some terrible misunderstandings. The Marshal will explain.'

'Misunderstandings!'

Henry's roar suspended the conversation for a minute or more. He was seated behind a table with Richard, both of them in full armour. Henry remembered another occasion in this city of Limoges when he had faced defiant sons across a table.

'Misunderstandings?' he repeated. 'We send two envoys and you butcher them. I came to parley with you and they shot arrows at me. Were these misunderstandings?'

'Yes, my lord King,' said William Marshal. 'I am sorry about the arrows. You were not recognised by one of our defenders.'

'The arrow lodged here – between the links. Another one wounded my horse. So much for misunderstandings!'

'I accept the blame, my lord.'

Young Henry had been cunning in his choice of William Marshal as a spokesman. A trusted knight and man of impeccable reputation, the Marshal had been appointed by the King as tutor to his eldest son. No-one could teach the martial arts with such authority. No-one could count on the respect of the King so confidently.

'If I might explain, my lord . . .'

But Henry was in no mood for explanations, even from the Marshal. He stood up, wincing at the pain from the old wound, and pointed to the castle in the distance.

'Geoffrey is in there with a thousand men. They've ravaged my lands for miles around. Is that all a misunderstanding as well?'

'My lord....' began the Marshal.

'Let *him* speak! He is not a child now. Let him speak for himself.' He sat down heavily. 'Richard and I are waiting...'

Young Henry came forward and there was deep anxiety in his face as if he were wrestling with his emotions. He suddenly unbuckled his sword and threw it aside.

'I *have* sworn an oath, father. I took the cross. When this is all settled, I will go on my crusade. It is too late to stop me now.'

Henry looked bemused. A son in rebellion against his father, now a crusading knight. He blinked at the Marshal.

'I shall accompany the Young King, my master, to Jerusalem.'

Richard looked envious, Henry seemed alarmed.

'The war is over,' promised the crusader. 'Geoffrey will make peace. He wants that, too. Here at Limoges we shall talk of peace. Our armies will be disbanded and we will swear allegiance to you.'

Young Henry spoke with an almost religious zeal. He persuaded his father that the rebellion was at an end.

Soon after the start of Lent, Geoffrey and young Henry left the castle of Limoges and pillaged the holy places of St. Etienne, St. Martial, and St. Valerie. They stole the most sacred relics to pay their mercenaries and the fighting continued.

Young Henry did not live long to see it. Struck down by severe dysentery, he breathed his last on a bed of ashes at the Château Martel near Limoges. The heir to the throne of England was dead and Henry was bowed down with grief.

Geoffrey the Fair, his father; Geoffrey, his brother; William, his firstborn; Thomas, his friend; Rosamund, his lover; Matilda, his mother; Louis, his lord and adversary; and now young Henry, his anointed successor. All dead, all missed.

Richard became heir to the throne of England and the

balance of power within the family shifted once more. The Devil's children soon found another reason to squabble.

Despite all evidence to the contrary, Henry retained a naive faith in the family gathering as a means of promoting harmony and of making major decisions amicably. Early in the year 1184 he brought his surviving sons and their mother together once more. Around a well-laden table at the palace of Westminster, he arranged a family that had long ceased to honour and respect him. Eleanor hated him, Richard distrusted him, Geoffrey resented him, and John, now sixteen, disliked him enough to flatter him.

'You will understand that you have come here for a purpose,' said Henry, briskly. 'The arrangements to be made following Henry's death. I have had time to think about the future.'

Eleanor sat next to Richard and took his hand. Alys was not at the table and her fiancé showed no interest in seeing her.

'When the division of my lands was made, John was a child. Nothing was done for him. They even coined a name for him.'

'John Lackland,' grinned the youngest son. 'They noticed.'

'I am going to put that right now.'

Eleanor stiffened, suspecting what was in his mind. Geoffrey was apprehensive, Richard piqued, John hugely delighted.

'What do I get, father?' he asked, merrily.

'Richard is my heir now. He takes England and Normandy, Anjou and Maine ... Geoffrey and Constance keep Brittany.'

'What do *I* get father? John Lackland.'

There was a pause while Henry looked steadily at Eleanor.

'John will receive Poitou and Aquitaine.'

It was the stab of a knife to mother and eldest son.

'That is not funny, father,' asserted Richard, rising from his place. '*I* am Duke of Aquitaine.'

85

'You will get England,' reminded his father.

'England! Who wants England? It is a land of hovels and pigs and whores!' Richard was indignant. 'Poitou and Aquitaine are mine. I fought for them. My blood has soaked into their soil, and their soil is in my blood. Forever.' He knelt before his mother. '*Maman* gave them to me. Now I give them back to her. Here is my homage to the finest lady in the world – for the lands in all the world that I love the best.'

'Lovely speech!' said John with sarcasm. 'We should clap.'

Henry repeated his decision to make John the new Duke of Aquitaine but Eleanor did not hear him. She was holding a Court of Love in the Poitiers of her imagination and her golden knight, Richard, was pledging himself to her. Poitou and Aquitaine with their hills and valleys and forests were safe. Her knight would ensure that.

'Keep them for me, my Richard,' she said, kissing his forehead.

'I will, *Maman*. Until you return.'

'Keep them for me.'

'You will never see them again!' bellowed Henry. 'Never! Do you hear me? Never!'

The knight did not disappoint his lady. Arduous years of subjugating the Aquitainian barons had been an excellent preparation for a military commander. Richard had mastered the arts of warfare and shown qualities of bravery leadership that were to become legendary. Even with the help of the envious Geoffrey, John had no real hope of claiming his inheritance. The Duke of Aquitaine demolished all opposition and John's nickname stuck.

John returned to England to sulk and idle and make nuisance of himself to Alys. Geoffrey withdrew to his dukedom and lived for the tournament once more. He took one fall too many in the lists and was trampled to death by the horses.

Two sons left, two eaglets in the fresco, two children of the Devil.

'He was your son, Henry. Are you not sad?'

'I never liked Geoffrey,' admitted his father. 'Too selfish and cynical. Now my *other* Geoffrey – there's a proper man!'

Alys had met Henry's illegitimate son, the loyal, efficient Geoffrey the Bastard, now the Chancellor of England.

'But a father should love all his sons,' she insisted.

'Father loves me,' said John, chirpily. 'Do I get Brittany now?'

Alys moved away from him in disgust. John's attentions had been growing more and more irksome. She loathed his strutting self assurance, his sly tricks, his boldness with her.

'It brings me one step nearer the English crown,' observed John, breezily. 'Now if Richard could fall in a tournament ...'

'You are horrible!' she said, involuntarily.

'I know. But you will learn to love me, Alys. You will have to.'

There was a cup of poison in the way he spoke. Alys turned to Henry in desperation. He could never marry her to John?

'Well ... no, Alys ...'

His uncertainty brought the fire to her cheeks.

'I would never marry him. I want you, Henry, and I will be your queen. Eleanor is old. She will die soon and then we can marry.'

The simplicity of her vision had kept her the mistress of a middle-aged man for well over ten years. Henry was evasive.

'I have to think of all the possibilities, Alys. One thing I want before I die is to bring the crowns of France and England together. If we could have a child ...'

'You always talk of that. Never of love. You only want a child so that you can play your marriage games again.'

John sniggered, recalling his betrothal to Alys of Maurienne. The child had died soon after and Henry's diplomatic triumph had been nipped in the bud. John now found it a comical situation.

'Constance is pregnant,' noted Henry. 'Geoffrey may have a son from beyond the grave.' He stroked her hair. 'We shall have a son. I am still alive, Alys. Even with this leg, I am still *alive.*'

'Princess of France,' she sighed, 'and I am your whore. My brother Philip wants me to marry Richard.'

John burst into mocking laughter.

'Leave Philip to me,' reassured Henry. 'I will manage him ... Your hair, Alys. Still so lovely ...'

John was not laughing now. He was watching intently, feeling his father's lust for her stir in his own loins.

Philip Augustus, King of France, was a very different man from his father. While Louis had been gentle, ineffectual, almost apologetic in his kingship, his son was shrewd, calculating and unscrupulous. Louis had looked at the Angevin empire with mounting unease and sought to contain it: Philip regarded it with unrelenting hatred and set himself to destroy it. The old King of France had dreamed of celebrating mass among the saints of heavens: his young successors dreamed of becoming a second Charlemagne.

'Excuses! Always excuses!'

Philip's face was dark with resentment.

'Listen to me, Philip—'

'I have listened to you far too much, Henry. No more excuses. Alys must marry Richard now or there will be war between us.'

Henry's temper flickered for an instant but he controlled it. Still a martyr to restlessness, he limped up and down in front of the blazing fire, reminding himself how much he loathed this pompous young man. It had been so much easier to deal with the fumbling Louis. Henry tried his delaying tactics once more.

'If we meet again in three months—'

'No!' interrupted Philip, adamant. 'You gave your word. Alys was to marry or you would return her dowry. The Vexin – and this castle of Gisors.'

'I will not give you Gisors,' retorted the other. 'I have spent a small fortune on its defences. Two and a half thousand pounds. If you want Gisors, you will have to take it from me.'

'Then Richard must marry Alys,' said Philip, turning away.

'He must not!' Henry was forced to use his last argument. 'I will not allow it. There is a reason.'

'She is your whore,' suggested Philip.

'No! It is something else. About Richard himself.'

'Well?'

'I think you know, Philip.'

The King of France coloured, and tightened every muscle. There was murder dancing in his eyes as the other continued.

'Richard is at your court day and night. And why? Because you turned my son against me. You told him I planned to marry Alys to John and that sent him running to you. Yes, I know the subtle way you work, Philip. Sowing discord between Richard and me. That suits your purpose.'

'Come to the point!'

'He lives with you, Philip. Every day you and he eat at the same table. At night you share the same bed.'

'I would kill any man who slandered Richard. Even if he were the King of England.'

His hand was on his sword but Henry moved fast, holding him back against a wall for a moment. Henry had killed more than one man with his bare hands and he remembered now the satisfaction it had given him. He released Philip and spoke firmly.

'I do not want war – God knows! But if you threaten me ...'

He got no further. There was a loud knocking on the door and it swung open on its hinges. Geoffrey the Bastard strode in, pushing away the guards who tried to restrain him.

'I am the Chancellor. I must see the King . . .'

Geoffrey crossed the vast room at speed and Henry dispatched his guards with a wave.

'Majesties,' began Geoffrey, almost out of breath. 'I seek your leave to interrupt this conference. The Archbishop of Tyre is on his way to Gisors to see you. An outrider from his escort reached here just now.'

Geoffrey was so shocked by the news he was carrying he was trembling violently.

'Jerusalem has fallen to the infidel. Her knights are now in chains.' His next words were a croak of disbelief. 'The tomb of Christ itself may yet be taken.'

While the two kings tried to absorb the impact of the news, Geoffrey came forward and knelt before Henry.

'My lord King. My true father. As your bastard son let me redeem my honour. Let me take the cross.'

Henry, still coping with the implications, only half-heard him. Philip refused to accept the news.

'Rumours,' he said. 'There are always rumours.'

'The Archbishop will be here within the hour,' promised Geoffrey. 'Then you will learn the truth.'

Henry had made his decision and announced it with reverence and determination.

'It is God's sign. For peace between us!' He grabbed the reluctant Philip by the arm. 'We are the greatest kings in Christendom! We have a sacred trust! I will go to England to raise an army. Join me – to save Christ's citadel!'

Philip was defeated by circumstance. He had to give his agreement to Henry. The latter laughed.

'God mocks our folly. This is a sign from heaven . . . and to think we might have fought over a girl . . . !'

The news which had stunned all Christendom filled Richard with the light of certainty. It was the call for which he had been waiting for so many years and it spoke directly to his religious impulse, to his love of battle, and to his high sense of honour. Righteous indignation fired him, military glory enticed him, and the chivalric ideal guided him like a star. With characteristic haste, and without seeking his father's permission, Richard took the Cross in November, 1187. He swore to relieve the Holy Land at once.

But the Holy Land was forced to wait. Domestic feuding kept him in Poitou and Aquitaine for another year. When the war spread to the lands of the Count of Toulouse, Richard fought with such manic fervour that Toulouse itself seemed about to fall. Alarmed at this prospect, Philip of France intervened and invaded Berri.

Once again Henry bore arms against France and defended his empire with something like his old vigour. Berri had been Alys's dowry and it had great emotional significance for him. The war raged and the Holy Land remained in the hands of the Saracens. The two kings felt the weight of disapproval bearing down on them throughout the rest of Christendom. A peace conference was called at Bonmoulins in the autumn of 1188.

Henry was met by a rude shock.

'What are you doing here, Richard?'

'He stands with me,' said Philip, smugly. 'Richard and I have had private talks.'

Henry had come to face the King of France and was now forced to parley with his own son and heir as well. Richard had been won over by the craft and malice of Philip, who knew how to play upon his fears and to exploit the affection which the Duke of Aquitaine had for him. Henry felt the whip of treachery lash him once more.

'Stand with me, Richard,' he ordered.

'I met Philip on the way, father. I thought it would offend, if I avoided him. Since it is peace you seek – and out of courtesy– I joined his party.'

Henry did not accept this bland assurance. He noted that his son stayed beside Philip, flanked by the soldiers of France. His suspicions were confirmed at once.

'My wish is for peace and justice,' said Philip with beguiling smoothness. 'You must be true to your word, Henry. The marriage of Richard to my sister, Alys, in return for the

Vexin. Also . . .'

Henry sensed what was coming and his armour was suddenly a great weight.

'Before the marriage, I demand that you return to Richard his lands – Aquitaine and Poitou – together with Maine and Anjou. And that the vassals of these lands do homage to him at once as Duke of Normandy and as heir to England.'

'These are the terms, father.' Richard was determined.

'For God's sake, Richard, can't you see?' argued his father. 'Philip is trying to come between us. You have seen it so many times before and still it happens.'

'These are the terms, father.'

'Richard is anxious to go to the Holy Land,' added Philip in clipped tones. 'When he comes back, he does not want to see his brother John sitting in his place. Make his inheritance secure now. Marriage and full recognition.'

Henry was not listening. He was looking at the fresco which he had had painted at Winchester cathedral. Richard was the eaglet at his breast, gnawing its way to his heart.

'Stand with me, Richard!'

It was a final bid and it was in vain. Richard unbuckled his sword and swore allegiance on his knees before King Philip of France. Henry could do nothing but fume and bluster as his eldest son received the kiss of peace.

'What do you say to our peace terms?' asked Philip with a complacent leer. 'How do you answer, Henry?'

'With the sword.'

The two armies kept their distance for little over six months before hostilities were resumed at Maine. Philip and Richard led a strong invading force and chased all before them. Old, weary, unequal to the physical demands of warfare, Henry was forced to limp away himself like a wounded animal. To cover his retreat he confronted his enemies with a wall of fire at Le Mans, but the wind changed and the city of his birth was burned to a cinder.

It was an omen.

'Do you hear me?' His voice was faint, hoarse.

'Yes, father,' said Geoffrey the Bastard. 'I hear you.'

He crouched beside the litter on which the dying king was stretched out. William Marshal, head bowed, watched.

'Ranulf de Glanville, my justiciar, has the treasure keys ... Send mercenaries. Call my knights to service. I shall avenge myself ...'

He pulled weakly at a ring on his finger. It bore the insignia of the leopard. Henry handed it to Geoffrey.

'Take this, Geoffrey. You have been the best of my sons. The only one conceived in love. What I cannot repay, may God repay for me.'

The fever tightened its grip and he closed his eyes against the oppressive heat. Delirium visited him for a moment and the faces of those who had been closest to him floated before him – Eleanor, Thomas, young Henry, Richard, Geoffrey. Loved ones who had hated him, trusted ones who had betrayed him.

'Are you all right, father?'

The solicitous voice of Geoffrey brought him back.

'I hope that God makes you ... the greatest in the land, my son.'

'If God will restore your health, father, I ask for nothing more.'

Henry fought for his breath then found a final reserve of strength to motion William Marshal to him.

'My lord King ...'

'I sent to know the list ... the names of those who have joined my enemies. You have those names?'

'Yes, my lord ...'

The great lion had at last fallen and there were many who wished to be there for the kill. Henry wanted to know their names to pronounce his dying curse upon them. Only Geoffrey the Bastard would never turn against him. And John. It was some consolation in a world now full of enemies.

'Shall I read the list, my lord?'

But Henry had drifted off again for a few moments, his

mind possessed by thoughts of death. He remembered Geoffrey the Fair, on the banks of the Loire; young Henry at Château Martel; Geoffrey beneath the hoofs of horses; Thomas on the blood-covered stones of his cathedral. He pondered the manner of their dying.

'My lord....'

'Read the list ... Whose name is first?'

William Marshal looked down at the list and blanched.

'Christ help me!'

'Well...?'

'The first name on the list is your son's. Count John.'

Henry Plantagenet closed his eyes for ever so that the last of the devil's children could not peck them out.

An epic reign was over. A restless, dynamic, single-minded man who had forged a great empire was now just another corpse on the slab of history.

He died at Chinon on July 6, 1189, and his body was taken to the Abbey Church at Fontevrault for burial. Richard came to see the body but he did not stay for long. He was King of England now and he had somewhere else to be.

CHAPTER SIX

The procession began at the palace of Westminster and made its way to the Abbey along a path of woollen cloth. At the head were the clergy, bearing holy water, crosses, candles and censers, chanting as they went. Priors came first, then the abbots, then the bishops, all lending dignity and propriety to the occasion in the full splendour of their vestments. In the midst of the bishops were four barons, each carrying a golden candelabrum. Next came Godfrey de Lucy with the King's Cap of State, John Marshal with his golden spurs, William Marshal, now Earl of Pembroke, with the golden sceptre, and William Fitzpatrick, Earl of Salisbury, with the golden verge.

'This is heavy,' complained John. 'I shall be glad to put it down.'

He was one of three earls who came next in line, each with a golden Sword of State. John glanced over his shoulder, past the six barons carrying the royal robes and insignia, past William de Mandeville, Earl of Essex, bearing the great, jewelled crown of gold, to Richard himself.

'He does love this sort of thing. Father hated it.'

Richard was flanked by two bishops and covered by a silk canopy that was held aloft by four more barons. He did not look at the solemn procession in front of him or at the laity who walked behind him. His eyes never left the crown.

'It is always dark in here, even in the day.' John had passed through the portals of Westminster Abbey. 'And always as cold as death.'

It was not only his flippancy which set him apart from those nearest to him. Almost alone among the barons, he was not wearing the white cross of the crusader.

They had reached their places before the altar now and the coronation could begin. Baldwin, Archbishop of Canterbury, stood by in readiness as Richard approached the faldstool to kneel before a copy of the Gospels and the relics of many saints.

Richard took the oath with an easy sincerity.

'In the name of Christ, I promise these three things. To keep peace, honour and duty towards God and holy church all the days of my life. To do right justice and equity among my people. To banish evil laws and customs that have come into the kingdom, and to make good laws and keep them without fraud or ill intent.'

The bishops began to chant the litany, answered by the choir. Richard rose and moved to one side so that acolytes could remove his outer garments and leave him wearing only breaches and a shirt which was bare at the chest. Baldwin took the vial of holy oil, raised it above Richard's head, then allowed the amber liquid to pour over him.

When his head, chest and hands had been anointed, Richard had received the divine sanction for his kingship.

He was now dressed again, a linen cloth and coif put on his head, a tunic and dalmatic on his body, gold buskins on his feet. Baldwin went up to the high altar, took the King's Sword of Justice from a bishop, and offered it to Richard.

'*Accipe gladium per manus episcoporum ...*'

Richard took the sword and stood still while golden spurs were fixed to his heels and the royal mantle was fixed around his shoulders with a clasp.

John had become bored by it all and yawned, looking around for some distraction. He thought he saw something high up in the half-dark of the roof and he grinned.

The choir was singing with full voice as Richard approached Baldwin again at the altar. Grave and perspiring, the Archbishop spoke low.

'Pray to Almighty God that you may keep your oath and the vow you have made to take the Cross as a crusader.'

John saw it flitting again and stifled a laugh.

Kneeling once more, Richard looked up at the crucifix and affirmed his intention of keeping his oaths. Then followed a startling departure from established ritual as the new King, anxious to be crowned, got up and took the crown itself from the altar to give it to Baldwin.

The Archbishop staggered under its weight and some nearby earls – John amongst them – came to his assistance. But while the others steadied Baldwin himself, John put his hands upon the crown and was loathe to remove them.

Richard was on his knees again and Baldwin, helped by the earls, held the crown above his head.

'God crown thee with a crown of glory and righteousness ...'

John was looking up again, seeing it for the third time.

'... that thou mayest obtain the crown of an everlasting kingdom by the gift of him whose kingdom endureth for ever. Amen.'

The crown was lowered upon Richard's head but its

weight proved a problem once more, Richard almost losing it as his head bowed forward. The earls supported him and the crown was righted, enabling the choir to burst into 'Te Deum Laudamus.'

Sceptre in his right hand, rod in his left, Richard listened to Baldwin intoning in a reedy voice.

'The Lord bless thee and keep thee; and as He hath made thee king of His people, so He still will prosper thee in this world, and make thee partaker of His eternal felicity in the world to come.'

The kiss from the Archbishop, the turn to face the congregation, and Richard could now stand before his throne as King of England.

His moment of glory was spoiled. As he moved to the coronation chair there was a flapping sound from above and a flitter-mouse bat descended from the roof. It wheeled and swooped around the head of the anointed King until some of the acolytes tried to beat it away.

John was enjoying it all immensely now, pleased by the obvious discomfiture to his brother, delighted that the ordered calm had now given way to excited murmur.

When there was a sudden, unexpected, incongruous peal of bells, he could contain his laughter no longer.

'I did not see you there, maman.'

'I was there, my Richard,' promised Eleanor. 'I saw my knight crowned by Baldwin. He is getting feeble, your Archbishop.'

'He intends to come on Crusade with me, nevertheless.'

A look of concern came into the old woman's face and she took her son by the arms. She noticed that he was trembling.

'The cold,' he explained. 'England in September is not like Aquitaine. I miss the sun, maman.'

They were in his room at the palace of Westminster not long after the end of the coronation ceremony. Richard had changed into lighter clothes and was ready for the traditional banquet, where he could flaunt his kingship and relish all the pageantry of a royal celebration.

'Richard, do not go on a Crusade.' Eleanor was serious. 'I will get a dispensation from the Pope. John can go instead of you.'

'*Maman* ...'

'Yes, I know,' she sighed. 'Your mother is wasting her breath. You *must* go to the Holy Land. It is good and noble and dangerous. And your bravery against the infidel will be seen by the whole world. More fame, more legends. That is why you have taken the Cross.'

'It is not!'

Eleanor suddenly felt weary and lowered herself into a chair. She was wrinkled and white-haired now, a grandmother in her late sixties. But she retained the handsome cast of her features and the sparkling eyes. She also retained her grasp on the political aspects of the given situation.

'You must marry, Richard. You are past thirty now and at the peak of your manhood. You must marry and have children.'

The subject did not seem to hold any appeal for him, but she kept at him.

'You are a king now. A king must have a queen.'

'There is always Alys,' he said, off-handedly. 'We have been betrothed long enough.' He shook his head. 'What a disaster – her life and mine.'

'Your father was to blame for that. And for so much else.' She showed alarm as he shivered again. 'Is it only the cold?' She became practical before he could reply. 'We must find you a wife, Richard. Soon.'

'I am still pledged to Alys,' he retorted with a show of petulance. 'If I break my pledge to Philip, I must give back the Vexin! Besides ...' He was reflective for a moment. 'Besides ... I do not want a wife. Marriage ... does not appeal to me.'

'England needs an heir, Richard. Your son.' Bitterness came into her voice. 'Geoffrey had a son. Do you want little Arthur to succeed? Never! I did not spend the last sixteen years in prison ...' She summoned up more voice. 'I did not suffer the last forty years to see a child of Constance of Brittany inherit my lands – or worse, have them revert to Philip Capet in default of an heir.'

She got up and took his hands in hers.

'Go to the Crusade but put it off for a year. You could have ensured your succession before you leave.'

He shook his head then kissed her hand with gentle lips. There was something else that she had been waiting for months to ask him.

'How did he die?'

'Geoffrey the Bastard was there. He could tell you.'

'They say that blood gushed from his nose at Fontevrault when you stood by his tomb.'

'It may have. I did not stay long. He was my father and I paid my respects. That is all.' He considered. 'I did feel some guilt.'

'So that is why you wish to rush off to the Crusades. As a penance for your guilt over your father!'

'No, *maman*. I want glory, yes. I want to serve God and rescue the Holy Sepulchre, yes. But there is something else. If I go, Philip goes and it puts a moratorium on our quarrels. Also ...'

'Go on.'

'Do you remember all those stories you told me about your own Crusade: I listened for hours when I was a child. How you rode into Antioch with golden boots at the head of Queen Eleanor's Guard, your troop of Amazons.' They laughed together, then he was in earnest. '*Why* did you go?'

'Because of Bernard of Clairvaux. He set us all alight with his preaching. For the first time – the *only* time – my soul was stirred by a man of the church. I had to go.'

'You told me what St. Bernard said ...'

'He was Abbot Bernard in those days. Louis revered him.'

'His words to the crusaders – "... you now have a cause for which you can fight without endangering your soul; a cause in which to win is glorious and for which to die is but gain." I have never forgotten, you see. And *that* is why I am going.'

'Religious fervour? No, you have too much of the troubadour in you.' She began to wonder. 'They call you Richard – Yea and Nay because your word is your bond. Give me your yea or nay, Richard. Is that *really* why you are going?'

'Yea ... *and* nay.' He was light-hearted again. 'The banquet will be starting. Come, *maman*. I am ready to be King now....'

The coronation banquet was disfigured by violence. Richard had issued a proclamation forbidding Jews to attend the celebrations, knowing that anti-semitism was rife when a Crusade was being preached. But some of the wealthy Jews of London, wishing to honour their new King, brought gifts to the banquet. They were ejected by the barons and seized upon by the waiting crowd outside, who were instantly roused by the rumour that the Jews had been involved in a plot to murder Richard. The London mob fastened gratefully on to this excuse.

After killing or molesting the gift-bearers, the vengeful crowd stormed off to burn and wreck most of the houses in the Jewry. Many lives were taken, many scarred. The London massacre was to spark off similar actions in many other towns.

Richard was furious because the Jews were under his special protection – a privilege for which they paid dearly. Compassionate people bewailed the loss of life: the new King of England bewailed the loss of income. It summed up his attitude towards his realm all too accurately.

'Because he can raise money, *maman*.'

'But not William Longchamp, Richard. Not that scheming little crookback!' Eleanor spoke what most of England was thinking. 'You can never trust *him*.'

William Longchamp had been appointed Chancellor and the howls of protest were universal. An able, clever, manipulative man, William Longchamp had been working his way up through the royal administration for some time, making more enemies at each step of the way. Eleanor found the man cold, merciless and satanic.

'Geoffrey the Bastard was a better Chancellor ...'

Richard looked at her sharply. He had no love for his father's illegitimate son. Geoffrey might one day be a rival to the King himself and he lacked the one capacity that Longchamp had.

'He can raise money. Crusades are expensive, maman. William will help me to finance our holy undertaking.'

'But how? By selling off crown lands to the highest bidder. He is another Stephen.' Eleanor was rueful. 'Scotland has gone already – what would your father have said to that? Anyone but Longchamp, Richard. Turn your back on him and he will sell London.'

'*I* would sell London,' he said, simply, 'if I could find anyone rich enough to buy it.'

After only a few months in England, Richard sailed from Dover for France. The Crusade occupied all his thoughts and the enterprise depended on his partner.

'Stop fiddling with that machinery, Richard.'

A heavy cold made the King of France immensely sorry for himself as he sat huddled in quilts inside an old mill at Gue St. Rémi. March winds whistled outside and rainclouds threatened.

'There must be a way to make it work,' insisted Richard, studying the huge stone mill-wheel. 'To come back to my point ...'

Philip had been back to that same point a hundred times. He decided to come to terms. 'If I go to the Holy Land, will you—'

'Damn you for a woman, Philip! If, if, if! There is always an "if" with you. Listen, I will do everything *for* you. Will that make it easier?'

'Marry Alys.'

'As soon as we return from the Holy Land.' He was amused at Philip's surprise. 'I mean it.'

'And will you keep faith with me and not forsake me if I am in need, for my life?'

'Yes. And we shall share our conquests, one with the other. And if either of us dies, the other shall have his treasure and his army.'

'And if I should not return ... ?' asked Philip.

Apprehension welled up in him. He was a competent but undistinguished soldier, having none of Richard's belief in his own invincibility. Unlike his companion, he had no great compulsion to go to the Holy Land at all. The words of St. Bernard did not ring in his ears.

'If you should not return, Philip, I swear to defend your land as if it were my own.'

'I swear to that ... and peace between us.'

They exchanged a kiss, then Philip became malicious.

'Do you practice condescension on your grooms?'

In answer Richard returned to the machinery in the bowels of the mill and put his shoulder to it. He began to heave with all his might and Philip grew fearful.

'You'll break something and I shall have to pay for it. Leave it alone! This is my mill, it is on my land. Leave it alone!'

As he tried to pull Richard away, the latter gave a final push and the wooden lever shifted with a groan. Immediately the whole mill came to life, the wheels turning with increasing speed, the whole building starting to vibrate.

'It is a Devil!' shouted Philip, jumping clear.

But Richard was fascinated by it. He watched the millstone grind into its stone base with relentless force and marvelled at the power and noise and rhythm.

'Listen – it is like an army on the march! Such strength, Philip. Such power. It could hurl huge boulders, or turn rivers, or grind men into worms – it is God!'

He grabbed his friend playfully and brought him close to the millstone. Philip was almost frantic with terror.

'You brought me here to kill me,' he screeched, falling to his knees. '*Mea culpa, mea maxima culpa ...*'

The wind had got up outside now and it drove the mill on with a savage command, making the wheels race as if they had some devilish life of their own. In the crunch of stone and the creak of wood and the tremors that now shook the place, Richard seemed to find a strange kinship.

He was a Devil child welcoming a brother, seeing the beauty of destruction in the great rolling millstone, hearing the voice of evil grind and rasp.

'Flesh is evil – matter is evil – the world is a wicked creation! Life is evil – birth from the Devil – death is from God – death is the only way to good!'

Philip was muttering prayers incoherently as Richard hauled him up from the floor.

'Do you want to live for ever, Philip?'

The King of France stared into the jaws of death as his head was held close to the now shuddering millstone. Richard did mean to kill him and he was powerless to resist. He waited for the push into eternity, for the Devil's crushing embrace. Suddenly, the machinery stopped as Richard flung himself against the lever.

Philip was exhausted with fear, Richard laughing and panting and leaning against the massive white stone.

'I meet you at Vézelay at Easter.' Richard was heading for the door. 'And keep the truce of God!'

The King of France pulled his quilts about him and turned to the first of his soldiers who came into the mill.

'He is a Devil. Worse than his father. I thought for a moment he was going to rape me!'

The soldier was quite baffled at first but he had a good story for his companions later on.

Eleanor stood in the choir of the Abbey Church at Fontevrault and stared down at the mottled stone effigy of her husband. He was sleeping peacefully on his back in royal attire, eyes closed, face serene, hands – for once – still. A crown was on his head, a sceptre in his right hand, a sword lying to his left.

Henry II, King of England for thirty-five turbulent years, at rest on a pillow of cold stone.

An abiding hate had brought Eleanor to her husband's

tomb but it had left her now. She saw the youthful Henry of Anjou, riding into Paris with a sprig of broom in his bonnet. She saw the impetuous Count, galloping to her castle at Poitiers to honour his pledge. She saw the ardent lover taking her to their wide bridal bed.

> If all the world were mine
> From the sea to the Rhine
> I would give up all its charms
> If the fair Queen of England
> Lay in my arms.

The song had been sung the length and breadth of Europe in her honour and it haunted her again now. He had made her Queen of England and laid the world at her feet in token of his love.

Her reverie ended abruptly. There was no love in that heart of stone. Henry had ridden with the Devil in a ceaseless search for power. She had been one of the victims of his lust for greatness.

She carried the burden of her hate out of the Abbey.

Richard knelt in the cathedral at Tours to receive the scrip and staff of the pilgrim. His crusade had now begun. When he leaned on the staff it broke. Had he been present, John would have sniggered.

The bat, the unexplained peal of bells, the broken staff. Undaunted by these and other omens, Richard I, King of England and appointed saviour of the Holy Land, led the long column of crusaders on its joyous progress through the streets of Tours. Resplendent in full armour and wearing the white cross with a fierce pride, he sat astride his destrier and rode over a path of flowers which dancing girls were laying in his way.

Drums rolled, hearts pounded, voices were strong.

> Men of every Christian country
> Join in one communal stand
> English, Norman, French and German,

Bear the Cross, the common brand.

A parade, a spectacle, an army on the march, a mission. This was his true element and he rejoiced in every moment of it. Let cowards receive their gifts of distaff and wool and know they were merely women. Bravery itself, Richard would lead other brave men to the supreme test of their mettle.

> Hear them coming!
> Hear them waking
> Every good man from his bed!
> Hear them drumming!
> Earth is quaking!
> Shaking with crusaders' tread.

A cause in which to win is glorious and for which to die is but gain. Prestige in battle and a plenary indulgence. Fame on earth and a place in Heaven. England could look after herself.

> Glory, glorious crusaders!
> Christian soldiers bound for Zion!
> *Anglicorum Rex Ricardus,*
> *Duc des Normands, Couer de Lion!*

Behind him he left England, before him he saw God.

William Longchamp, Chancellor, bishop of Ely, justiciar for the south of England, stayed at home and paid for all this courage and good intention. He was thorough and remorseless, taking his court, his clerks and his dwarfish body to every town and city of the realm. Longchamp sold everything – royal manor houses, castles, lands and forests, decrees in equity, patents, offices. England was turned into an open auction.

There was scandal and complaint but the Chancellor was in no way deterred. He was free to increase his popularity because he was unchecked by rivals. Geoffrey the Bastard, much to his own disgust, had been elected Archbishop of York and forced to take priest's orders, thus rendering himself ineligible for kingship. Richard had further curbed his ambition by banishing him from England for three years. John suffered the same fate at the hands of his brother, but he was at last allowed to shed his nickname of Lackland. Richard granted him vast lands in the Midlands and the West Country, as well as the Norman county of Mortain. Marriage had made John the Earl of Gloucester and an unfaithful husband. His brother hoped that his new-found wealth would soften John's envy and disaffection.

So England suffered and protests went unheard. Eleanor was no longer there to raise her voice against the Chancellor. While Longchamp provided his King with money, she sought to equip him with a wife.

'Berengaria! Berengaria! Mother of God – it's the Queen of England!'

'Here in Pamplona? Never!'

Princess Berengaria and her nurse leaned out of the window of their tower room. Down below in the courtyard, Eleanor, poised but travel-sick, was being helped from her horse. The young Berengaria had a naïve charm.

'Why has the Queen of England come to see father?'

'Why else?' giggled the nurse with excitement. 'Because the King of Navarre has a beautiful daughter.'

The beautiful daughter blushed instantly and brought her delicate hands quickly to her face. The nurse adopted the patronising smile of the worldly-wise and instructed her young charge.

'Queen Eleanor is a very old lady. She would never travel all the way to Pamplona unless she had good reason. She has come to arrange a marriage. The Queen of England has a handsome prince called Henry.'

'He died years ago,' said the girl with scorn. 'Your troubadours are out of date. The Queen has only one Henry now and that is the King, her husband.'

Berengaria's own information was out of date. The kingdom of Navarre was distant from the centre of great events. Berengaria's view of what happened in France and England was a mixture of gossip, fairy tale and childish speculation.

'Henry may be dead,' said the nurse, easily. 'But the Queen has other sons. There is Richard.'

'Richard!' She almost swooned at the sound of the name. 'I saw him once when I was two. A Prince among Princes ... Richard!'

Richard was riding south with his crusaders, heading for the port of Marseilles. He had assembled a huge fleet from England, Normandy, Brittany and Aquitaine and sent it round through the Straits of Gibraltar so that it could await him at Marseilles. Ignoring the traditional overland route to the Holy Land – through the Balkans and the Byzantine Empire – he planned to sail on his crusade via Sicily.

On the ride south Richard found time to call in on Bertrans de Born, the knight of Limousin who was the finest minstrel of his day and the devoted vassal of Eleanor, former Duchess of Aquitaine. The warmth of their mutual affection kept the two men talking happily for hours, exchanging songs and poems that each had written and reaffirming their dedication to the Code of Conduct of the true knight. Richard put an arm around his friend.

'Come with me on the Crusade.'

'No, Richard.'

'Come on, come on.' Richard tried to cajole him. 'Why ever not?'

'I must not leave my poor parents.'

'Not even for God?'

'God has managed without me for forty years,' he rejoined, wryly. 'You go, Richard. You *need* to go.'

'But God has lost his lands,' argued the other.

'Where was God when I lost *my* lands?' asked Bertrans with sudden bitterness. He relaxed, laughed. 'You have grabbed everything on earth, Richard. Go and grab yourself a place in heaven. Go and spread death. Make life on earth a hell.'

Richard sat back and sipped more wine. He recounted the episode in the mill at Gue St. Rémi yet again.

'Philip thought I was going to murder him. He thought I was a Devil.' He paused, vulnerable before a friend. '*Why* am I going, Bertrans?'

'To be Richard Couer de Lion ...'

'But *why*?'

'To please your mother with your list of triumphs.'

'It is not enough.' Doubts crowded in upon him. 'I took the Cross because I had to and because my soul was stirred when Jerusalem fell to the infidel. I want to go, Bertrans. I need to go. But I am no longer sure why.' He hunched his shoulders. 'What do I *believe*?'

'What does any man believe?'

'I am in earnest, Bertrans,' he said with passion. 'At Tours it was easy. The blessing of the church, the banners, the lances held aloft, the music, the jubilation, the spirit of self-sacrifice ... We all believed then. But now ...'

Richard was no valiant commander at the head of an army of God now. He was a pensive man, looking into a troubled soul, questioning the faith that was dictating his life. Bertrans made a suggestion.

'Go to find out why you go, Richard. The answer is in the Holy Land itself.' He got up. 'More wine?'

'I know why you will not come,' said Richard, his playful smile returning once more. 'You are afraid. We shall have to find a distaff and some wool for our Bertrans.' He prodded him as he teased. 'He is afraid to fight. Afraid to be a man.'

Bertrans responded by jumping at his friend and the two wrestled happily on the ground for some minutes. Richard gave Bertrans a kiss then got to his feet again. It was time to resume the Crusade.

'I meant to say, Richard ... your mother passed through Limousin, heading south-west like the swans in winter.'

Richard sighed and knew his mother's purpose.

Stiff with rheumatism, Eleanor carried out that purpose in the conviction that she knew best for her son. She was in a draughty room of the palace at Pamplona, seated opposite Sancho VI, the fat, slow, deaf King of Navarre.

'It rained at St. Jean Pied de Port. It rained again at Roncesvalles. It rains on at Pamplona.' She felt her aches. 'I bring rain wherever I go.' She was aware of his deafness. 'Rain! It is raining!'

'Oh yes.' Sancho had appalling teeth. 'Rain.'

Eleanor felt that this dark, dank, thick-walled room had been specifically designed to appeal to her rheumatism. She decided to get on with the business discussion at once and spoke slowly and loudly at the portly monarch.

'I have come in the hopes of arranging a marriage.'

Sancho chuckled and his pot-belly bobbed up and down under his gown. He had already worked things out for himself and his glee was largely self-congratulation.

'I know, your grace.' His teeth affrighted her. 'My son and your very lovely daughter. I give a father's blessing.'

'Son!' He had no difficulty in hearing the exclamation. 'I am not looking for any son. I have had enough bother with my own. Besides ...' She suppressed the fond mother in her. '... my youngest daughter is plain. Very lovely in some ways – but plain.'

Sancho sat with wrinkled brow and tried to adapt his thinking to this new situation. She enlightened him at once.

'You and your Queen had a daughter ...'

'My wife is dead,' he said, cheerfully. 'I will show you the mausoleum I had built for her, your grace.'

'I thought this was it ... Now, listen to me, Sancho. I come about your little girl, Berengaria. Your daughter – my son, Richard.'

'Marriage?' He was surprised but delighted. 'Yes, yes. When they grow up.'

'I thought she had grown up. Berengaria!' She pointed

to a servant near the door. 'Fetch the Princess, man!'

The servant ran off and she turned back to Sancho, who was chuckling merrily to himself again.

'I must see this Richard of yours, too. Where is he?'

'Gone to the Holy Land.'

'Him, too?' His face crumbled. 'That is very sad, dear lady. We are in God's hands then.' He looked up, brightening. 'Ah, my daughter ...'

The Princess Berengaria entered shyly with her nurse, the latter fussing with the girl's hair and clothes.

'Berengaria,' beamed Sancho, on his feet, 'I wish to present you to the Queen of England who has recently lost her husband.'

'Oh!' Unsure of the appropriate comment, Berengaria settled for a graceful curtsey.

Eleanor appraised the girl with a mother's determination to find someone worthy of a son. The girl was small and dark with a pleasing olive complexion. She had a slender, attractive figure and its posture suggested diffidence. Her dusky hair was parted in the middle so that it lay smoothly on her head, framing the round, gentle and quite enchanting face. Eleanor spotted a defect.

'Stop squinting, girl. Men do not like girls who squint.'

'Stop squinting!' urged the nurse in a whisper, before retreating at Eleanor's approach.

'Show me your teeth.' She would never ask this of Sancho. 'Now your hands.' Eleanor seemed satisfied so far. 'You are painfully thin but we can see to that. One question. Are you a virgin?'

Berengaria looked offended and the nurse crossed herself several times. King Sancho did not seem to find the question out of place at all and answered it without hesitation.

'Oh yes. It is hereditary. All our girls are virgins – and some of our boys, too.'

'My father has answered for me, your grace,' said the girl with dignity. 'He was spared me the silence which my rank and name would have returned to such a question.'

Eleanor was impressed by the girl's air of modest reproof.

She considered for a moment and then came to her decision.

'I want you to marry my son, Berengaria. I have come to take you to him as soon as possible.'

Berengaria lost her composure and looked around for the nurse's support. The pace of life in Navarre did not usually admit of speedy decisions and she was fearful. There was another anxiety.

'I do not wish to marry your son, John.'

'John?' She turned to Sancho. 'Why is she talking about John?' She was facing the girl again. 'John is married to Isabelle of Gloucester. In a manner of speaking. He is now in Normandy plotting with Geoffrey the Bastard.'

'Bastard?' Sancho was disturbed. 'My daughter is to marry a bastard?' He was bewildered now. 'Please explain, your grace.'

'It would take far too long,' sighed Eleanor. 'The point is that the Princess will not marry John or Geoffrey the ... let us forget him. No, Berengaria ...' She went up to the girl and announced to her the great good fortune that was to befall her. 'You will marry my son, Richard, King of England!'

'Richard!' Berengaria was swaying with joy.

'King of England?' Sancho had heard that bit. 'A King and Queen.'

'To breed a line of Sanchos, Sancho!' She looked around with misgiving, then out at the rain. 'To bring this streaming mountain into the family! But he must *have* a wife.'

'Richard ... Richard ... Richard ...' Berengaria needed no persuasion. 'I saw him once. I loved him. I will make him love me.'

While his mother was wife-hunting in Navarre, Richard was standing among the Greek ruins at Marseilles and staring out into the pellucid Mediterranean. There were few vessels to be seen. Richard's fleet of over a hundred ships had not been waiting for him in the harbour as planned. It had been held up by the King of Portugal, who had persuaded the sailors to help him in his fight against the

Moors of Spain. Ten days had passed at Marseilles and still there was no great expanse of canvas on the horizon.

Richard was not annoyed by the delay. He had spent the ten days in a haze of languor and contentment. The boy's name was Milo.

'What are you doing, Milo?'

The boy, fifteen, was fresh-faced, brown-skinned, the epitome of boyhood. He was an urchin from Montélimar and Richard had found him irresistible. Milo was an angel, his innocence a joy.

'I am writing that letter you taught me.' Milo had been drawing with his finger in the hot, yellow sand. 'You promised my mother that you would teach me to read and write. And I want to learn.'

'You shall learn, Milo.' Richard had never seen such smooth skin. 'What are you doing now?'

'The same letter. You only showed me one.'

'Here is another, Milo ...' Richard let his finger displace sand. 'Come and see.' The boy moved closer to him. 'Now I have taught you two letters.'

'How many are there?'

'Eighty or ninety.' He laughed at Milo's pained expression. 'It is a pity to teach you anything and spoil your perfect innocence.'

Milo copied the letter in the sand, then rolled over on his back and put his hands behind his head. He was dressed only in breeches.

'You did not tell my mother you were a king,' he recalled. 'She thought you were just another crusader wanting ...'

'Wanting what, Milo?'

'My mother is a whore,' he said, easily. 'She is well-known back in Montélimar. I am the son of a whore, my lord.' His face puckered. 'Why did you bring me with you?'

'I told your mother – so that I could do better by you than she ever could. Educate you properly, feed you well, dress you ...' He was fascinated by the boy's narrow shoulders. 'I shall treat you like my own boy, Milo. You shall be page and son to me.'

Milo pulled himself up and leaned on one elbow, drawing again in the sand. He gave up and looked defeated.

'Eighty or ninety?'

'We have plenty of time,' reminded Richard. 'Since we have been in Marseilles, we seem to have all the time in the world.'

'I thought we were going on a Crusade.'

'We are.'

'We ran here. Why are we waiting?'

'My fleet has not arrived.' There was an evasive note in his voice. 'We shall go when my fleet is here.'

'You could hire ships from the merchants of Marseilles.' The boy had been talking to someone. 'Your Archbishop did. He has gone on ahead while you stay here.' There was simple curiosity in his eyes. 'Why, my lord?'

Richard could not hold the truth back from him now. It was the moment to tell him, here in this timeless place among the ruins.

'Why, my lord?'

'We are waiting for the King, Milo.'

'And why is he waiting?'

'Because he is in love.' He was kneeling beside Milo. 'In love.'

The boy was non-plussed. What he had heard did not accord with his idea of a king. Faint annoyance stirred him.

'A king should not have to wait for anything,' he argued.

'What can he do?' asked Richard, levelly.

'What he usually does.'

'It is not a usual situation!' Richard was irritable. 'What do you imagine a king "usually does", Milo?'

'He shouts for what he wants and someone brings it.' There was a disarming simplicity in his manner. 'Is that not right?'

'And what do they ask in return?' pressed Richard.

'Nothing. But sometimes they get a kick or a slap from the king. If they deserve it. A king asks, then takes.'

'He can hardly go about saying "I am in love", Milo.'

'He would not have to shout very loud.'

There was an awareness between them now and it made Richard's voice grow soft and searching.

'And if he shouts . . . they will bring?'

'Themselves, I suppose.' He was suddenly uneasy under the King's burning gaze. 'I do not know.' He recognised something he had not seen before and his voice faltered. 'There is nothing else . . . is there?'

'Why ask me!' yelled Richard, the mood broken. 'I started to teach you, but apparently you can teach me *everything*!'

Milo's tears welled then streamed. He ran off across the sand.

A soldier summoned Richard into the courtyard of the palace that night. He felt it was a matter of some urgency. Richard was only half-awake.

'I would not have bothered you, my lord King, but he was one of your own pages.'

The corpse lay broken and twisted on the ground.

'They found him below the town wall. He tried to jump. It is very high, my lord. He must have been trying to run away.'

Richard reached down and turned the boy's head over so that he could see the face. It was Milo, blood trickling from his nose. He held the boy close to him for a long time.

On the next day Richard hired ships from the merchants of Marseilles and set sail for Messina.

CHAPTER SEVEN

King Philip of France watched moodily from the quayside as the English fleet made a ceremonial entry into the port of

Messina. When his own vessels had slipped into harbour a week before, they had been met by indifferent stares or muttered curses. Yet that same polygot community which had resented his arrival was now according the tribute of its rapt attention to the approach of the King of England and his crusaders. Malevolence ate further into Philip's soul.

Ostentation may have marked Richard's first appearance in Messina but he had in fact journeyed to the island in a leisurely and relaxed way. After sailing from Marseilles in a hired merchant ship, he called in at Genoa and Rome before disembarking at Naples. From there he went overland to Salerno, a renowned centre of medicine, in order to consult doctors about the ague which was now troubling him with increasing regularity. He was not cured. Hearing that his fleet had finally reached the island of Sicily, he moved south to join it before making a spectacular entry into Messina.

Trumpets warned of his coming and then a hundred and more galleys put into port, fine vessels painted in different colours and hung with shields and standards and pennons. Richard himself, attired magnificently, stood on a raised platform in the leading ship so that all Messina might see him.

Philip saw him and scowled. When Richard came ashore to greet the French King, he was met by cold hostility.

The welcome which the citizens of Messina had given the English crusaders did not last long.

'Come here, you little fox.'

The man was drunk, excited, waving a bottle as he lurched after her through the arches. A Sicilian carnival was making the night ring with its noise and music and dancing.

'Wait for me ...'

He was disobeying orders in coming to the carnival celebrations, but the lure of cheap wine and dark-eyed Sicilian girls was too much for him. She had stopped in the shadows of an arch now and was smiling after her with flashing teeth.

'Now then, my—'

Before he could even touch her, many hands were laid upon him in the darkness. He was beaten, robbed and stripped. The naked body was left in the dust as his assailants went back to join in the tarantella. The crusader was one of several killed or mutilated that night.

Outside the Chapel of Reginald de Moyac, a Sicilian boy hid in a doorway. He was wearing a gaudy costume for the carnival and his face was covered by a mask. A big, powerful man with red hair crept up and grabbed him playfully, making the boy scream in surprise. He turned to see the crude lionskin which the other was wearing and recognised the hair. It made him stop struggling, remove his mask and droop his eyelids whorishly.

Richard pressed him against the door of the Chapel, kissed him full on the mouth, then thrust against him. The rotting timbers of the door gave way and man and boy fell into the Chapel. In an instant the boy had regained his feet and vanished. The King of England lay sprawled in a thick layer of dirt and bat droppings. It was no ceremonial entry this time.

The chapel was small, dimly-lit and almost filled by the tomb of the first crusader – a great, black, cold Angevin. There was the stench of decay in the air.

Richard struggled to his knees, his hands and costume fouled with the mess. He began to tremble with the chill of God and looked up at the crucifix on the wall. By the light of two flickering candles, the eyes of Christ pierced and accused him.

Overcome with contrition and trembling more violently, he hauled himself up on the side of the tomb and then pulled at his lionskin. There was a tearing sound and he ripped it off completely, standing naked before God.

The eyes of Christ continued to pierce and he could stand their accusation no more. Falling to the ground, he grovelled and cried and held his head low in submission.

'*Cela touche à la folie*,' observed Philip, as they approached the siege-tower. 'Not to be seen since Christmas? Living up there like ... Simeon Stylites! Does *he* want a sainthood as well?'

The Black Monk who accompanied Philip said nothing. They were at the base of the siege-tower now, walking under its massive, rough-hewn beams of wood.

'Is it the affection of madness, or the madness of affection,' continued Philip. 'I might be more convinced if he was not, at the same time, intriguing with his sister, Joanna, the Queen of Sicily.'

He began to ascend the first ladder, then thought better of it.

'You go first.'

He stepped down and let the Black Monk go up the rungs in front of him, relying on the weight of the church to test the ladder for safety. All seemed secure and he started the long climb.

'He knew his mother was going to Navarre! At the moment he was swearing loyalty to me! That is why he is hiding up there!'

The higher they climbed the narrower became the beams, the more unsteady the ladders and the sharper the tug of the wind. As they neared the top, the King of France looked down and saw the whole of eternity stretching out below.

They went on and clambered up into the bare structure of a room – wooden platform, one wall, hide roof – which surmounted the huge siege-tower. Richard was kneeling on the floor, gaunt, filthy, abject, dressed in a soldier's tunic and sackcloth leggings. A scourge lay beside him on the floor and the Black Monk noted its bloodied thongs with approval.

Philip regained his breath after the exertion of the climb then crossed the bare room to stand over Richard.

'You are like Thomas Becket – you take pride even in your humility, on top of a siege-tower in case nobody would notice!' His words fell on Richard like strokes of the scourge. 'Self-denial is the worst sort of pride – the Father here would tell you if he had not taken the vow of silence. It is the sin of self-hate, Richard, refusal to accept God's goodness, Christ's powers of redemption. Yes, your old heresy.'

Richard's head fell to his chest and his body sagged, but Philip did not spare him.

'What a traitor you are, Richard – Yea and Nay. You swear faith and then make a web of alliances against me. A sister in Saxony, a sister in Spain, a sister here in Sicily ... and the queen-spider, your mother, sits and spins.'

The sting of this last remark made Richard whip around and glare. He got up and moved to the edge of the platform, leaning against a thin wooden strut.

'I will not go to Acre without you. We begin the assault together.' He was peeved by the lack of reaction. 'I know where she is and who she is bringing with her. That old woman, who has outlived her time, crossed the Alps in mid-winter with the Devil's blessing, for the good brothers would not go out in the snow.'

Richard started, genuinely surprised at the news. Philip's sarcasm continued.

'I am not surprised that you are silent. The last word you spoke was a lie.' He saw that he had kindled a reaction at last. 'You swore to keep your vow to marry my sister, and the old queen – God and St. Bernard curse her! – is bringing you a princess of Navarre. You are false, Richard. False to your father, false to Alys, false to me!'

With amazing agility for one who had been weakened by excessive fasting, Richard leapt up and seized Philip by the coat, dragging him to the edge of the platform and thrusting him out so that he was suspended over space.

Philip was white with terror.

'You *lie*, Philip!' shouted Richard.

'I swear that your mother is coming. I swear. Father – tell him.'

The Black Monk, in some confusion, indicated that he

could not speak. Philip looked down again and feared for his kingdom.

'On my soul!' he cried out.

'On your soul, I am not false,' said Richard, with vicious emphasis. 'Alys was false, with my father. Alys bore my false father's child. Release me from my vow, Philip, or I will release you.'

His strong arms urged Philip further into space and the King of France conceded the argument with a whimper.

'I release you.' He was pulled back on to the platform. 'I release you, Richard ...'

The Black Monk came to his master to see if he could be of any aid and was waved away. Philip waited long enough to regain some of his dignity and then struck back.

'You will give me proof. You will return the Vexin and Gisors ... Richard, for what you have just done, I could renounce your fealty and become your mortal enemy.'

Richard turned away, angry, dissatisfied, weary.

'Take what you like and go,' he said.

In his mind's eye he saw his father and felt an affinity. As King and Black Monk descended the ladder, Richard spoke quietly to himself.

'*Par grace, mon père*! Now for all purposes, I am Henry. The only result of self-sacrifice is the sacrifice of self.'

The room in the palace of Messina was large, sumptuous and an example of all that was best about Moorish taste. Spring sunlight gilded the furniture and ornaments and enabled two of the women to bask in deep chairs.

Queen Eleanor was talking to her daughter, Joanna, widow of the King of Sicily. Berengaria was wearing an uncomfortable head-dress and sat perched awkwardly on a pile of soft cushions.

Joanna, a striking woman in her mid-twenties, had her mother's grace and regality. But she had none of Eleanor's abrasiveness or forthright manner. Gentle of speech, she remembered her own wedding.

'My dowry was a gilded chair and table, two gilded

trestles to support the gilded table, four-and-twenty cups of silver, four-and-twenty dishes of silver ...'

'Joanna – *tais-toi*.'

'I had to leave it behind,' Berengaria blurted out, apologetically.

'What, child?' asked Eleanor.

'My mountain. I could not get it over my mountain.'

She fidgeted with her head-dress, dislodged it and earned a sharp rebuke from Eleanor. Joanna at once came to her assistance and fixed the head-dress back in position again. Berengaria was nervously grateful. After a long time in the company of the outspoken Eleanor, the girl found Joanna both soothing and refreshingly feminine.

'Oh!' One look was enough and she had to avert her eyes.

Richard had come into the room looking like a young god. It was some months now since his self-imposed penance atop the siege-tower of Mategriffon and he had regained much of his weight. In his bright eye and clear face, there was no suggestion of the spiritual crisis through which he had been. He was Eleanor's favourite son again, her dashing knight, elegant, poised, manly.

After greeting him with a kiss she did not waste words.

'She is young but that does not matter if she can have children. Her teeth are sound and she is still a virgin. You must marry her before Lent. I am not able to stay.'

Richard was confidential, urgency in his tone.

'Maman, have you looked at her?'

'John and Geoffrey have broken their promises and returned to England. Longchamp has made himself even more detested than I thought. I am much needed in England.'

'You could have chosen somebody with ... something.'

'She has something – Navarre.' She was caustic. 'Do you want to marry for love, as I did? Folly, Richard.'

'We shall lose Gisors and the Vexin if I marry her.'

'Not if we keep Alys.'

'Philip *knows*, maman.'

'What can he do about it in the Holy Land? Perhaps he

will become a saint. Louis always wanted one in the family.'

'As long as Philip's away,' he mused, 'what can brother John do except build castles in Gloucester and frighten the Scots?'

'Leave John to me. I leave Berengaria to you.' She prodded him forward with her stick. 'Go on.'

'Does she understand?' he asked and got another prod.

Richard came over to Berangaria who did not dare to look up. Her attention was fixed on his feet. A third prod indicated that Richard had to make some declaration. He remembered something.

'What did you say her name was?'

'Berengaria ... the Princess Berengaria.'

She felt an upsurge of confidence and raised her head sharply to see into his face. The head-dress wavered again, she lost her balance, and the daughter of Sancho VI came sliding towards Richard's feet amid an avalanche of cushions. Joanna laughed, Eleanor turned away in exasperation and Richard felt a desire to be kind to the girl. He knelt beside her.

> 'There was a Princess of Navarre,
> Who could not see very far.
> She made a pet out of a flea ...
> And kept a pig for company.'

'That is a dreadful story!' she protested.

'Yes, but she was the only one who came well out of it in the end.'

Richard the Lionheart showed his teeth in a broad, winning smile and the little Princess Berengaria of Navarre was in love.

Acre had to be taken. It was the essential first step in the repossession of the Holy Land. The chief port and the largest town in the kingdom of Jerusalem, Acre had fallen to the might Saladin in 1187 and he held it securely for the next two years. Then Guy de Lusignan, King of Jerusalem, gathered a small army together and laid siege to Acre, pitching his camp a mile to the east on the hill of Turon. Guy could never hope to take the town with his modest forces but, sustained by his own bravado and reinforced by a steady trickle of crusaders from the West, he managed to complete the landward blockade. Denied access to the town, Saladin encircled Guy's camp and subjected it to a series of lightning raids.

The siege army was thus besieged itself. All that Guy could do was to hang on grimly for the arrival of Philip and Richard. Only with their support could a stalemate be broken.

The King of France arrived in April, 1191, and immediately helped to strengthen the maritime blockade of Acre, thus cutting its supplies off completely. Though afraid to attempt a general assault before Richard arrived, Philip was not idle. He set up a number of siege engines and battered sections of the wall with rams, concentrating on the area around the Accursed Tower. Again, a mine had been started.

All this was done in the face of enormous danger and discomfort. Apart from the stern defensive actions of Acre itself and the threat from the marauding hordes in the hills all around them, the crusaders had to cope with baking heat, flies, lizards, snakes, bad food and water, and disease. Philip had reached Acre during the period of the *khamsin*, the hot winds from the south which created swirling sandstorms of unendurable viciousness.

Hacked by swords, pierced by lances, consumed by Greek Fire, split by hooks, stuck by arrows, blinded by sand and tortured by disease, the crusaders of France had second thought about their venture. Armour which had been light in Vézelay now became an oven of lead, bodies which had been young and strong now became fevered and weak, spirits which had soared to the marching hymns now sunk low.

Acre had to be taken but the price of its fall was high.

*

The pavilion of the King of France was a dark cave of rest in the furnace of the desert. Outside, two soldiers cut meat off a dead horse; inside, Baldwin, Archbishop of Canterbury, stood in battered armour beside the ragged banner of St. Thomas. The prelate's voice was hoarse with fatigue.

'Your men watch us go out, they watch us return. The lords of France pass by us as Pharisees passed by sinners.'

Beneath a pile of towels and quilts in the coolest corner of the pavilion, something stirred. Philip, King of France, face blotchy and head swathed in a towel, peered at Baldwin in pain.

'Do you know what I've got?' He raised his head from his litter and looked at the doctor. 'What have I got? Tell him what I have got.'

'The arnoldia.' A pause followed the confident diagnosis. 'Though some physicians might call it leonardie.' Private anxieties nudged him. 'Let us pray that it is the arnoldia because I cannot cure leonardie.'

'All men suffer,' chanted Baldwin. 'It is glorious to suffer for God. It is more glorious to fight for God – if the soldiers of France would fight.'

'The French will fight under their king!'

The speaker was the proud Duke of Burgundy, one of Philip's principal lieutenants. He was scornful of the Archbishop, who had come ahead of Richard to Acre with a portion of the English army.

'We will fight when our Lord and King is recovered,' he added.

Baldwin broke into prayer and laid his battle-weary soul before his God. Philip was resentful.

'Stop preaching at me! I am here at least! Where is your King? Where is Richard? In Cyprus!'

He sat up and tore off the towel from his fevered brow. Great tufts of hair came away and Philip was hysterical.

'Richard has taken Cyprus! And I am here! Dying of the arnoldia.'

The doctor was a stickler for accuracy.

'With your grace's permission, if you are dying, it is leonardie.'

Richard stayed long enough in Cyprus to conquer the island and to marry Berengaria. The conquest was brilliantly conceived and carried out with vigour : the marriage was not his idea and it was undertaken without pleasure. The valiant commander was no loving husband.

The wedding took place in the chapel of St. George at Limassol. Berengaria, still shy and diffident, wore a yellow bridal dress. Richard, detached from the whole proceedings, wore a vest of rose-red, ornamented with crescents of solid silver.

When the service was over, Berengaria was crowned Queen by John, Bishop of Evreux, who was a long way from his see in Normandy. After the coronation, Richard took his young wife out into the bright afternoon to look at Mount Olympus.

Berengaria thought of her father. She was tentative.

'If we should ... if we should have ... if we should have *it*, shall we call it Sancho?'

'What?' He was only half-listening. 'Oh, I see. *Dieus!* Call him what you like. Anything but Henry.'

She looked up into his eyes and her love for him surged. Taking care not to squint, she smiled her devotion. He seemed embarrassed.

'Something is wrong?'

Punctilious about that kind of thing himself, he expected the same standards of excellence in others.

'Yellow does not suit you.'

Berengaria, Queen of England, began to squint. She felt the distance between Cyprus and Navarre. Sancho, her father, had always liked her in yellow.

'Do you see that great mountain?' He was pointing. 'It is called Olympus. The Greeks of the island say that it is heaven and the gods live there. It is not true.'

'My mountain has a name, too,' she said, wistfully. 'It is called Monte Perdido – because it is lost.'

She stood before an indifferent husband, lonely, helpless, doomed. If he sensed the tragedy of her situation, he did not mention it.

That night they talked frivolously for a long time to stave off the moment of going to bed. When they finally lay in the darkness, not touching, Berengaria thought about her mountain. Richard's mind was on Milo.

The English fleet sailed south-east for Acre and arrived in time to intercept and scuttle a Saracen supply ship. It was an important victory because fresh supplies would have added months to Acre's chances of holding out. On hearing of the loss of his ship, Saladin, a man inclined to prophecy, was heard to say — 'Oh God Almighty, now have I lost Acre!'

It may have been lost but it still needed to be won.

Richard was welcomed ashore by a cheering crowd. The legendary conqueror of Taillebourg was a master of siege warfare. He would soon bring Acre to its knees. As they saw the mighty siege-tower of Mategriffon being unloaded from a ship in sections, they took fresh heart and remembered their vows as crusaders.

Death and disease were among the first to welcome Richard.

'*Richard!*' It was a scream of horror and she positively leapt out of the bed. 'Your hair . . .'

They had been sleeping in his pavilion and the Queen had been first to wake. She had looked at his noble face, so loving in repose, and given it a gentle kiss, running a hand through his hair as she did so. It had come out by the roots.

'My what . . . ?'

He was half-awake and faced by a jabbering wife who was trying to dress herself in a state of panic. Her eyes were his mirror and he was horrified at what he saw. His face and chest were covered in scaly blotches and some finger-nails were rotting.

Hubert, Bishop of Salisbury, came in, saw the King, then hustled Berengaria out into the waiting arms of Joanna. The

French doctor was sent for and diagnosed leonardia and announced that it would be fatal. Hubert at last had a moment to deliver his message.

'Baldwin is dead, my lord.'

Notwithstanding the French doctor's certainty, Richard fought back hard against his fever, which was malarial in its effects. He refused to submit to its rigours and had himself carried about from place to place so that he could superintend the siege.

Richard discontinued any attempts to ram the walls. He saw at once that long-range fire was needed and set up his balistas and mangonels at strategic points. What made the mangonels particularly effective was the fact that he had brought from Messina some huge, flint-like boulders. One of these was hurtled with such venom on to the wall that it splintered and claimed the lives of twelve men.

While English crusaders manned their siege engines, French miners managed to penetrate the defences and burrow under the walls. They knocked their wooden props into position and awaited the signal to set fire to them.

If the garrison of Acre was worried by all this, it was horrified at the sight of Mategriffon being assembled piece by piece in readiness for a major assault. The monstrous siege-tower, now mounted on wheels, was a castle in itself, a timber giant who would soon come knocking on the town gates to demand entry.

Richard himself, still seriously ill, involved himself totally. His men had pushed close to the wall and built a screen of mantlets – hurdles covered in hide. This shelter was used as a protection for sharp-shooters and Richard liked to be among them, shivering on his silken litter, and picking off defenders with his cross-bow.

'I killed him. Straight through the brain!' Richard was delighted.

His arbelester was winding and loading his crossbows for him. Richard took the next one from him and selected a target.

'My father lived for hunting. Deer, mostly. I prefer Saracens.'

Another hit seemed to satisfy him and he asked to be carried back to his pavilion. On the way he yelled aloud to his soldiers.

'Four gold besants for every stone taken from the walls!'

His arbelester spoke against a policy of recklessness.

'My lord, last week you offered three and a lot of young men got themselves killed.'

'For the good of their souls!' sneered Richard, a new cruelty etched deep in his face. 'Put me down ... Drink.'

They were back in the pavilion now. Someone brought him wine and then the men left to resume the assault. Joanna came to Richard and indicated a silent Berengaria, who sat as if in a trance among the cushions. The King ignored his wife and talked about the Crusade with heavy sarcasm.

'It is all for the greater glory of God. All the working of Divine Providence. All this death. That is what Christ is all about. Signior God, you should be pleased with Acre – God's acre of saints! We restock heaven.'

'Give her a moment's peace.'

Joanna waited long enough to see that he had calmed down and then left. Berengaria remained motionless.

'What did you do today? Berengaria!'

She looked at him, a child waking from a sad dream.

'I wished.'

'I wished too, my queen. I wished that the siege would end, that we would march to Jerusalem, that we would sail home and have four sons and three daughters.' He was moved by her unhappiness. 'What did you wish, my sweet?'

'I wished it would rain.'

That same day the town of Acre capitulated at last. Richard the Lionheart had scored a signal triumph. He could now divide the booty.

'I will take the cross, Philip.'

'As your lord, I ought to have it.' He looked up at the crucifix on the wall. It was cracked beyond repair. 'A cross can not be divided, Richard.'

'Half the city, half the money, half the prisoners. When Saladin gives up the Cross and our people, we release them. That was the agreement.'

They were both on litters under quilts, two fevered kings haggling over the day's takings in the palace of Acre.

'Which part of the cross would you have, Philip? Hands or feet?' He considered. 'You can have it – if you will agree to stay here with your army for three years.'

'I am ill,' moaned the French King. 'My doctor advised me not to stay here.'

'He advised me to die.' Richard was amused.

'I respect his opinion,' muttered the other.

'Speak up, Philip! Tell me about these rumours. That you're making preparations to return to France.'

'I am *ill*.' It was the groan of a hypochondriac.

'To break your vow, your faith, your honour as a Christian king your duty to man and God – if it was true, you were no better than the Saracen who did *that*.'

He pointed to the defaced crucifix on the wall.

'I have heard from Paris that my son is ill,' said Philip by way of explanation. 'You cannot make me stay.'

Richard leaned over from his litter to confront his old enemy.

'Swear you will keep the truce of God with me, while I am on God's business here and you are on your own at home. You will not hurt Normandy, nor any of my lands, nor my people. In peril of your soul.'

Philip nodded to his soldiers and his litter was borne to the door with speed. Richard's men were too fast for him, rushing the other litter there first and blocking the exit.

'Swear!' ordered Richard.

'I do not have to,' bleated the other.

'Swear, Philip! In peril of your soul!'

'I swear it.'

There was a peevishness in his voice which did not bode well for the sincerity of his vow. On impulse he got up off the litter, shed his quilts, and stood above Richard in full armour.

'You see?' he boasted. 'I did not have to swear.'

Philip and his men left the palace at speed. Richard himself threw his own coverings aside and stood up on strong legs.

'You did.'

Triumph over the Saracens had been matched by triumph over his fever. Richard strode out into the courtyard of the palace to survey the captured town. His eye ran proudly along the English banners, then ruefully along those of the French. He stopped.

'Tear that standard down!'

Planted alongside the English and French banners was the tattered standard of Duke Leopold of Austria. Leopold, who had brought only a tiny retinue to Acre and who lacked the money to attract others to his colours, was now staking his claim to a share of the spoils. Richard was insulted by the arrogance of it.

'Tear that standard down! Throw it in a ditch!'

France and England took all of the booty between them. Duke Leopold of of Austria was humiliated and ignored. He had a good memory.

King Philip of France departed as quickly as he could from a place he had loathed and a Crusade for which he had no more stomach. His vow to Richard seemed less binding with each mile he went. The French army had been left under the command of the Duke of Burgundy, a haughty man who nevertheless tempered his soldiering with a degree of compassion.

'Kill them?'

'Saladin has not paid his money on time,' said Richard without emotion. 'He has let us see the True Cross but not returned it. He has let us speak with our prisoners but not released them.'

'Even so, my lord—'

'Kill them.'

'Three thousand men?' It was the Duke's last plea for mercy.

'We could never feed them all and they would only keep us here in Acre. We must march on to Jerusalem.' He looked away to the east to make sure that Saladin was watching. 'Kill them!'

On a sandy hill outside the town of Acre, the Christian ranks moved into line. The mounted cavalry dipped their lances, the light cavalry, the Turcoples, loaded their bows, the massed infantry unsheathed their swords. The Moslem prisoners, bound together by cords, could do nothing to escape their fate.

Horses charged, arrows sailed, swords removed heads with gruesome ease. It was a systematic massacre and Saladin's army could not stop it. When the work was done the blood of three thousand men soaked into the sand.

Richard took a pleasure in what he saw. It was a side of his character that his queen, the gentle Berengaria, had not been told about.

On the march to Jerusalem Richard had more opportunities to exercise his military genius and his seasoned cruelty. He took Haifa, then Caesarea, then continued south along the coast towards Jaffa. The army marched along the shore so that its right flank was protected by water and by the fleet. Saladin and his vast forces trailed the crusaders every inch of the way, harrying them whenever possible. Richard gave strict orders for his men to march in close formation and to ignore all provocation.

By September of that year, 1191, Saladin saw that he could only demolish the Christian army in a pitched battle. He had the advantage of being able to choose the battle-ground and settled on the plain of Arsouf. A nearby wood offered good cover for his men. Saladin's army was three times as large as Richard's and he felt that a combination of superior numbers and surprise would win the day.

But he could neither surprise nor out-general Richard.

The King of England gave the order for the advance towards Arsouf and almost a hundred thousand crusaders marched doggedly on. The Templars were in the van, followed by the Bretons, the men of Anjou, and King Guy with his Poitevins; in the fourth division came the Normans and English, guarding the royal standard; behind them were the French contingents under the Duke of Burgundy; in the most dangerous position of all were the Hospitallers, bringing up the rear.

On the plain of Arsouf, Saladin attacked with terrifying force, bent on avenging the massacre at Acre. His archers sent down a rain of arrows so thick that it blackened the sky; his horsemen, supported by Bedouin and Nubian auxiliaries, pressed close in such deadly abundance that they seemed to engulf the crusaders.

Fighting was fierce and slaughter thrived. The number of casualties was enormous. At length it was the charge of the courageous Hospitallers, goaded beyond measure, that was to prove decisive. The Saracens and their allies turned tail and scattered.

Taillebourg had been impregnable and he had taken it; Saladin had been invincible and he had now twice beaten him. Richard's name became an emblem of fear. On the plain of Arsouf, the legend of Melech Ric was born.

That night he invited an Arab boy into his pavilion and forgot all about Milo.

Al Malec Al-Adil Saf-Ad-Din Abu-Bekr Ahmed was an amiable Kurd of middle years. Brother to Saladin, the smooth Safadin had been sent on a diplomatic mission to Jaffa, the latest city to fall to the crusaders.

'You fled from Jaffa,' reminded Richard. 'Now I hear that you have dismantled Ascalon.'

Safadin knew how to emphasise the weakness of an enemy.

'Your army is divided now that the French have gone back to Acre.' He smiled. 'You are only half the man you were.'

'Jerusalem is mine by right,' came the proud reply. 'My grandfather, Fulk of Anjou, was its king. That is more than you and Saladin can say.'

'You are probably right,' grinned the other. 'Nevertheless, Jerusalem now belongs to Mohammed. Even by your Christian standards, he who succeeds, succeeds.'

Richard waved a hand and sounded gracious.

'Let me have the country from Jerusalem to the coast.'

'And in return?'

'I would go away,' Richard promised.

'Whatever happens, you will do that,' said Safadin.

'*After* I have captured Jerusalem.'

'If Allah wills it,' added the other.

'Because God will have it so!'

Safadin was on his feet, arguing with a soft intensity.

'It is the hardest thing in the world to accept that you cannot change the world. Where is the man who will admit his own impotence – you, Melech Ric? – who will say God's will be done *whatever* it may be? That is the end of pride. But once accepted, it is also the end of punishment.'

'Then I will be punished because I cannot say "Amen" to everything.'

Safadin was very puzzled.

'You fight hard for a man who doubts his own cause.'

'He loves best who fears his love is false,' mused Richard, then he brightened. 'Are you married?'

'Four times.'

'It is a good alliance, an integration of interest, without the jealousy of blood, brother but in-law; I protect your interests, you protect mine.'

Safadin was looking at him in sheer amazement.

'I give you Jaffa, Acre, Ascalon, and you keep Jerusalem.' A studied pause. 'Why not marry my sister, Joanna?'

'You are mad!' chuckled Safadin. 'You are mad, Melech Ric. That is why Allah protects you.'

'Take care that he protects *you*,' admonished the other. '*My* sister, Safadin. A queen.'

'And a Christian.'

'The Pope handles these things very well. A few dispensations will cover it.' He displayed the dowry. 'I will leave the Holy Land by Christmas.'

Safadin saw the certain astonishment there would be on the face of his brother. He also thought about his four wives.

'I agree,' he beamed and straightened his turban.

Joanna was not pleased when she heard the news. It was the first time that Richard had ever heard his mild sister use bad language.

In the event, the marriage did not take place. Richard pressed on to Jerusalem but was unable to take it. He got within four miles of the city and caught his first sight of its majesty. He turned his eyes away quickly. Defeat made him humble.

'Those not worthy to win the Holy City are not worthy to look on it!'

Peace talks were held and a truce of three years agreed upon. The Christians held the sea coast and the towns they had captured. In addition they were given right of passage and access to Jerusalem and the Holy Sepulchre. But Saladin still ruled.

Promising to return in three years, Richard turned his back on Palestine with its fevers and sunstroke and sandstorms and death. In the autumn of 1182, having sent his neglected wife ahead of him, he decided to return to his neglected country. The King of England set out for home.

CHAPTER EIGHT

Too much wine and the burden of his guilt made it a deep and troubled sleep. He was peering into a void and his thoughts were racing.

'Here is the answer that was promised both by Catholic and the heretic. But is this emptiness hell or heaven? It is as dark as hell and as cold as heaven. Oh God, dear God! Let us not say at last there is no difference – all indifference as much this side of life as that side of death. All chaos, panic, madness, fear, despair ...'

'My lord ... ?'

'You must be dreaming, Richard. Death is too serious to be the subject of contemplation. The dead can hardly contemplate the dead. It is the negation of negation, and so by dialectic I am resurrected!'

'My lord ... ?'

William de L'Etaing heard his king talking in the dark and wondered if he was awake. A silence confirmed that he was asleep. William climbed gently into the large bed beside his master. Dark thoughts demanded expression once more.

'The indifferent difference remains. Yea? Nay? What matters God? What God matters?'

Richard was suddenly awake, sitting up in bed with a jerk.

'Reinfred?'

'No, my lord,' explained William.

'You are not Reinfred! Treason! *Aux armes!*'

He threw himself on the hapless William and tried to strangle him. Only the intervention of the other three servants – two on the floor and the third, Beaton, in bed – saved a life. Panting and afraid, William fetched the candle from the table and held it up to his own face. Like the other servants, he was bearded, desperate, exhausted.

'Lord King, I am William de L'Etaing, your servant.' He moved the candle from face to face. 'We are all your servants.'

Sadness made Richard's question a whisper.

'Where is Reinfred?'

Reinfred had been the Arab boy who had helped the King to celebrate his victory over Saladin at Arsouf. And to console him over his defeat at the hands of Berengaria in Cyprus.

'Reinfred stayed in the Holy Land,' said Beaton.

'Holy Land?'

Richard was totally confused. He could not remember where he had been, where he was going, or where he was now. The only thing that he could remember was Reinfred.

'We are in Freisach, my lord,' reminded William. 'This was the last room in the inn.'

'But how did we ... ?'

Beaton took up the story, re-arranging the bedclothes as he did so.

'We came across the mountains, my lord. Through the Pontebba Pass. We were shipwrecked near Aquileia – the storm separated us from the fleet.'

Memories began to form again in Richard's mind. He thought of Acre and a standard thrown in a ditch.

'Austria? Does the Duke of Austria—?'

'Nobody knows who you are, lord King,' reassured William. 'We are travelling like pilgrims returning from the Holy Land. If we can reach Saxony ... your sister's dukedom.'

Richard was wide awake now, smiling at his own bewilderment, glad to be among loyal servants. He looked out through the tiny window.

'It is nearly dawn. We must go on.'

They pulled on their rough, hooded tunics and their breeches with cloth leggings. Only his fine gloves distinguished Richard from his companions. They began to roll up their small packs.

'I have never travelled like this before,' said Richard with contempt. 'On foot like a mean man. We must find a Jew and borrow and buy horses.'

'How will he know that you will repay him?' asked William.

'He will have a cousin in London!' sneered Richard. 'Riders! Soldiers!'

Beaton was at the window and gave the alarm. There was a clatter of many hoofs on the stones outside and the sound of men dismounting, Richard blew out the candle and told his men to keep quite still. They waited in the dark with their hands upon their weapons.

Heavy footsteps climbed the narrow stairs and then the door opened without ceremony. Two soldiers walked into the room with lanterns. They were followed by a man of slim build and dark colouring.

'*Sind Sie Deutcher?*' he asked, brusquely. 'Where are you from? *Italiano? Frankreich? England?* By the order of Count Frederic of Pettau, all pilgrims on this road must be examined.'

'Excuse me, sir . . .' began William.

'Norman!' snapped the man.

'Yes,' returned William with dignity, 'and like my companions returning from the Crusade, I am protected by the church.'

The man appraised them for a moment then dismissed his soldiers. He came to take a closer look at Richard and the servants edged around to get between him and the door.

'It is said that Richard, Duke of Normandy, is in this country – and in great danger from the Emperor of Germany and the Duke of Austria whose men are looking for him.'

'What harm have I done them?' Richard was casual.

'What harm have my cattle done me but I sell them to the butcher. A Frenchman called Philip.'

'Seigneur Dieus! Poor Richard!' He moved away from the man's searching gaze. 'But I do not suppose you would know him even if you saw him.'

The man's voice dropped to an urgent whisper.

'I am Norman — Roger de Argentan. It is twenty years since I last saw you, my lord.' He knelt down. 'God protect you, lord King! You must fly!'

'On foot?'

'Take my horse!'

'The boy can ride with me,' decided Richard, an arm around Beaton, the youngest of his servants. 'Let us go.'

In his haste he had ignored the probable fate of his other servants but they seemed to accept this and helped him with his pack. Roger stood close to the open door and raised his voice.

'I can see you are travellers. *Enschuldigen Sie bitte!*'

He went out with Richard and Beaton, led them to the courtyard of the inn and found his horse.

Two riders mounted and took the road towards Vienna. Three servants watched from an upstairs window. The King had always shown a preference for Beaton.

The dungeons of the castle were deep in the bowels of the earth. No natural light penetrated and the dampness of the stone walls was extreme. Lanterns hung in a few cells but darkness was eternal in most. A pungent smell of decay and excrement filled the air and the sound of suffering was not muted.

The best carpenter in Vienna had built the rack and his handiwork had been above reproach. Stout timbers had been cut in the forest above the city, the ropemaker's art had been employed, and the result was a machine of exquisite torment, able to break a man of iron in two.

There was a thin, pallid, young body stretched upon the rack now, running with sweat in the freezing cold of the cell. The gaoler whistled happily as he went about his work, adding another inch or two of agony and then looking with professional care to see any splitting of sinews, or tearing of skin, or dislocation of joints.

It was a healthy body which lay naked before him and

he was methodical in its destruction. He picked up a pair of fine gloves and dangled them in front of the boy's death-white face.

'Where did you say he was?'

Beaton could master the pain no longer. He had been captured just outside Vienna by Duke Leopold's men when he was buying wine for his master. The extravagance of his spending had belied his disguise as a poor pilgrim, and he had been arrested by alert soldiers and brought to the hands of the torturer.

'Where did you say he was?'

Beaton began to talk and talk and Richard's fate was sealed.

Eleanor spent that same winter of 1192 at Oxford Castle, a place that harboured many memories for her. She and Henry had spent several family Christmasses there and this was the very fortress from which Matilda, her redoubtable mother-in-law, had once escaped from Stephen and his siege army. Eleanor smiled at the thought of the Empress slipping out of the castle at night and wearing white robes in the deep snow.

Another memory jolted her and she stopped smiling. Her youngest son, John, had been born at Oxford.

'Can he sing anything happy?' complained John.

'Of course ... Blondel.'

'That last song was like a dirge,' said John.

'It was a sad song,' corrected Eleanor, 'because I am in the mood for sadness.'

'Christmas is a joyful time,' retorted John, sourly. 'Minstrel!'

Blondel needed no more urging. His lute-strings now danced and his fine tenor voice celebrated Christmas.

> 'Hey ho! be merry,
> Pluck the red berry,
> And the white,
> Our Lord was born this night.

The red is for his precious blood,
The white is for his mother's love
Hey ho! be merry,
Pluck the red berry,
And the white,
Our Lord was born this night ...'

While the minstrel continued to fill the room with music,
Eleanor stared into the heart of the fire and confided her
anxieties.

'I suspect Philip.'

'There is a mouse in the larder and you suspect Philip,'
he joked. 'He is suspect in perpetuity.'

'What has happened to him?' asked Eleanor, anxiously.

'Accept the truth, mother. The most likely explanation is
that Richard – *poor* Richard, that is – was drowned. So I
should be King.' The thought cheered him. 'Did you get
your Christmas present this morning? It is an abbey to
retire to.'

'You are not a king,' she snapped. 'Just a nuisance. I
sometimes wonder who was the fool I slept with when I
conceived you.'

'Did you hear that, *mon père*?' asked John, looking up.
'Your youngest, your Benjamin, the apple of your eye!'

'No, you are Henry's son all right,' she conceded with a
sigh. 'You have the family ingratitude.'

Blondel had finished his song and was awaiting instruction.

'I have the family brains, mother, all of them. I did not
go off crusading and let father's empire fall apart.'

'No, you stayed at home and kicked it, hoping it would.
In your place, Richard would have seized England and
invaded Normandy. All you do is to chase out Longchamp,
the only man in England smaller than you.'

'If Richard is dead, mother ...' he warned.

'You can bury me,' she replied. 'But he is not.' She put
her head back and sang. 'Now winter open up your
prison ...'

Blondel joined in at once, accompanying with the lute.

> 'Release the captive spring
> The Son of God is new arisen
> In all his glorying!'

John took up the song with a somewhat raucous voice.

> 'Lost in the deep,
> Lost in the deep,
> Lying in Abraham's buzzy.'

He drank heartily as the minstrel sang on alone. Geoffrey the Bastard entered in a hurry with two letters.

'News at last!'

'*Grace à dieu*! Geoffrey, dear Geoffrey,' she said, getting up from her chair. 'What does it say?'

'It is a letter from Rome. Sealed by Pope Celestinus.'

'The Pope himself!' She was excited, all the more so because John was not. 'What has happened to Richard?'

'I have been absolved from my vow not to return to England,' said the prelate in the family. 'It is now official.'

Bitterly disappointed, Eleanor sank back in her chair. John's mocking grin returned.

'This letter has taken over a month,' noted Geoffrey.

'*He* has taken two and still not arrived.'

Geoffrey looked at the old woman and felt pity for her. Then he remembered something.

'There was a letter from Würzburg for you.'

Eleanor took it uncaringly and gazed into the fire again.

'My eyes, my heart, my life, my love, my son ...'

High in a tower in the castle of Dürnstein, the King of England lay sprawled on a pallet, picking lice from his body. He was wearing the same rough clothes in which he had been captured some months before. Filthy, bearded and long-haired, he was in no way recognisable as the debonair Prince who had ridden in so many tournaments, as the handsome bridegroom who had been married in Cyprus, or as the dashing commander who had joined the charge at Arsouf with a cry of ' St. George for England!'

Heavy chains were attached to his wrists and ankles, chafing the skin until it flaked off. Richard had learned to accommodate the irritation. What chafed him now was the sheer boredom of being locked away in the tall angular room. Deprived of company, he had taken to talking to himself.

'Richard, King of England, Duke of Normandy and Aquitaine, Count, son of his father – am I such a one in your sight, dear God?'

He picked some more lice from his chest.

'When the body of the blessed Thomas Becket was stripped of its hair shirt after death, the saint was found to be covered in lice. It was regarded as a sign of his holiness.' He considered. 'A louse in the morning, proud with blood, then pinched between your thumb and forefinger with no more care than it takes you to breathe. Why, then, let us rejoice! For as you have lived on a king, I have lived on a God.'

He snapped his fingers, leaving a smear of blood where a louse had been held. He examined it with care.

The faint sound of a lute drifted in through the window. He heard it but dismissed it as a trick of his imagination. Since music was pleasure, he was denied it.

'Now winter open up your prison, *ai Dieus!*' he sighed, then sat up. 'This remorse will kill me! Mary, Christ – take pity! I am a mother's son.'

The music was closer now and had words to it.

> 'March is the month of merry-making,
> Cuckoo, cuckoo, cuckoo,
> Field and wood and fallow waking,
> Cuckoo, cuckoo ...'

He knew the voice, he knew the song. It was Blondel. He struggled to his feet amid the clanking of his chains and moved towards the window.

> 'Trees with budding breezes shaking,
> Cuckoo, cuckoo, cuckoo,
> Earth with bursting branches breaking,
> Cuckoo, cuckoo ...'

He had tried in vain to see out of the high window. Instead, he called out as loud as he could.

'Cuckoo, cuckoo, cuckoo ...'

There was a pause and then the minstrel's voice replied.

> March wind, March rain, March man forsaking,
> Cuckoo, cuckoo, cuckoo,
> The thirst of March with passion slaking,
> Cuckoo, cuckoo ...'

He was crying now and shouting in desperation.

'Cuckoo! Cuckoo! God! Take pity on me, God! Cuckoo!'

Crossing to the pallet, he flung himself down and wept until he became conscious that Blondel had stopped.

'You make me shame myself. Abase myself. To know you. My Lord – have you thought to drive me to such ends I will rebel against you? Can man love God? Can God?'

He listened intently once more but the minstrel had gone.

After a long and exhausting search among the castles of the German Empire, Blondel had finally located his King and friend. The minstrel could now return to England and report to Eleanor, who had despatched him on his mission. Richard began to weep again. His prison cell was now as lonely, silent and cheerless as it was intended to be. Leopold, Duke of Austria, had seen to that.

It was a rare thing for Philip to laugh so much. He read the letter once again and giggled.

'His Potence! His Imperial Highness! His Exaltedness! These Germans think they rule the world! Emperor Henry indeed! He is no king.'

'He has a king in check,' reminded John with a leer.

Philip's amusement vanished and he looked at John steadily as he shook his head.

'But I am next!' protested the other.

'Young Henry was a pretty man,' mused the King of France. 'And Geoffrey of Brittany. I loved Geoffrey – and Richard, before he became King.'

'You do not have to sleep with me, Philip. Just make me Duke of Normandy.' He saw craft in Philip's eye. 'Why not?'

'Richard is gone, no heir, the dukedom reverts to me ...'

'No! No! It is mine! My father's! Mine! God's tits, you—'

'Yes,' interrupted Philip. 'The same stable, the same foul-mouthed, foul-tempered, greedy, sly Plantagenets. Take Normandy, on condition.'

'Anything!'

'You return the castles of the Vexin and you marry Alys.'

'Agreed!' He had no compunction about discarding his wife. 'One thing. How can we be sure they won't release Richard?'

'Who can pay such a ransom?'

'Mother will try,' he said, with pursed lips. 'How much is it?'

'A hundred thousand marks.'

John stared, then smiled, then rocked with laughter.

'Mother will never raise a hundred thousand! That is twice as much as he raised himself for his Crusade. I am safe! Who would buy Richard for a hundred thousand?'

Philip was coldly envious of the asking price. Spite made him turn on John.

'Will you do me homage for Normandy?'

'Anjou, Aquitaine, Brittany and Normandy,' consented John, amiably. 'When are you going to get them for me?'

'Get them yourself!'

'I will. I will.'

John was well satisfied with his visit to Paris.

A covered wagon rolled along the road through Württemburg. Inside, a fat guard in the livery of the Austrian army kept watch on a manacled prisoner. The fat guard spoke no French but this did not deter the prisoner from trying to hold a conversation.

'*Diabolus!* For what God? What end?'

The guard looked blank and shifted the axe to his other shoulder. The prisoner tried to explain his attitude towards religion.

'I went crusading to the Holy Land for God. I was not suffered to adore him. I was lost, betrayed, captured, imprisoned. My lands, for all I know, taken, myself going to death.'

A troop of cavalry gave chase to the wagon which immediately stopped. The prisoner emphasised his point.

'After all that, whose side would *you* be on?'

The canvas at the back of the wagon was pulled back and some soldiers looked in. Though the prisoner feared for his life, it was the fat guard who was hauled out, his axe wrenched from him.

Henry VI, Emperor of Germany, dismounted from his horse and clambered up into the wagon, closing the canvas after him. For a long time he stared at the prisoner with a mixture of relief and gloating. The Emperor's position had been critical and his throne had been in danger. He was surrounded by enemies both inside and outside Germany – the Welfs, the ruling house of Saxony; a powerful group of Rhenish princes in the north; the Pope; and Tancred, the usurper of the crown in Sicily.

With all these the prisoner was closely associated. His capture represented a great deal to the Emperor, who had therefore been annoyed by the tardiness of his vassal, Leopold of Austria, in transferring the prisoner to him. The Emperor had now arranged that transfer himself. What he was now looking at in the back of a covered wagon was his security of tenure.

'I am going to give you a kiss,' said Henry.

'How much will it cost me?'

'A hundred thousand marks.'

'You must be the most expensive whore in history.'

As Henry leaned forward to kiss his gift from Heaven, a guard looked in and asked about the fate of the fat Austrian. The prisoner was still enough of a king to order summary execution.

'Kill him,' said Richard.

Hubert Walter, Archbishop of Canterbury, Justiciar, soldier, diplomat, personal friend of Richard and nephew to Ranulf de Glanville, was given the job of raising the ransom money. With control of Church and State, he set about raising the enormous sum without delay. Eleanor, now seventy-two, was always at his elbow to count the money as it came in.

'How is it going, Hubert?'

'There was never such a willing sacrifice as Englishmen are making for Richard. Poor people bring their rings and buckles, the abbeys empty out their silver and gold, the Cistercians give their wool crop, Normans and barons bring out their spoils of golden things. No king was ever so beloved, my lady.'

'None ever cost so much!' observed Geoffrey the Bastard. 'Nor loaded England with such an unnecessary burden.'

'A good cow needs milking.' Eleanor was blunt. 'Besides, the English have a sense of duty and pay taxes willingly.'

'They do not pay to bring Richard back,' argued Geoffrey. 'They pay to keep John out.'

Eleanor's reading of the situation was radically different.

'Richard is the ideal king – a soldier, a crusader, a hero. Here long enough to excite admiration, gone long enough for ministers to be blamed for bad government. He is great.'

'He is still costly,' asserted Geoffrey.

'He is King.'

The Archbishop of Canterbury, as usual, had the last word.

What John had thought an impossible task Hubert and Eleanor accepted as a sacred charge. The hundred thousand marks was eventually raised and it was time to haggle with the Emperor. Philip, shaken by the likelihood of Richard's release, offered to pay twenty thousand marks for each month that the King of England remained a captive. Richard himself was now far more comfortable in his imprisonment. A life free of the cares of kingship, and the duties of a husband, had a lot to recommend it.

Henry VI, Emperor of Germany, was sufficiently tempted by the offers from Philip and his ally, John, to postpone the date set for release. In February, 1194, he summoned a meeting of the Princes of the Empire at Maintz. Eleanor was invited, as were envoys from Philip and John. The fate of the King of England was in the balance.

'Richard!'

She hardly recognised him when they met in the Imperial Palace. Rich food and a slothful life had made him fat, sleek, almost puffy. His hair and beard were curled, he stank of perfume, and his clothes were uncharacteristically gaudy. Though only thirty-six, he looked much older.

'What have they done to you, Richard?'

'Three years since we met in Messina, *maman*. We have not been apart so long.' His attention was caught by the ransom money, a huge pile of silver. 'A hundred thousand marks. I could have bought Jerusalem from Saladin.'

'Saladin is dead,' she said. 'He died with nothing.'

Surprise at his changed appearance was giving way to resentment.

'How is everyone in England. Well?'

'Poor – but well.'

'Berengaria?' She had not been invited to Maintz. 'Where is she?'

'At Fontevrault. She is well. No children to bother her.'

He ignored the sarcasm and the anger in his mother.

'John?'

'Oh well. Plotting with Philip against you but – very well. *Dieus!*' she exploded. 'What has happened to you? Where is my son in all that frippery? You're in the colours of a Venetian barber. Belled like a wether! A ringed gelding! Curled like a sow's tail. Fat! Where is my Richard?'

'I am growing old,' he said, apologetically.

'*I* am old, Richard. I am too old. But I am not too gross, too greasy, too – whorish! We were in misery until we heard that you were captured. We slaved to amass your ransom – collecting, begging, praying, entreating, extorting! For *you*!' Disgust welled up in her. 'And I thought I was the Queen of England!'

Richard was embarrassed and felt justly rebuked. He was rescued from further attack by the arrival of Henry into the now crowded room. The Black Monk, Philip's envoy, was at the Emperor's heels and Richard became alarmed.

Henry called his prisoner across for private conference and told him that Philip and John had offered a ransom of one hundred and fifty thousand marks so that he could become their prisoner. After much discussion with Eleanor, Richard announced that the extra fifty thousand marks would take another year to collect. Henry saw a solution.

'I release you today, providing you do me homage for your kingdom of England and pay five thousand pounds a year.'

'I cannot suddenly turn the English into Germans!'

'England was once part of the Roman Empire,' reasoned the other. 'Why object to it becoming part of the Holy Roman Empire?'

Richard looked back to Eleanor for guidance. She gestured towards the gold circlet around her head. He took it from her, knelt before the Imperial throne and offered it to the over-joyed Henry, who was able to impress all his princes with his power. Henry handed the crown back to Richard, who put it on.

Five weeks later Richard was a free man, his mother was satisfied, the Emperor of Germany was content, England was jubilant. Philip took the news badly and sent word at once to John. His message was short and explicit – 'The Devil is loose.'

As soon as he was loose, the Devil visited a cathedral. After leaving Maintz with his mother, he travelled up the Rhine to Cologne, where Eleanor insisted on a guided tour of the old cathedral. Byzantine architecture was not to Richard's taste that morning and he found the visit boring.

The guide conducted them into a chapel.

'The Chapel of the Three Kings, erected some years after the cathedral by Otto, Archbishop of Cologne, to contain the bodies of the Three Kings – entrance three half-pennies.'

'Kings were cheaper then,' commented Eleanor, ruefully, as her son paid the guide. She saw the relics. 'Ah!'

Richard was more interested in catching up on the political situation in England. He pressed for details.

'John tried to get us to release Alys for him. When he failed, he tried to raise a rebellion in the north. That failed, too, so he fled to Philip. Nottingham is holding out.'

'John could not subjugate a convent!' said Richard.

'But he would *try*,' she added. 'You will have to fight, Richard.'

The guide was ready to continue and stood near the collection of holy relics, speaking with a kind of reverential off-handedness.

'The bones will cure fungus, swollen knees, itching crotch, the piles, bad backs, ringscab, running eyes and leprosy.' He paused. 'For half a mark.'

Eleanor showed great interest but her son was contemptuous.

'They've been touched by so many sick, they contain all the diseases they are supposed to cure!'

'Have you anything for lassitude?' she asked, with a sidelong glance at Richard.

The guide produced the blackened mummy of a dog.

'Caesar's dog, faithfully followed his master on all his campaigns and never once closed his eyes. Called Brutus.'

'He did Caesar little good,' she observed, tartly. 'Something for a soldier.'

'A military gentleman?' He had just the thing. 'Charlemagne's great toe. Sir, that is the toe that conquered the world.'

'Poor great Charles. The wonder of mankind, a touch for a foolmaker!' He became wry. 'What part of *me* will be displayed to dispense what miraculous qualities? What will they say?'

Eleanor was thoughtful for a moment then lowered her voice.

'Have you the cure for infertility?'

'Faith moves mountains, lady, but at your age ...'

'For a lord I know,' she replied.

While the guide looked through the relics, Richard wandered round the chapel and his soul was sickened by what he saw. He looked up and his thoughts were bitter.

'Dear Lord, why turn apothecary? Wasn't death your greatest gift? Men will crawl after existence, arms outstretched, mouths agape, eyes rolling, imitating the demons that torment them. But the greatest gate of death, the magnificent masterpiece, the triumphal arch through which we should ride as on chariots – what? – denigrated to a sewer, shrunk to a gut, and we sneak out like turds.'

The guide had shown something to Eleanor.

'Attila's pizzle?' she asked.

'It never failed him.'

Eleanor took the twist of gristle and then prodded Richard with it. He looked baffled.

'What was that for, *maman*?'

'The benefit of mankind,' she said, drily.

England was not able to detain its King for long. Of the castles held in John's name, only Nottingham showed any fight and its resistance was short-lived. Richard arrived there in March, 1194, fat, sluggish, but still master of siege tactics. He stormed the outer gate immediately and convinced the doubting garrison that he really was their King.

Surrender followed and he spent the rest of the day hunting in Sherwood Forest.

His main priority now was the recovery of those Norman lands which he had lost during his long absence. The campaign would be costly and the money, inevitably, had to come from England. A country which had been squeezed and squeezed again to finance his Crusade, then crippled by taxes to provide his ransom money, was now to be hard-pressed a third time.

In view of the new tax burdens he was placing on his kingdom, and because his subjects had seen so little of him, Richard arranged an important ceremony at Winchester Cathedral in April. It was a crown-wearing, an occasion of pomp and splendour, attended by all the notables of the realm. The pageantry appealed to Richard and the political implications were not lost on Eleanor.

As they entered the great nave and walked solemnly towards the high altar, he thought about the fresco which his father had painted nearly twenty years before. He was the eagle now. His mother was thinking about Henry, too.

'I last wore this crown with Henry. In the very early days. It has grown much heavier since then.' She remembered someone. 'Should I have sent for Berengaria?'

'You are the Queen, *maman*.'

'What is wrong with her?'

'Nothing.'

While a King and a Queen marched in the regal procession with frozen smiles of majesty, a mother chided her son without being able to look at him.

'Divorce her.'

'She has been hurt enough,' he said, recalling the Crusade.

'You must have children. Mon Dieu! I had four sons. Where are my sons?'

'Gone to the Devil!'

'Young Henry was too young. Geoffrey had bad luck. And John ...'

'John is John,' he muttered, with an air of finality.

'There is Geoffrey's son, Arthur ...'

'Odd how we are no good at making families.'

'And he is the son of a whore.'

'It does not seem important to me,' he confided. 'To have issue. It sounds obscene.'

'Who will *succeed*?' she hissed.

'Flesh of one's flesh. The whole idea is revolting.'

'*I* am your mother,' she reminded.

'How I cannot conceive,' he mused. 'In bed.'

'In blood. A river of royal blood that runs through time as the Loire runs through Touraine!'

They had reached their positions now and turned to face the assembled congregation. It was the last time most of them would ever see their King. When he left England the following month, he was never to return.

Count John had been lying low in Normandy since his brother's release from prison. He had incited armed rebellion in England, seized Norman lands, plotted ceaselessly with King Philip of France. When he heard that Richard had arrived to a tumultuous welcome at Barfleur, therefore, he knew the extreme danger of his position. He decided that there was only one course of action to pursue.

'Here? In Lisieux?' Eleanor could not believe it.

'In arms?' asked Richard.

'No, my lord – in fear.'

The speaker was Robert de Alençon, at whose manor house the King and his mother were dining. Robert had been immensely careful in his preparations, loading the huge oak dining table with all manner of tempting foods. The last thing he wanted was violence on such an occasion.

'So John has come crawling!' sneered Eleanor, now used to the idea and realising that it was very much in character. 'What will you do, Richard?'

'He *is* my brother,' he sighed. 'In any event, *maman* ... it would be either John or Arthur.'

'I will not let that poxy Constance be queen!' declared Eleanor, banging the table. 'Call John.'

Richard sent the nervous Robert de Alençon to fetch his

brother and assessed this latest move.

'John has the family virtues of greed and inconstancy – his crime is failure.'

His voice was firm but his mind was uncertain. The doubt which had plagued him in Limousin, in Messina, and in the Holy Land, had left its footprints upon him. He now had the habit of doubt and could not be decisive in this situation. Forgiveness or retribution? Generosity towards a younger brother or anger towards a vicious foe?

John came slowly into the room, dirty, unshaven, dishevelled, and blubbering. Twenty-seven years old, he was crying like a baby as he fell to his knees in front of Richard.

'Stop that!' ordered his brother. 'And get up! ... Come on. Give me a kiss. Come on, John. A kiss.'

Still sniffing, John obeyed and found himself subjected to a long, punishing kiss. When he broke away, his lip was covered in blood. Richard was laughing.

'That was how father used to kiss us. So that we would remember.'

'John,' commanded the steely Eleanor, 'kiss mother.'

He pulled a face but did as he was told. He then sat at the table, saw the food, and began to help himself, cutting off large portions of the salmon which was the main dish of the evening. Eating, drinking and growing in confidence every minute, John talked volubly about what had happened.

'It was Philip's fault. He tricked me – you know what he's like. He said you were as good as dead and so our dukedoms reverted to him ...'

He tried the wine and was impressed. It took the apologetic note out of his voice.

'Well, I could not let him get away with that, could I? So I agreed to his terms – trick for trick –to give up Gisors – I did *not*, he took it – and marry Alys.'

The salmon was excellent and disappearing at speed. John put in a scornful laugh.

'Who would marry Alys? Would you? No – nor me! And then, you came back and listened to my enemies! It was too late. If I was wrong – forgive me. But I had no intention of rebelling against you, Richard, you must know that.'

Richard had already stopped listening and Eleanor was now yawning. Both had seen John in action far too many times before to pay any heed to what he said. Undaunted, John gobbled down more salmon and persuaded himself that he was not to blame at all.

'In fact, Richard, *you* were at fault, leaving a weak government in England. One thing to be said for father – he put strong men in government and kept the barons down. You went to the Holy Land and nearly lost England. If it had not been for me ...'

Eleanor was now dozing off. Richard was looking weary. John threw in some false modesty so that all his virtues should be on show.

'If it had not been for me ... but no, I refuse to take the credit.' He waved a knife at Richard. 'You do not pay enough attention to England. It is the only land that is absolutely ours! You think it is a bank for your crusade, your ransom, your campaign – England is the crown!' He became even more self-important. 'Luckily, I realised that and diverted Philip's attention to Normandy.'

John sat back, pleased with this new version of events and almost convinced of its factual basis. He sipped more wine, ate the last of the salmon and then leaned across to Richard.

'I like England,' he said.

CHAPTER NINE

Imprisonment may have sapped his strength but freedom soon restored it. Enforced idleness gave way to frantic activity as he sought to reclaim his lost Norman possessions. Richard Coeur de Lion was a king and a soldier once more.

The devil was truly on the loose.

After the meeting with John at Lisieux, he took his army south to relieve Verneuil, cutting Philip's supply line and forcing his men to retreat in disarray. Within a month he had marched further south into Touraine and recaptured the fortress of Loches. Philip invaded Touraine from the north but Richard was once again a match for him. The French army was put to flight so comprehensively at Fréteval that it had to abandon its camp. Rich booty was taken, including valuable military equipment and a sizeable amount of Philip's treasure.

Verneuil, Loches, Fréteval. Three more victories for Richard, three fresh wounds for the King of France to lick. Morale was high among Richard's men. They marched triumphantly into Anjou and camped for a night in Fontevrault.

Richard and a few others chose to sleep in the Abbey.

'God is good, just, merciful and mysterious,' complained Richard. 'Philip got away.'

'It would have been a good prize,' agreed Mercadier, captain of his mercenaries. 'Philip's head would look better off its shoulders.'

Soldiers had brought in bedding and Peter the Chaplain had lit a few candles. Richard became introspective.

'Nothing is complete, whole, finished.' He unbuckled his mail surcoat. 'My crusade, my life, myself ...'

Mercadier made no reply. He was already asleep. Peter helped the King to pull off his leather acton and saw that his shirt was soaking wet underneath. A hard ride under a hot sun had made them all sweat.

'*Dieus!* I stink,' said Richard, peeling off his shirt.

There was a slight breeze and he stood in it so that it could dry his face and body. It was cooling, soothing, almost seductive.

'My lord, you will catch a cold,' warned Peter.

The Chaplain lay down beside Mercadier and disappeared into the folds of his cassock. Richard, after taking off his mail leg-pieces, decided to sleep between the two men. He wriggled down under the quilts and glanced each way in turn.

'Between Scylla and Charybdis ...'

How long he slept – or whether indeed he still was asleep – Richard did not know, but he found himself standing in the middle of the nave and looking down towards the choir. The candles had now burned out and the moon had come up, filling the Abbey with coloured light through the stained-glass windows.

Someone was standing beside his father's tomb. Richard felt neither surprised nor frightened when the figure approached him with a bandy-legged swagger. The man was big, well-built and dressed in rough clothes and curt-mantle. In some areas of light he looked quite ghostly but in others he was recognisably Henry.

'Hello, father,' said Richard, quietly.

'Richard Yea or Nay.' He did not seem pleased.

'You are from hell,' decided the son.

'If that is where you are.'

'Your sins are visited on me, not mine on you. Because you cursed me, my father, I am partly in hell. You called on the devil and cursed me. I am not a whole man. I am crippled.'

'You are not crippled because I cursed you, Richard – God knows! I cursed you *because* you were crippled.'

'I was not.'

'Blasted in the spring, lamed in the bellox, before you were a boy.'

'I had a shaking fever as a child,' he recalled.

'You had a hating mother as well. She hated me. So did you.'

'I hated you for what you did to her!' snarled Richard.

'I lay with her,' mocked Henry. 'You could not.'

'*Dieus!* I could kill you!'

'*Dieus!* You did.'

Henry looked back at the stone effigy and shook his head.

'Not a remarkable likeness.' He came close to Richard, whose body was now glistening with sweat. 'You were a big, strong lad, I grant you, but heartless. That is your trouble, Richard – no heart.'

He turned and began to swagger back towards the tomb. Guilt prompted Richard years too late.

'Father, forgive me.' Henry walked on. *'Please!'*

Henry was at the tomb now and leaned against it. Richard moved up the nave to join him and looked into his face. Henry shrugged.

'The legacy of guilt goes with the crown. Beggars and kings cannot be choosers.'

'Answer a question, yea or nay!' Richard was desperate. 'Is there a God?'

'Yea, there is a God.'

'Where?'

'Nay,' smiled the other. 'One question, one answer.'

Richard was shaking with cold now and flushed with fever. He grabbed at his father's cloak.

'Is there a God here?'

'Here, and hereafter.'

Richard fell to his knees beside the tomb and whimpered. 'Forgive me, father! Forgive me!'

Henry looked down at his son and spoke with measured contempt.

'Without God – what are you? Richard, you are a whore. You sold your honour to Philip for my crown. You sold my crown to pay for your crusade. You sold out the crusade to save your pride, and gave up the Holy Sepulchre rather than risk defeat. You sold *yourself* for a king's ransom.'

He was standing right over Richard now as the latter continued to shake and sweat and whimper.

'Honour – crown – crusade – ransom ... all that is left is you! You whore. You whoreson whore. Give me a kiss. I never could resist a whore.'

He pulled him up and gripped him in a hard, brutal embrace. Putting his hand behind Richard's head, he forced him into a grinding, savage, uncompromising kiss of hate.

When Peter the Chaplain awoke at dawn the King was no longer beside him under the quilts. He began to walk down the nave in search of him and was stunned by what he saw. Richard was lying full-length on top of the stone effigy of his father, in a rigid embrace. His lips were pressed down hard on the cold lips of stone.

'Suscipe Flos florem, quia flos designat amorem ...'

Berengaria was singing softly as she came into the yard with a handful of wild flowers.

'Illo de flore nimio sum captus amore,' sang John in reply, and she giggled.

'Wherever did you learn that?'

'In a monastery ... I came to call you.' He showed her two large white eggs he had just collected. 'Breakfast.'

They strolled across the yard, scattering hens and geese and a single, lugubrious duck. A horse neighed in its stall. It was springtime in Normandy but there was a decided nip in the air. Berengaria was glad when they walked back into the old house and found a fire crackling away.

'How is he?' asked John, going to a tankard of wine which was warming over the fire. 'The paladin.'

'Better – worse,' she answered, looking up. 'Why ask me?'

He cracked the eggs and dropped their contents into the tankard, watching to see the wine curdle. Then he turned back to her and felt a strange pang of sympathy. She seemed as lonely and unloved as ever.

'You should be Queen of England, Berengaria,' he said, quietly.

'I am.'

'No – mother is queen. Mother will *always* be queen.'

'I am married to a King of England and I have never been there.' She was wistful. 'Are there mountains in England?'

'Some, mostly in Wales.'

'Then I will be Queen of Wales,' she said with almost

childish glee. 'Queen of the mountains of Wales.'

'I think they have a king of sorts,' he muttered.

'Good. I am a queen of sorts ...' She saw him out of the corner of her eye and withdrew her hand as he tried to grab it. 'Brother John, you already have too many bastards.' He looked ashamed. 'Did you learn *that* in the monastery as well?'

He lifted the tankard from the fire and offered it to her.

'Nice!' she complimented, sipping the concoction.

'I can do *some* things well,' he argued.

Her sad face went darker for a moment and she looked up again.

'When Richard was very ill, it was quite like Cyprus – only he was ill. Now he is better.' She frowned. 'Why do you not live with Isabelle? She is still your wife.'

'Gloucester hath lost her charms.' He sat down. 'No children, not my fault. I think we are doomed to die out – we Plantagenets. There is only little Arthur left, big Arthur now. Father used to swear that we had the Devil's blood in us.'

'*Dios!* Do not joke about such things!'

'We have to – or we might begin to believe it.' He was serious. 'Can a woman love a man like Richard?'

'I saw him once in Pamplona. He came to fight in a tournament and I thought he was Roland. Roland once wanted to cross my mountain in winter and made a great big breach in it with his sword.'

'That sounds like Richard!'

'Roland had a friend called Oliver.'

Before she could say any more, Richard himself came clumping down the narrow staircase. He was trying to get into his armour but found it too small.

'Must have shrunk!' he decided, throwing it aside.

'Who needs armour?' asked John. 'There is a truce. Make peace, live happy, keep a pig.'

He went back out into the yard and left them alone. Berengaria had started to load the table with milk, cheese, bread, butter and bacon. Richard slumped into a chair.

'In the Holy Land we used to breakfast on dates.'

She sat opposite him and watched him begin his breakfast. He became conscious of her gaze after a while.

'Richard, do you want to divorce me?' she asked.

He broke off more bread and stuffed it into his mouth.

'You?'

'I asked you first.' She bowed her head. 'You have reason because I have no child. It is my fault. It is always the woman's fault.'

'Berengaria, do you want to be divorced and go back to Navarre?' She shook her head and started to cry. 'Then why did you ask me?'

She shrugged, sniffed, ran the back of her hand under her eyes, then found an excuse.

'You never crowned me Queen of England.' She raised her head. 'I am a Princess. My family is as old as the mountains . . .'

'*Dieus!* Is that all?' He was amused.

His smile could still make her love him.

'It does not matter now, Richard. I will wait.'

'*Maman* has been Queen for so long,' he explained, gently. 'If God had wished us to have a child . . .' He got up. 'I will give you this house and land so that you can be independent. You can live here while I go on campaign.'

'But there is a truce . . .'

'Truces never bother Philip too much. You wait.'

He was about to caress her but drew back. As he went upstairs, she remembered something he had once told her in Messina.

> There was a Princess of Navarre,
> Who could not see very far.
> She made a pet out of a flea,
> And kept a pig for company.

She had no appetite for breakfast and began to clear the things off the table.

'*Nunc florem, Flora dulcissima, semper odora . . .*'

She was now standing by the fire, singing to herself and dropping the wild flowers into the flames one by one.

The truce expired and war began again in earnest. It was a hard, costly, wearisome war of attribution, full of raids and counter-raids but lacking a decisive pitched battle. Neither side had the upper hand for long and both committed atrocities which shocked their own supporters. Philip had taken a particular dislike to Richard's Welshmen and their longbows. He rounded up three thousand of them and had them slaughtered to a man. In retaliation Richard blinded fifteen French prisoners and sent them to their king. It was a brutal, shameful, futile war which nobody could win.

The Treaty of Louviers ended it in January, 1196. Negotiations were conducted in an old barn amid muck and straw and smell. It was the one building in the area left standing. The other farms had been burned to the ground and the nearby hamlet destroyed.

'What do they offer?'

Richard peered over a cattle stall into its neighbour, where Hubert Walter and the Black Monk pored over a document. Philip and his men occupied another stall and in another, all alone, was Alys. Richard was in a bitter mood.

'Well?'

'The King of France gives up all claim to lands which he has captured in the last war,' explained Hubert. 'In return for this, the King of England gives up the castle of Gisors and the whole of the Norman Vexin.'

'All right! All right!' Richard was graceless.

Philip heard him and answered from his stall, taking care not to look at his adversary.

'It was never yours! It was my sister's dowry, which you forfeited when you broke your oath and rejected her!'

Alys felt embarrassed to be the bone of contention between the two kings. She tried not to listen as Richard stamped up and down in his rage.

'*I* broke! You broke the truce of God and took Gisors when I was in the Holy Land! And you tried to bribe the German Emperor to keep me! Take it! Take Alys back — I have no use for her.'

A French soldier approached her stall as Richard roared on.

'Take the Vexin but do not think to take another inch of Normandy or Aquitaine!'

'I am your overlord for Normandy and Aquitaine,' asserted Philip, shuffling in his straw.

'What!' Richard's temper was now equal to his father's. 'Oh lord! Seigneur! Sieur! What? No Frenchman sets foot in Normandy, Anjou, Poitou or Maine, Berri, La Marche, Auvergne or Gascony! These are my lands! I dare anyone to say he is lord of what is mine!'

The challenge sent many hands to their swords on both sides, but the Kings kept their soldiers in check. Richard waved at Alys and she was taken to Philip, whom she tried to embrace.

'Not now,' he said.

'After twenty-three years — when?'

Alys, well-thumbed pawn for so many years, was hurried away. Hubert and his counterpart came out of their stall with papers. The Treaty of Louviers was now accepted fact. All that remained were a few formalities between the two Kings.

'Does the war go on?' screamed Philip.

'After the Nativity!'

'I will not fight till after Lent.'

'When you like and be damned! Philip, keep your word!'

Philip and his men went towards the door at the far end of the barn, where he turned to deliver his Parthian shot.

'You are so sworn and forsworn, so crisscrossed with oaths, the Lord has made a little broken pitcher of your soul ... for the Devil to drink from!'

'Let him drink!' said Richard, grimly. 'If he will come and kill you.'

As the King of France left the building at one end, Richard stalked out of it at the other. He felt the need to put his arm round someone and the first available person was John. His younger brother had been eavesdropping on the negotiations.

'Poor Alys!' sighed John.

'She has been in captivity of one sort or another since she was six months old. What a life!'

'Father would have married her,' suggested John, mischievously.

Richard took his arm away and strode towards his horse. John scurried after him, worried about his future.

'You have given away Gisors and the Vexin. How are we going to protect the road to Rouen?'

Richard mounted his horse and looked down.

'We are going to build a castle, John. The strongest castle ever built this side of the Holy Land. On a rock, in the Seine, at Les Andelys....'

Château Gaillard was a masterpiece of military architecture. It stood on a spur of rock that rose three hundred feet high out of the river, south of Rouen. At the lip of the rock was an octagonal fort with walls ten feet thick and a ditch dug out of solid stone. Behind this was the fortress itself, an awe-inspiring structure with a great citadel that echoed the conformations of the spur. The walls of the inner ward were an innovation. They were constructed in a series of semi-circles so that enfilading fire could always be obtained in the ditches between these protrusions. The parapets of the walls were crowned with narrow corridors that jutted out, thus allowing boiling oil and missiles to be dropped through the holes in the floor.

Château Gaillard made the road to Rouen secure. The building of it was a labour of love to Richard and he supervised operations throughout the whole year it took to erect.

It was indeed one of the strongest castles in Christendom. It was also yet another reason to bleed England's tax-payers.

Philip was at once alarmed and envious when the fortress was completed and delivered himself of a boast – 'I will take it though its walls were made of iron.'

'I will keep it though its walls were made of butter ... Château Gaillard!' Richard raised his glass. 'We toast you!'

'Château Gaillard!'

It was a Plantagenet Christmas party at the new castle and they were all in festive mood for once – Richard himself, Eleanor, John, Hubert, William Marshall, Mercadier, William de L'Etaing, and Arthur, a boy of thirteen. They were all gathered around the fire in the Great Hall and Richard could talk of nothing but his castle.

'What do you think of my present, *maman*?'

'Built to last,' she conceded, age making her croak.

'For ever!'

'Do not be impressed by the idea of permanence, Richard. It can be very unattractive if one's condition is not quite ...'

'St. Edmund's hair is still growing,' remarked John.

Arthur shook with laughter at his uncle.

'It is true,' insisted John. 'Our patron saint, dear St. Edmund, has hair and fingernails that still grow – after three hundred years. Imagine – growing quietly away. Inside his tomb.'

'Edmund is a saint,' said Richard, grandly. 'He is entitled to a little eccentricity. Saints and kings.'

He smiled at William and Eleanor was displeased.

'Now you've built your castle,' she croaked, 'will you make peace with Philip?'

'No, *maman*, I will make war as it has never been made before in France – as I made war in the Holy Land.'

'It is Christmas!' protested John.

'We are united and surround the Île de France – *I* am the continental King and Philip rules an island in my ocean!'

Hubert Walter put in a word for his ailing country.

'My lord, England has paid these last four years, ten hundred thousand pounds towards the wars. Military service keeps Englishmen in Normandy and Aquitaine ...'

'Hubert, it is Christmas,' said Richard, reprovingly.

They all sat around the fire for a long while without speaking. The oldest among them broke the silence.

'It reminds me of the old days – no wit, no music, only heavy breathing. I have had enough of the company of men.'

'You are not eighty yet,' noted John.

'I shall go to Fontevrault in the New Year,' she mumbled.

Richard looked around benignly, wanting everyone to be happy in his Château Gaillard. He noticed Arthur and felt an impulse of generosity.

'Arthur ... when you are older, I will make you a present of something larger than Brittany.'

'Will I be king?' asked the boy.

The relaxed mood was suddenly replaced by one of tense uncertainty. Everyone in the room was going to be deeply affected by Richard's answer and all waited with anxiety. John, most anxious of them all, began to perspire freely. Arthur repeated his question.

'Will I be king?'

'Yea – and nay.'

There was a general feeling of relief all round and John even started to chuckle. Then a door opened at the far end of the room and servants ushered in a visitor. Hubert was on his feet at once to greet the Papal Legate.

'A cardinal from Rome,' said William. 'There must be news.'

'The Pope has had a baby,' quipped John.

Hubert brought the illustrious visitor forward and all could see the state of consternation he was in.

'The venerable father Cardinal Peter of Capua,' introduced Hubert. 'Tidings are bad.'

'King Richard,' said the Cardinal with something resembling desperation, 'there is war again in the Holy Land. The truce you made has been broken, Jaffa is taken and twenty thousand Christians have been slaughtered. All that remains to God is the harbour of Beirut.'

'Who broke the truce?' asked the perturbed Richard.

'A band of Germans. The infidels then slew every Christian in Jerusalem and came down to the sea.'

'Christ, the Son of God, aid us and his Holy Sepulchre ...' said Richard to himself, trying to cope with the news.

Hubert was praying, Eleanor was grieving, John was smirking. The cardinal delivered his message from Pope Innocent.

'His Holiness sends the same message to the King of France – where then is your God? You ravage each other's lands when God's land is ravaged by pagans. Where is your God? You war in Christendom and slaughter Christians as Saracens to yourselves. Where is God? He commands you in the name of Christ crucified to make a truce between you and to join your armies and conquer the Holy Land for the Cross of Christ.'

Tears were streaming down Richard's face.

'God forbid that I should glory, save in the Cross of our lord Jesus Christ!'

It was the best Christmas John had ever had.

Bertrans de Born was overjoyed to see his friend again and called for wine. They sat on a bench in the castle yard and talked happily about old times.

'I hear that you finally made peace with Philip.'

'We made peace so that we can make war in the Holy Land.'

'But have you considered the year, Richard?'

'What year?'

'Don't kings count years? 1199 – the last year of the century. Next year, we are bound duodecimo, sold by the dozen, a twelfth of the great gross! We reckon by inches and apostles! We are rounded, finished!'

'What do you predict?'

'Something foul,' cautioned the other. 'Evil is predictable. Mercy comes as a surprise. A bolt from the blue. God confounds us, the devil always does what we expect.'

'I will not predict, I will predicate,' said Richard. 'A Crusade, a second Crusade, this time to complete God's work.' He leaned back in the spring sunshine. 'It will be the best army and the best campaign that I can assemble and devise. Now I know what to do – the key to Palestine is Egypt, not Beirut and Damascus. The road to Jerusalem is from the south.' He shared his vision. 'You should see the silver towers, the white walls, the domes of precious pearl. Holy Sepulchre, the Cross where God was nailed as a banner to his people, the heart of the world, Bertrans.'

'What am I doing in this dunghill when you can show me heaven?' wept Bertrans. 'I will follow you, Richard. I will follow you ... Papiol!'

'More wine?' The servant's head had appeared at a window.

'My sword! My shield! And some more wine!'

'What do you want your sword for?' asked the servant. 'Cook is using it.'

'Hang the cook! Hang you!' He was on his feet. 'Hang the lot of you! I am a gentleman.'

Richard got up and placed a consoling arm on his shoulder.

'You are a prince among poets and an admiral of soldiers and a friend of kings, but ... I must manage without you.' He went on quickly as the other looked crestfallen. 'I cannot afford to pay you. There's not a penny in the treasury at Chinon.'

'Then how can you talk of a Crusade?' came the truculent reply.

'I am on my way to Limousin,' said Richard, conspiratorially. 'Count Aimar of Limoges is my liegeman. One of his knights, a man called Achard, has a castle at Chalus.' Bertrans was bewildered. 'Not a month ago, his ploughman turned up a piece of gold. Achard went to look and found a great hoard of treasure – an emperor, with his wife and daughters, all gold, seated round a gold table.'

'Ai, Dieus!'

'Now they are trying to keep the gold from me. I am going to Chalus to get it. After that – we shall lay up treasures in Heaven.'

'I will come to Chalus!' announced Bertrans.

'No – Chalus is mine. Come and see me when I return.'

They took leave of each other and the paunchy Richard walked away, leaving the frayed, unkept Bertrans behind. Papiol rushed up with the sword and Bertrans noticed its blackened end. It was the final indignity.

'Someone's been poking the fire with it!'

The castle of Chalus stood on a green hill above the little River Tardoire. It was late March and there was blossom everywhere. Birdsong filled the air and added to an impression of romantic tranquillity.

Then Richard and his men arrived and pitched their pavilions. To the conqueror of Taillebourg the tiny fortress presented no problem. There were less than fifty people inside the castle and they included some women.

'Achard has gone, my lord,' said William de L'Etaing. 'They say there is no sign of the treasure.'

'The treasure is here,' asserted Richard. 'These people lie like the devil.'

'They say you will not attack as it is Lent,' continued William. 'But in any case they will surrender if you promise to spare their lives.'

'I'll crack this walnut this afternoon.' Richard was impatient.

'My lord!' William was upset. 'Next week is Easter.'

'The best time ... for a siege.'

William was deeply hurt by this attitude.

'They *yield* the castle to you!'

Richard ignored him and addressed his remarks to Mercadier, captain of the *routiers* who made up the bulk of his forces.

'It was at Easter, twenty years ago, that I took four castles in Angoumois. The last of them was Taillebourg. I was only twenty-one, Mercadier.'

William tried to speak again but Richard walked away with his captain. The King was not to be deprived of the pleasure of taking by storm a castle that was ready to surrender. William brooded for a while and then returned to Richard's pavilion. He noticed something which disturbed him. The King's helmet and shield were still there.

As Richard and Mercadier stood near the castle to assess its weaknesses, a bolt from a crossbow came whirring through the air.

'Dieus!'

It struck him between the neck and the shoulder where the mail was unlaced and open. Its impact made him stagger back and grunt with pain. Mercadier supported him and looked up at the battlements. There was an arbelester on top of a tower. Richard saw him.

'Take that cursed castle and hang every man and woman in it! Except the man with the crossbow!'

He stumbled back towards his pavilion as William came rushing up with his helmet and shield. Richard pushed past him.

'The devil take you!'

He left William to suffer the insult and found his way into the pavilion. Sitting down to steady himself, he pulled his mail surcoat off with care, more annoyed than concerned about what had happened.

The wound was in his left shoulder and he explored it gingerly with his right hand. Then, taking hold of the shaft firmly, he began to pull it out. The pain was intense and he winced but he tugged bravely on. Suddenly, the shaft snapped and came away with a gush of blood.

Richard looked down at the broken shaft and shuddered. The barbed head was still buried deep in his shoulder.

Eleanor came at once when she heard the news. She found a number of people in his pavilion – doctors, priests, lords, soldiers – and had to push her way to the side of his bed. One of the doctors was covering up the wound but she saw the hideous expanse of blackened flesh up his left side.

'Richard!' It made her reel.

'*Maman* ... forgive me.'

She was looking at a death-mask, a pale, anguished ghost of a man. She fought back her tears and asked for the truth.

'Have they done everything?'

The doctors nodded gravely and moved away. By the time the surgeon had finally removed the bolt, gangrene had set in. There was no hope and Richard knew it.

'The Great Seal. Brieuse must take the seal to John.'

'You have decided?'

'Not if you say nay.'

'Arthur has fled,' she said. Back to Philip. It has to be John.'

'Give three parts of my treasure to John, the fourth part to the poor,' he whispered.

'So *much*?'

'There is not much,' he confessed.

'There is so much treasure and pride in you,' she urged. 'I never knew a king, my son, so loved and praised for his courage, his Crusade. I never knew a king his people would give a farthing for, and for you they gave their treasure. You *have* a treasure, a golden treasure ...'

Her emotions would no longer be denied and she sobbed bitterly. It made him feel the full weight of his pain and guilt and he tried somehow to stop her.

'*Maman*, do you remember Caesar's dog?'

'What nonsense!' A smile through tears.

He was still for a moment as if fighting off some inner demon. When he spoke he was much weaker, fainter, paler.

'The Abbot of Charroux, the young one, wants me to be buried in Poitiers. I said that he could have my tripes.'

'Richard!'

'Rouen can have my heart and the rest of me ...' He thought about the night he had spent in the Abbey. 'The rest of me can lie in Fontevrault at father's feet.'

'You did not kill him,' she whispered.

'I did not save his life,' he mused. 'I wanted to go back to the Holy Land but my pilgrimage ends here.'

'Mine, too ...'

She straightened his hair, caught sight of the tainted flesh again and closed her eyes tight in pity.

'*Laudate Nomen Domine ...*'

The chanting of the mass began outside the pavilion and he knew that his time was now short.

'Berengaria ... ask her to pray for me, maman, pray for my soul.' His voice was fainter than ever now and she put her face close to his to hear the next words. 'I love thee, as I have never loved man or woman ...'

The chanting was louder now and a small procession entered the pavilion. Panic showed in Richard's face as priests gathered around his bed and the smell of incense sharpened the air. Eleanor looked up in her grief and prayed.

'God let me die instead of him! Send me to everlasting hell and let him live!'

She sighed at the hopelessness of the bargain, then found Brieuse and Mercadier at her elbow. It brought out the Queen in her.

'Brieuse, go to Count John at Rouen, tell him to meet us at Fontevrault.' She grabbed him as he made to leave. 'Not a word of this must reach Arthur of Brittany or the French King. There will be trouble soon enough.'

Brieuse nodded, took a last sad look at his King, then left. Mercadier, who had fought with Richard in the Holy Land as well as in all his dominions, expressed his disgust

'The great captain of the world – in a dunghill like this!'

'In Aquitaine!' said Eleanor with pride.

William de L'Etaing, who had been standing close to the bed, now joined them with his King's last wish.

'He wants to see the man with the crossbow.'

Mercadier signalled to two *routiers* and they brough

forward a young man. Richard had enough strength to try to lift his head to see his assassin.

'You have killed me ...'

The young man, who had been trembling at the thought of the punishment that awaited him, now found a token defiance.

'You killed my father and my two brothers, and you are going to kill me.'

He was fair-skinned and clear-eyed and no more than sixteen. Richard found himself thinking of Milo and of Reinfred. Here was such another boy.

'I forgive you ...' He summoned up more volume. 'I pardon the boy. Let him go free.'

'To the end!' muttered Eleanor in exasperation.

The young man could not believe what he had heard and began to laugh with sheer relief. He turned away and walked out of the pavilion, only to find a mailed glove on his shoulder.

Mercadier had followed him with a few of his men and Mercadier had no mercy at all in him.

'Flay him alive – then hang him!'

Mercadier went back inside the pavilion in time to see the final moments of the man he had served so often and so long. Richard's eyes were closed now, his breathing gentle. His prayer joined those of the priests who were gathered around him.

'Christ, Christ, Christ ... let me kill Saracens in heaven!'

He had been a soldier to the last.

Bertrans de Born was heart-broken when he learned of the tragedy. William de L'Etaing had brought him Richard's horse and now left him alone to measure the depth of his sadness. Bertrans put his head against the horse's neck and felt a grief that was beyond tears.

'Ah Richard – you were the best King of all. You were the courtliest knight that ever carried a shield. And you were the truest friend to your lover that ever rode a horse.

And you were the most generous man that ever killed his enemy. And you were the prettiest poet that ever couched a lance ...'

He remembered the talk which he and Richard had had on the eve of the King's departure for Marseilles and the Crusade.

'And you were the most faithful of unbelievers that ever asked God for his mercy.' His eyes searched the heavens. '*Ai Seigneur Dieus*, pardon him because he has great need of it. Do not think what he did, but what he might have done.'

From a window in his royal palace, Philip looked out on a sunlit Paris and felt happy in his new world.

'Envy, avarice, murder, perverted lust, and pride – the hatred which has ruled twice five years – all these blown with a pin!'

He turned back into the room to see two boys playing.

'Louis!' The boy with the pointed chin ran to him. 'You will be King of France.'

'Yes, father.'

'King of all France, Normandy and Aquitaine.'

'What about Arthur?' asked a sullen Louis. 'He says that he is now King of England.'

'He is what *I* make him,' emphasised Philip. 'Arthur – kneel!'

The other boy obeyed at once and Philip gave him more commands.

'Stand up – kneel – stand up – kneel!'

When he had exercised Arthur to his satisfaction, he looked into the grinning face of his son.

'King of France – and King of England. After John.'

John stood in the Abbey Church of Fontevrault and could scarcely suppress his elation. In a tent of light cast by four tall candles, Richard lay upon his bier at the front of Henry's tomb. Hubert, William Marshal, Brieuse and many barons had come to pay their respects. John was in no mood for solemnity.

'God must be great to bring the great so low. Richard, no king on earth was ever higher than you were in his subjects' eyes, for men admire magnificence in a king more than justice, mercy, policy, or peace.' He gazed at the effigy on the tomb. 'My father was a better king than Richard, but no-one mourns for Henry, everyone for Richard. Which shall I be?'

Disapproval was all around him but John blundered on.

'A Henry or a Richard? Shall I make laws or wars? A reign of uneventful prosperity or turbulent glory? No-one remembers peaceful kings, but who forgets a tyrant?'

Hostility hemmed him in now and he met it with a warning.

'Well, lords, let me tell you — I am for peace. Your hunting days are over now and you must settle down to shepherding your sheep.' He put a hand on the stone Henry. 'Father made the empire out of nothing. He had the little country of Anjou and a big sceptre.' John laughed obscenely. 'He ploughed Normandy, forked England, and dibbled Aquitaine!'

He was annoyed that nobody appreciated his joke.

'No king has held as much land as we three Kings since Charlemagne!' he boasted.

'My lord,' said Hubert, sternly, 'look at your father's tomb and your brother's corpse. What do they hold? God has seized their land, amerced their monies, and taken full account for mort d'ancestor. Their dues are paid to God.'

The barons had formed a dark, almost menacing circle around John now and he was on the defensive as the Archbishop continued.

'You hold your lands from God. You hold your sovereignty from God's church and the election of your nobles, who put aside your elder brother's son, Arthur ...'

Hubert pointed a finger to complete his admonition.

'As your nobles owe homage to you for what they hold from you – John, you owe homage to God.'

Resentful but cautious, John pretended to be cowed and

nodded his head at Hubert. William Marshal stepped forward.

'My lord, will you stay here tonight or go to Chinon?'

'You go to Chinon,' murmured John. 'I will stay here with my grief.'

He waited quietly until they had all left him and then glanced round furtively to make sure that he was alone. John then knelt before the altar and put his palms together.

'Lord God. My lord, I swear you fealty, homage, and service – in return you give me all my lands to hold in peace. This is a contract between you and me, Lord God – no church, no barons. Amen.'

Having made his private pact, he walked back to the tomb, lay down beside it, wrapped his cloak around his small frame, and dozed off to sleep in the company of a father and a brother.

King John was fully aware of the threat posed by King Philip, and the weapon with which he fought it was marriage. Blanche, the Castilian grand-daughter of Eleanor, was married to Louis, son of Philip. As the young couple retired to their nuptial couch at Piramor, John was gleeful at his own cleverness.

'Blanche of Castile and Louis of France ...'

'Louis of France and Blanche of Castile,' corrected Philip.

'We are of the same family now. What a good augury for the new century! Let us have a hundred years of peace. Give me a kiss.'

Philip sensed that his moment of triumph had come. He could make John do what neither Henry nor Richard had ever done.

'Kneel!'

'I am a crowned king, Philip. And we are as good as brothers ...'

'Kneel!'

'Oh all right,' sighed John, kneeling. 'Anything to keep the peace.'

'Stand up!'

John shrugged and started to get up again.

'Kneel!'

The command was imperious and its tone offended John.

'Kneel!'

He was being tested and the realisation brought a sudden rush of blood to his face.

'*Kneel!*' howled Philip.

The veins on John's face stood out, his eyes contracted in their sockets, his nostrils flared, his whole body vibrated. It was a rage of frightening intensity and it made the curse from his mouth like escaping steam.

'The Devil take you and your issue, and the blood of the innocent be on your head!'

A new reign had begun.

CHAPTER TEN

The Abbey Church at Fontevrault was graced by a new century, a new king, and an old woman.

In the early summer of the year 1200, King John stood in a small garden beside the Abbey while his mother toyed with some memories. John, a hawk upon his wrist, was scanning the blue, cloudless sky for game. Eleanor, seated upon a bench, was too old to be deterred by the fact that he was not really listening to her, and talked for the simple pleasure of it.

'I used to watch the English river running through the water-meadows at Windsor, as grey as silk. It passed like time with hardly a movement – the tremor of a leaf, a kestrel hovering in the sky. At evening the horsemen came plashing across the river, calling to each other – "Ha! What a run she gave us!" What a run! At night the owls hooted and all the meadows were silver in the moonlight.'

Distance had lent considerable enchantment to the view

and her surviving son was the first to remind her of the fact.

'You never liked England,' he said, stroking the back of the hood of his hawk.

'I do not like or dislike any more,' she sighed. 'I remember or I forget. Glorious days in Poitiers before you were born, which were dry and never still – dancing in sunlight, my children. And before.... *ai Dieus! Toujours la même chanson!*'

'You remember so much, mother. And so well.'

There was a sundial within her reach and she leaned across to trace the hours with her hand, the great ruby rings of France and England loose upon her old fingers. John was still paying more attention to the hawk than to her.

'Time overtakes us like a tide,' she mused. 'All distances from sea to sea are only islands in a sea of time. A man can travel endlessly but he will never out-travel time. All journeys end in empty places.'

His shadow fell across the sundial and the mood of nostalgia perished. She looked up and spoke sharply.

'At least you can have children. Divorce Isabelle of Gloucester.'

'I will divorce Isabelle and keep Gloucester.' He seemed pleased with the notion. 'Whom shall I marry?'

'The Princess of Portugal.'

'Oh, for the empire, like Richard,' he mocked gently.

'Richard was an empire in himself – you are yourself in the empire.' She sat back, considering. 'You, the last of the brood, the cuckoo – how will you rule the roost?'

'I am my father's son,' he said, peevishly. 'It is mine.'

A flight of geese went honking overhead. He loosened his hawk and held his wrist up.

'I have taken the oath of homage from every freeman from Scotland to the Pyrenees. Before God!'

He slipped the hood from the hawk and sent it soaring into the sky with a yell of encouragement. Eleanor showed no interest.

'Why do you dislike me, mother?'

'I hardly remember you. I can never forget Richard.'

She turned back to gaze through the archway into the Abbey. The stone effigy of Richard now lay beside that of his father, and still she grieved. John accepted her words as a challenge.

'I will bring in a hundred years of peace. I will be remembered long after Richard.' He became confidential. 'That is between you and me.'

His hawk had now caught its prey and he was content.

'I will go south,' he announced, 'to Lusignan and Angoulême, to Périgord and Agenais, Toulouse and Gascony. And I shall marry – someone.'

In the castle of Lusignan two old enemies were sinking their differences and groping towards friendship. It was the worst moment for them to be interrupted by the arrival of an uninvited guest. Hugh, the corpulent Lord of Lusignan and Count of La Marche, was suspicious.

'I do not like him, Ademar,' he confessed. 'I have never met him before. I fought his brother often enough and always got beaten. Well, he is Duke now and I bend the knee for Lusignan as you must for Angoulême.'

'What is he doing at Lusignan, Lord Hugh?' Ademar of Angoulême was tall, thin, ambitious. 'At this particular moment!'

'He said he was on his way to Portugal to look for a bride.'

'What liars the Plantagenets all are! He knows very well that your son is about to marry my daughter. I think he wants to stop the marriage. Divide and rule.'

'I hate a crafty man,' declared Hugh. 'With Richard, he would be out there battering down my walls, and he would get in, hang a few serfs and say – "*Dieus*, Hugh, how fat you are getting!"'

'What have you done with Duke John?' asked the slimmer man.

Hugh indicated a lighted window across the courtyard.

John and two servants could be seen quite clearly. Ademar, as unruly and rebellious a baron as any in his time, sighed.

'Pity there is peace!' He watched John's profile. 'They say he is the biggest liar of the lot.'

'Geoffrey was the biggest. He lied like the devil. What a family, Ademar!'

'He is the last of them,' recalled the other, thoughtfully.

'Eh? No, if he went the Duchy would revert to his mother, who must be a hundred! After her, Philip of France will get it. Do you want to be ruled by a Frenchman? A foreigner from Paris?'

Ademar was always ready to consider any possibilities in a situation. He nodded.

'I can see advantages in it.'

'Only if you are related to him,' said Hugh. 'And you are going to be related to me ... ah!'

His exclamation was caused by the entry of Ademar's twelve-year-old daughter, Isabelle. She was exquisitely beautiful, rose-cheeked, delicate. Nature had spared her any resemblance to the sharp-faced Ademar. Isabelle of Angoulême made the widowed Hugh gasp and remember his manhood.

'I think I shall marry you myself!'

It had not taken John long to find out all the details of the impending marriage. As he stood at the window of his room and looked across the courtyard, he could see Hugh and Ademar laughing and embracing as friends. John spoke to his valet, Petit.

'Why does Ademar want Lusignan?'

'The Lusignans are good fighters, my lord. Good men to have on your side in a war.'

'If Angoulême and Lusignan combined against me – God's teeth! – even Richard could not have beaten them.'

'They must not combine, then,' opined Petit, simply.

'I thought I came here by chance,' said John, still at the window, 'but if God wants me to prevent this marriage ...'

He paused, transfixed by what he saw. The two men had disappeared from the window and their place had been taken by a miniature Venus, a sprite, a fawn, a flower-fairy, a creature of sun-like radiance, a goddess. John stared at the neat figure in the tightly-fitting gown of scarlet and gold that allowed her dove-like shoulders to peep through. He was Henry seeing his Rosamund for the first time, Richard meeting Milo.

When she saw him watching her, she was curious, her curiosity quickly making way for a coquettish modesty, which was displaced in turn by a sly amusement. John had identified her at once and put the seed of an idea into his mind. He smiled, waved, gestured, communicated and laughed until she was laughing with him.

Across the narrow courtyard of the castle of Lusignan King John of England and Isabelle of Angoulême laughed away a marriage contract.

'I must speak to Ademar,' decided John. 'At once.'

'What is the matter with you?'

The crying from inside the curtains was quite piteous.

'What *is* the matter?' demanded the bridegroom.

'I do not like you,' came the sobbed reply.

'Too late now,' observed John, philosophically.

He sat on his treasury chest and pulled his nightshirt around him. They were in a room in the Tower of London and its thick, stone walls, dingy banner, and guttering flambeau did not add up to a romantic setting. There was an oppression in the air which she had noticed at once.

'I do not like it here. The Tower of London is a prison.'

'Yes.'

'And you do not like me!'

She peered out of the curtains in her shift and was miserable again when she saw her husband. Her tears made him defensive.

'I do like you, Isabelle. I made you Queen before your thirteenth birthday. To marry you I had to divorce another

Isabelle – that took some arranging.' He touched her hair. 'I love you! Surely you understand that what we do together means I love you?'

'No,' she replied, sulkily.

'Well it does.'

'I was happy in Angoulême then you put me in prison.'

'We *live* here,' he reasoned. 'The Tower happens to be safe.'

'I want to go home, back to my parents.'

Her sobbing started again and John looked around for something to distract her. He jumped off the chest, opened it up, and began to display its contents.

'Isabelle, look! Here is your crown. You did not have that in Angoulême. Put it on. I shall put mine on.'

He posed in his nightshirt with the crown of England on his head and the sheer absurdity of it made her giggle. Isabelle got out of bed and took her crown while John lifted regalia from the chest.

'This is the crown of the Dukes of Normandy – the coronet of Aquitaine – my sceptre – my ring as Count of Poitou – the crown of the Empress Matilda, my grandmother ...'

He became fascinated by the range and glitter of the jewels and took them all out until they were in a great heap on the floor. When she knelt beside him, he began to put the things on her until she was bedecked with gold, silver, rubies, pearls, diamonds. The effect was dazzling and he could do nothing but sit and gaze at her in adoration.

> 'Red gold her hair,
> Pink pearl her flesh,
> Two eyes of amethyst,
> Rubies her lip upon I kisst.'

And in the midst of his treasure, he kissed her softly. 'Now it is my turn,' he said, greedily.

There was a note of hysteria in his voice as he grabbed at rings, chains, sapphires, diamonds, jewels of every kind, until he was bespangled like an Eastern emperor. John was a King who would always outshine his Queen.

Hugh of Lusignan was disgruntled. He had been tricked and betrayed and was now kept waiting. Hugh stood in a room in the royal palace with a group of Poitevin barons, the blackness of his face contrasting with the gay, almost lurid colours of their attire. He had come to Paris in search of justice and revenge and the King of France was making him wait.

'In the time we've been here,' he muttered, resentfully, 'we could have sacked Angoulême, hanged Ademar from his tower, raised an army and besieged Bordeaux, spread war like dung and grown blood-red daisies! Go to law! I would as soon go to hell!'

At the far end of the room, Philip, coifed like a hawk, sat in a chair and listened to the Black Monk with keen interest. From inside the dark cowl the voice came out harsh, passionate and whispered.

'From this act of lust comes their destruction. The father seduced your father's wife, engendering the brood in incest and adultery. Each was tainted with lust – for power, for land, for the glory of this world – festering as a venereal sore upon the fair body of France. Under judgement of God, note well, my son, without issue – saving the boy, Arthur.'

Philip ran the tip of his tongue around his lips.

'The tyrant, Henry, aggrandized using the deceits of law. The perverted heretic, Richard, used the sword. By God's grace both burn in hell. The last voluptuous Angevin, John, has offended both law and sword.'

The Black Monk gripped his master's arm like an eagle.

'John abducted the young girl from the custody of her legal guardian to whose son she was pledged. When the man, who is his liegeman, appealed for justice, he was refused. This offends feudal law.'

'How does this serve me?' asked Philip, now impatient.

'It is your solemn duty as John's overlord to see that he

answers for his default. You summon him to appear before your court. If he comes, he acknowledges he is your vassal. If he refuses, he is condemned a recreant and contumacious vassal and his lands are forfeit!'

Philip wetted his lips once more.

'More than that – the lords and knights who have sworn him homage are released from their oaths and service. He is alone and you will destroy him.'

'I never heard you speak to such effect,' said Philip.

'Pray God I will not talk again!'

Philip looked down the room to see the surly Hugh and his companions fretting even more.

'These will be mine,' he grinned, 'these dogs that have tasted the blood of a King.'

The carcass of a stag, struck with an arrow, lay in the middle of the floor. A serf, arms bound, stood before a bench, flanked by two of the King's foresters. The clerk behind the bench was toneless.

'Pleas of the King's Crown, assize of Nottingham, the year from the incarnation of our Lord 1201, in the month of October.'

King John was in no hurry to begin proceedings. He was pacing up and down as he read a document. The clerk waited, the serf waited, Hubert Walter, William Marshall and Brieuse waited, the stag waited. At length the clerk tried to move things along.

'John Dol is charged with taking venison in the royal forest of our lord the King in ...'

'Let him wait,' interrupted John.

He finished the document then started to read it again.

'Lord King, give me justice,' pleaded the serf.

'Archbishop,' said John, ignoring his namesake, 'the summons is unjust. I am to attend the court at Paris, yet there is an established agreement that, as Duke of Normandy, I always meet King Philip on the boundary between us.'

Hubert tried to be tactful.

'With respect, my lord, you are not summoned as Duke of Normandy but as Count of Poitou, where the alleged offence took place.'

'You would never have dared to talk to Richard of alleged offences,' snarled John. 'It is a lie!'

'Mine, too,' urged John of Dol.

Hubert was calm and rational.

'King Philip can demand the presence of that part of you that is Poitou, my lord.'

'Which part do you suggest I send?' joked John. 'My head is England, my heart is Normandy, my belly is Anjou ... and I need the rest because I am married.'

The foresters laughed with him and even John Dol rose to a snigger. William Marshall and Brieuse were shocked by the King's flippancy and looked to Hubert to speak for them.

'If you do not attend,' warned the Archbishop, 'you must have another answer ready.'

'I will give him the old English answer.' John was still laughing. 'Blow for blow – like King Richard and King Henry.'

'Henry was a good king,' argued John of Dol, grasping at any chance to defend himself. 'He was not too particular about the forest laws.'

John quelled him with a look then crossed to his barons.

'We must go to Normandy, Marshal. Muster the army and meet us at Portsmouth the week before Easter.'

William Marshall, Earl of Pembroke and the most respected soldier in the realm, broke the news quietly.

'There was a meeting of the earls at Leicester ...'

John began to look angry, dangerous.

'By common consent they said they would not cross the sea until you restored their rights.'

'What rights!' blustered John. 'Every man thinks of his own interests and calls them rights.' A hissed aside was aimed at the Marshal's ear alone. 'Pick out the most outspoken and take hostages from their families – so they observe *my* rights.' He was full of bluster again. 'Good

King Henry knew what to do with rights – he gave them to me!'

He was about to storm out of the court when the clerk intervened.

'Lord King, John Dol is charged with taking venison.'

'He is guilty.' It was an instant verdict. 'Read out the sentence.'

'Whoever shall commit an offence in the King's forest with relation to his venison and shall be attainted for the same, he shall be at the mercy of the King for the loss of his eyes and his virility.'

John Dol's hand moved protectively to his groin. The King gave him a glance then headed for the door.

'He did not ask for mercy – give him justice.'

The two foresters pushed the serf out.

Summary justice was dispensed in the French court as well. When John failed to appear in Paris to answer his summons, all the lands which he held of the King of France were declared forfeit. Philip commanded Arthur, now a boy of fifteen, to kneel before him and made him Duke of Aquitaine, Count of Poitou and Count of Anjou.

'Not Normandy?'

'Mon Dieu!' Philip was shocked. 'Another greedy Plantagenet, with those cursed hands that grab all!'

He did not disclose his plan to make Normandy an integral part of France.

Like his brother and his father before him, King John raised an army to defend his French inheritance. He set up his headquarters in Le Mans, a city with strong Plantagenet ties. From this base in Maine, he was able to watch developments in both Normandy and Aquitaine, both of which were soon stained by blood.

In the summer of 1202, he found himself kneeling in the chapel of the castle at Le Mans. In the adjacent Hall, William Marshal and Brieuse, veteran soldiers in full armour, idled the time away by playing dice. Brieuse threw first.

'Two aces – two angels, as Richard used to say. Would he were here to say it!'

'He would not be here,' asserted the Marshal. 'He would be in Château Gaillard defending Normandy. He would be in Poitou putting down rebellion. The last place he would be is here in the middle – in Le Mans – on his knees.'

'This is war and no war,' agreed Brieuse. 'Fear losing Normandy or Poitou and he will lose them both ... Your throw.'

While his commanders were passing the time at play, John was gazing at the jewelled cross in the chapel as if trying to hypnotise it. He was remembering a night in the Abbey of Fontevrault when he made a bargain with God before settling down for a sleep between two dead kings. There was a sense of menace in his prayer.

'Almighty God, I have sworn fealty to you; you are my lord and let me keep my lands. It is a contract between me and you on pain of forfeit. I have not failed you, God be with me, men are against me, God be with me ...'

He was so absorbed in his contemplation of the cross that he would not have heard what was being said about him next door if it had been shouted in his ears.

'Betrayal is in his character.' William Marshal was gloomy as he rolled the ivory dice. 'At the end, he betrayed his father. He betrayed Richard and fled to Paris. And the first thing he does as king is to steal a girl and betray his host – and his wife! He keeps failing.'

'Richard behaved the same way before he was king,' reminded Brieuse. 'As for the girl – it would have been madness to let Lusignan marry Angoulême. And have you seen her? John is no fool.'

A page entered to announce the arrival of the senseschal of Anjou and a breathless William des Roches came in.

'Where is the King?' he asked.

Brieuse pointed towards the chapel and raised a hand

when the newcomer tried to walk in that direction. The panting seneschal sat down and the page was sent for wine.

'Well, des Roches?' asked the Marshal.

'The world is turned upside down. Once Anjou was the centre, the keep, the bastion. Now it is the front line. I am fighting Bretons, and Lusignans, and now Arthur is leading a French army in Touraine.' He glanced towards the chapel. 'He needs to pray.'

'When Richard was ransomed, the situation was worse than this,' offered Brieuse.

'John has lost the legal battle,' sighed the Marshal. 'Men who were once loyal now refuse to serve him. Men who were rebels now justify rebellion.'

'He is still King Henry's son,' said Brieuse.

'Arthur's claim is good,' conceded the Marshal.

William des Roches was sullen as he examined the possibilities.

'Your lands are in England,' he muttered, enviously.

The page brought a flagon of wine and goblets on a pewter tray. There was a clatter as he put his tray down on the table and it disturbed John in the chapel.

'Who is it?' he called.

'William des Roches, my lord.'

'Any news?'

'They have captured Angers.'

Still on his knees in the chapel, John began to feel his wrath stirring once again. He got up, face red and swollen, glaring at the cross. The solemn contract had been made on pain of forfeit. He grabbed the cross, stuffed it into his pocket, and left at speed.

Irreverence occurred at Fontevrault, too. Arthur had attacked with an army of Lusignans and French and put all to flight. Inside the Abbey, nuns ran and hid at his approach, not stopping to see that he was wearing a sur coat emblazoned with leopards.

Arthur looked at the tomb of Henry, then at that of

Richards, his uncle. He remembered the Christmas at Château Gaillard when he had asked if he would be King of England. And he remembered Richard's evasive answer. Raising his sword in a sudden frenzy, he brought it down upon the stone with a jarring clang. Fingers on Richard's right hand were severed by the blow and fell to the ground.

Hugh of Lusignan was openly disgusted.

'In the Holy Land one morning, Richard rode out of our camp alone and came back with the heads of seven Saracens hanging from his saddle – cut off with that hand.'

With a rough tenderness, Hugh tried to gather up the fragments and put them back in position on the effigy. Arthur was unrepentant.

'I am your lord now.'

'He was a *lord*, my lord. *Dieus*, how I hated him. *Dieus*, how I loved him.' He regarded Arthur, thoughtfully. 'You are like your father, Geoffrey.'

'Did you know him?'

'I knew them all. Young Henry, Richard and Geoffrey. They were Devils at play and war. The world is a safer place without them but they dazzled.'

'How did *he* dazzle?' asked Arthur.

'He was the most accomplished liar I ever knew.'

'He was the Count of Brittany,' yelled Arthur, defiantly. 'A great soldier who was never beaten.'

'He never fought.'

Arthur was starting to work himself up into a Plantagenet rage when some Poitevin soldiers came in. They were empty-handed.

'She has gone!' roared Arthur, stamping.

'Of course she has gone,' said Hugh, sagely. 'She would hardly wait to welcome you.'

'Follow her!'

'Which way, my lord?' Hugh was mocking him now. 'North to Chinon, south to Poitiers. Queen Eleanor is old and light – she might have blown either way.'

There was a noise from behind the screen and the

soldiers went to investigate, reappearing with a young nun who had been crouched in hiding. Arthur had an opportunity to show his mettle.

'Where has the old Queen gone? You will be tortured. Your habit will not protect you. I shall order my men to tear it off.'

The nun looked at the boy and was unafraid.

'*Credo in Deum, Patrem omnipotentem ...*' she began.

'Poitiers is her city,' said Hugh, 'and that is where she has gone. Come, let us fight holy sisters and old women because Richard is dead and the light has gone out of the world.'

He led his Poitevins out of the Abbey and back to their horses. Arthur was left alone with the chanting nun and the broken hand of Richard. He ran quickly after Hugh.

The elderly cleric, Guy Diva, was praying for all his worth in his room in the castle keep at Mirebeau. A devout man in peacetime, he became even more assiduous in his devotions during war. He heard horses in the yard below, rushed to the window, and saw something which sent him scurrying down the stone steps.

When he entered the courtyard, Queen Eleanor was resting on her litter while four nuns stood in attendance. Vast amounts of baggage lay around and a captain was giving orders to a handful of men.

'Two on watch! The rest hold the gate below! Hurry!'

Guy Diva had a marked preference for the least violent solution to any problem.

'Captain, if we surrender immediately and do not give them trouble, I expect they will spare our lives.'

'I have sent a rider to Le Mans,' said the captain. 'Eighty miles away. Three, four days march. We can hold the keep ...'

The man was set on resistance and so Guy Diva went to the Queen instead. She was aching with rheumatism and with the discomfort of her flight from Fontevrault.

'*Quel aventura!*' she whispered.

'Your grace, we must surrender quietly,' he advised.

'How long have you been with me, Guy Diva?'

'So many years.'

'You are sacked.'

'I am a friar,' he protested.

'A sacked friar ... Captain! Put this old woman out!'

Fear of what might happen to him made Guy Diva hop about as if the stones were red hot.

'They will hang me! Let me stay here and die with you! Please!'

'*Seigneur Dieus!*' she snorted. 'What company for my last Crusade.'

She called the captain to help her up out of her litter and her fine grey robes were soon covering his hauberk. She felt the strength and closeness of a man again.

'Kiss me!' she commanded.

The captain promptly kissed the frail old woman full on the lips. She could now get down to the serious business in hand.

'What is their strength, captain?'

'A troop of cavalry and about fifty footmen, but they will have reinforcements on the way.' He weighed bravery against discretion. 'We cannot hold out for long, your grace. Maybe we should surrender.'

She jabbed at a bag with her stick and one of the nuns brought it forward, opening it for her. Eleanor's hands groped about inside the bag with an eager pride.

'I had a son, your King, who never lost, never yielded, never betrayed any man. Richard would have laughed at this.'

She pulled out a banner which had Richard's leopards upon it and clutched it jealously. Then she kissed it and handed it to the captain.

'Set him up – let them know that they will have to kill us all.'

The captain responded with a grin while the trembling Guy Diva crossed himself.

*

With all his faults, King John was no mean soldier. He lacked Henry's tactical sense and Richard's military genius, but he was nevertheless a very competent general in the field. None of his enemies could call him a coward and an emergency brought out the true Plantagenet fighting spirit in him.

When the news about the siege of Mirebeau reached him, John did not pause or dither. His army was riding south within the hour. They crossed the Loire, struck down through Chinon, and reached the besieged town long before they might be expected.

While her son was wreaking havoc in the town below, Eleanor, convinced of the nearness of death, was fondling old memories in a room in the keep. The captain, Guy Diva and the now frightened nuns were in attendance.

'One night at Woodstock, I could not sleep. I think it was the moon. I took off all my clothes and danced naked.'

'Do you want to be confessed?' asked Guy Diva, hopefully.

'Henry was not there. He could not have been.' Sourness claimed her. 'He put me in Salisbury Tower for sixteen years. I came out an old woman.'

'I do not believe that,' said the captain, gallantly. 'You are younger than the moon and twice as beautiful.'

She was about to thank him when they heard the creaking of a door below as it was pushed open. Footsteps pattered their approach and they prepared themselves for the worst. The keep had been invaded.

'Mother?'

John came into the room in an ecstasy of triumph, laughing, boasting, giving orders, strutting. Eleanor was astonished, the captain pleased, Guy Diva sent gratefully to his ancient knees. Activity filled the room as William Marshall, Brieuse and William des Roches entered, followed by a group of prisoners under escort.

'I captured Arthur,' bragged John. 'There is no more rebellion. What shall I do with Arthur?'

Eleanor looked across at the scowling youth and smiled grimly.

'He is a Plantagenet. Forgive him, promise him anything, give him nothing.' She was complimentary for once. 'You must have ridden like the Devil.'

'No – like father.' He turned around. 'Are you prisoners all Lusignans?'

'I am the only Lusignan here, my lord,' said Hugh. 'The rest are Poitevin dogs. If they had been from Lusignan, they would have made a better fight of it.'

'Hugh – Hugh – Hugh,' began John, walking around him. 'You old whore. Fight me because a girl preferred me to your son? I will find him a wife – you as well if you are still capable! On payment of a small fee.'

He reserved his ire for the Poitevin prisoners and now glared at each one in turn. Brieuse was at his shoulder.

'Recreants, oath-breakers, traitors. Your word was given before God and you offended God. I shall send you to England as a punishment. No Bordeaux wine, no delicious olives, no sunshine – no girls!' He spoke aside to Brieuse. 'Take them to Corfe Castle. I want to forget them. For ever.'

William des Roches, seneschal of Anjou, came up to the King.

'My lord, I will take Count Arthur to Chinon.'

There was something in his manner that alerted John. Seasoned in treachery himself, he could detect its early stirrings in others.

'May I remind you of your promise, my lord,' urged des Roches. 'I was to keep Count Arthur in my custody.'

'Only if you took him,' quibbled John. 'And you did not. Brieuse captured him in his nightshirt.' He laughed at Arthur, who was still attired for bed. 'I will keep Arthur.'

William des Roches suppressed his annoyance and turned to go.

'Des Roches,' called John. 'When you get home, send me your son – for his education.'

The seneschal left and John spoke to his mother again.

'Come with me to Rouen.'

'Winter. No, Fontevrault for me. I am half turned to stone as it is. And John ...' She was on her litter and he bent over to hear the whisper. 'Arthur is no threat. Philip is the enemy. Treat Arthur like a son ... Kiss me.'

He obeyed and she was carried out on a litter. John now approached the shivering Arthur.

'I will treat you like a son – take the traitor to our castle in Falaise in chains! He will learn what it means to be a king!'

Almost at once his manner changed to that of a solicitous parent.

'Are you cold? Here, let us go away ...'

He put an arm of comfort around Arthur and led him away.

Philip was furious at the capture of Arthur but he learned a new respect for John's abilities as a soldier. William des Roches went over to the French King and John's instinct was proved right.

John spent the winter at Rouen with his second wife. She loved him no better than before but she was nevertheless about to bear him a child. When the New Year came it brought neither comfort nor cheer for him. True to the Plantagenet tradition, he began to be disturbed by his dreams. Henry had been haunted by dreams about Thomas Becket; Richard's dreams had been a mirror of his spiritual unease; John dreamed of treachery against himself, of plotting, of intrigue, of assassination. He came to wonder if there was anyone he could really trust, and it was with this thought in mind that he visited Falaise.

'Well, Hubert?'

Hubert de Burgh was the keeper of the castle at Falaise.

'Nothing, my lord.'

'Nothing at all?'

They were in a dark passage outside a cell. John pulled

his furs around him and felt peeved that his prisoner had not been cursing him openly. Hubert was shaking his head again.

'Nothing, my lord.'

John attempted craft and tried to draw this reserved man out.

'I will be merciful. I should be merciful, I think.'

'Yes, my lord.'

'*Why?*' he snapped, and the other was caught on the spot.

'Arthur is only young. He was misled ...'

'If he is young, he has plenty of time to do it again, Hubert. He is a traitor taken in arms against his liege-lord. Any court would sentence him to death. It would only be justice.'

'That is so,' agreed Hubert without enthusiasm.

'It is so, Hubert and you would have to carry out the sentence. Open the cell.'

The heavy iron door was unlocked and John marched in. He pretended to sound indignant and horrified at what he saw.

'Are you trying to kill the boy?'

John grabbed the quilt that Hubert was carrying and threw it round the boy's shoulders. Arthur was still wearing the nightshirt in which he had been arrested some months before and it was now tattered, soiled and stinking. Gaunt, filthy, unkempt and blue with cold, Arthur was on a wooden bench, his wrists held by chains which ran to iron loops in the walls.

The cell was dry and light but the temperature was near to freezing. John managed to feel some genuine pity for the boy.

'I knew nothing of this,' he apologised. 'I spent Christmas at Rouen. I wished that you had been with us. Ask Isabelle. Did you have a good ... no, of course not. But it was not my fault.'

Arthur tried to edge away but his uncle had a hold on him.

'All you had to do was to talk to Hubert de Burgh. You should have said "Tell my uncle John that I am sorry. Ask him to forgive me." Do you think that I am inhuman? You are my nephew, my brother Geoffrey's son, my son now.'

'I am not,' said Arthur firmly.

'Because you rebelled against me,' accused John.

'If I am anybody's son, it is King Philip. I am going to marry his daughter.'

'No!' howled John, anger removing all trace of concern. 'We think that by marrying French princesses that we make ourselves secure. The other way round. Young Henry married Marguerite, Richard was going to marry Alys, I was going to marry Alys, even father was going to marry Alys! Do you think you are the first sprig of broom Philip has used to try and sweep us out?' He was waving his arms about now. 'He encouraged young Henry to rebel, and Geoffrey. Marry Marguerite and betray your father.'

'My mother was Constance of Brittany!' declared Arthur.

'Your mother would have been Philip of France if it had been possible. Geoffrey was up him often enough! Philip! Philip is deadly poison.'

'You rebelled against King Philip,' insisted the boy.

'A Plantagenet can *not* rebel against Philip. We are at war with him and always will be. Us or him, Arthur.' He let a promise dangle for a second. 'It is whichever one of us is King and Duke – me now, you after.'

John was disappointed that it got no reaction. He became more reasonable.

'Philip believes he is another Charlemagne. He wants Normandy, he wants Aquitaine, he wants Anjou. Arthur, he wants our empire.'

Months of imprisonment had not curbed Arthur's temper or given him an inkling about tact. His reply was immediate and blurted out.

'It is not your empire, it is mine!'

Rage made its way into John's countenance once again.

'My father was older than you, so I succeeded King Richard. King Philip only wants to do justice and—'

He was talking to thin air. John had gone out with Hubert and slammed the cell door after him with a clang of doom.

While Arthur was left to speculate on his fate, John was taking a more positive interest in it. A little distance from the cell, he was making his feelings known to Hubert.

'I trust you, Hubert.'

'Thank you, my lord.'

'How can you prove yourself worthy of that trust? By deeds, Hubert. Deeds do not lie.'

'No, my lord,' admitted the other, cautiously.

'He swore me fealty before God and broke his oath. He is a traitor and deserves to die.'

'If sentenced by a court . . .'

'This is a court. He is condemned to death.' He sensed a deep reluctance in the other. 'Hubert.'

'My lord?'

'You advised me to be merciful.' His tone was almost jocular. 'He is a boy and he will live.' John could not make Hubert speak. 'But not to try and steal from me again. I commute the sentence – to mutilation.' He came closer when he saw the shock on Hubert's face. 'If *he* had been caught red-handed with a buck, *your* eyes had stayed where they were.'

'My lord, he is your nephew!' implored Hubert.

'So he will live, blind, impotent, alive, to thank me.' His anger flared yet again. 'God man! You have done it before! Castellan of Falaise, warden of the forest! Have his balls out!'

John was off on his way along the passage and Hubert de Burgh permitted himself an assessment of the House of Plantagenet.

'From the Devil they came, to the Devil they will go.'

That same evening, when Arthur had eaten his meal off a metal platter and was moving towards his pallet, he preceived two visitors. They brought long, sharp knives and no light and moved about their business swiftly. Hubert was wrapped in his chains and pinned against the wall before he knew what was happening.

'Hubert, I'm sorry!' he screamed, as the knives cut. 'Ask my uncle John to forgive me!'

His sobs went unregarded and the men held his head back. Having done the first part of their task, they now went for his eyes with a fury that John would have approved.

CHAPTER ELEVEN

Spring brought hope, promise and a resumption of war. Armies which had rested throughout the winter now donned their armour again and tried to settle old scores with renewed vigour. Flowers were trampled and grass was bloodied throughout the length and breadth of the continental dominions. It was a revolt against nature, a denial of the burgeoning expectation of a new season.

Things went badly for King John from the start.

'He has lost the best part of his hereditary domains in Anjou and Maine to the Bretons and des Roches.'

Eleanor did not seem to be listening. He raised his voice a little and turned his face towards her.

'The castles on the frontier of Normandy are falling, some by siege, most by treachery and desertion.' Brieuse summed up his tidings in a sentence. 'Madame, your husband's empire is falling to the King of France.'

Eleanor, now in her eighties, body bent and wasted, hands like talons, face like parchment wrapped in a linen wimple, stopped beside the tomb and rested on his arm.

'I have renounced the world, Brieuse.'

'Your son needs help.'

'I left the Devil with some regret, the flesh with some

relief, but the world – how hard we cling to the world! A baby to its mother's finger.' She looked down at Richard's effigy. 'I can not help him. Let me be. I have travelled so long on my pilgrimage.'

She leaned on the tomb for support, her hands exploring the contours of her son's face with loving care. They came to rest on his forehead, the brow of her crusader-king.

Brieuse stared in admiration for a moment at this remarkable woman – wife of two kings, mother of two more, Queen, Duchess, diplomat, politician, crusader, Empress of the Courts of Love. He suddenly knelt before her on impulse.

'Some few of us were captured by a Queen. A yellow flower danced above our head and dared the world for Eleanor. We rode with the Young King in his hour. We sailed with Richard to the Holy Land. We wept for Richard at Chalus and ever since. Some few of us could not forget.'

'That was not bad for an Englishman with Norman blood,' she smiled. 'What has my cuckoo done now?'

Brieuse was on his feet again, talking quickly.

'Arthur was at Falaise when the rumour spread that he was dead. The Bretons raised an army. Hubert de Burgh, the castellan, swore that Arthur was alive but would not produce him for a deputation of Bretons. They marched into Anjou and King Philip attacked Normandy.' He was loyal enough to be hurt. 'Men have lost faith in the King.'

'Where is John?'

'At Rouen for Easter.'

'And Arthur?' She got no answer. 'Tell the King this. He must release Arthur and give him titles – Count of Brittany to pacify the Bretons, Count of Anjou to disarm des Roches. He must name Arthur as heir to Normandy and check Philip who then has no legal claim while Arthur is alive.'

'And if Arthur is dead?' he asked.

'Adieu. Adieu, Anjou. Adieu, Normandy. Adieu, Aquitaine. Adieu, England. Adieu, dominion of the world, Adieu, king ...'

*

The chapel in the castle at Rouen was veiled in white for Maundy Thursday. White light streamed in through the windows and fell upon the bowed heads of the celebrants, themselves all in white. The cross was covered in white and the choristers – now singing 'Gloria in excelsis' – were wearing their white surplices.

The chapel was in the centre of a network of galleries and passages, and it was down one of the latter that John was now coming in the white garb of a penitent.

When soured by bad news at Le Mans, he had questioned his contract with God; when lifted by good fortune at Mirebeau, he had renewed it; and now, at Rouen, racked by doubts and assailed by worries, he needed to examine the terms of that contract again.

He walked with William Marshal.

'Is that the truth?'

'Of course. I have just had remission for my sins. I am not going to start again on Maundy Thursday.'

'If Arthur is alive, my lord, where is he?'

'At Falaise.'

'Let him be seen. This secrecy makes men suspicious. It has the same effect as if the boy was dead. Men say so.'

'My enemies,' said John, dismissively.

William Marshal felt that he had earned the right to be blunt and honest with the King.

'They were your friends.'

John accepted the reproach without flinching, then detached himself from the Marshal and turned down another passageway. He could hear the voice of the priest echoing in the chapel.

'O God, from whom Judas received the punishment of his guilt, and the thief the reward of his confession, grant us the effect of Thy clemency; that as our Lord Jesus Christ in His passion gave to each a different recompense according to his merits ...'

'All but one,' noted John. 'My God, I keep faith with you, keep you with me.'

He went down a flight of steps in his bare feet until he

reached the lowest of the passages. There was a square of light in the floor and he knelt beside it to look down through an iron grating. He seemed at once reassured and alarmed by what he saw, secure in his purpose yet fearing the discovery of that purpose.

Black dominated the chapel on Good Friday and it reflected the darkness of a soul in which suspicion, hatred and dread had taken refuge. The cross was veiled in black and he watched with fascination as the priest slowly and ceremonially unveiled it – first the top, then the right arm, then the head. He was staring into the blind eyes of Christ and could not look away.

The service continued to the point where the celebrants, now in black, began to wash the cross. He was mesmerised as the ivory Christ was rinsed in wine and water. It was an image too powerful for him to contemplate for long – a corpse dripping with blood-red water – and the cross shimmered before him.

'Can I trust you, God?' asked John. 'God? God?'

That same night Brieuse was walking along the gallery above the chapel on his way to his room in another part of the castle. All was in darkness but he heard sounds which made him stop in his tracks. Someone was moving about in the chapel and muttering.

'Judas had the grace to hang himself, or went into a field and burst. His light is out, he is as good as dead, as bad, worse living.' The voice rose in reproach. 'Can you not keep your word any more?'

Brieuse knew the speaker at once and felt embarrassed.

More noises followed – a cupboard being wrenched open, a clink of glass, a loud gulping as he drank.

'You did today. Good health. Good health, God.' Another gulp and then the voice became a shout. 'I can not resurrect the dead, the living dead – *he* is not dead.' John was quieter. 'Traitors suspect, I committed mercy, betray me, in a moment of compassion, Bretons – what have I to do?'

Brieuse only dimly understood what his King was saying and he was uncertain what to do about it. He remained where he was as he heard the scrape of a chair on the stone floor.

'The King of France takes castles on his knees at prayer. God – why hast thou forsaken me? ... *Pater noster, mea culpa, mea maxima*, but not of that, not that, not that. All they want is to see him.'

There was a flare of tinder as he lit a candle and stumbled towards a passage with the bottle still in his hand. Brieuse descended swiftly and followed as closely as he dared. He heard the iron door of a cell being unbolted and opened, then found himself facing a grating in the floor. Still not understanding, Brieuse crouched down and inched towards the grating.

'Arthur – it is uncle John. Did I wake you? No, you do not know day from night down here. It is night, night.'

Brieuse could see a cell and a pallet and the familiar outline of Arthur. John was lighting torches in wall brackets and the cell was soon bright. Arthur was lying face downwards on the pallet until John nudged him.

'Did you sleep well? Answer me.'

The boy rolled over and Brieuse shuddered as he saw the black, shrunken, empty eye-sockets.

'It was not me,' said John, defensively. 'I had left Falaise. I do not know how it happened. Hubert has not talked yet.' He sat at the table. 'Believe me, Arthur, it has caused me as much trouble as it has caused you.'

Real compassion seemed to soften him and he poured out two cups of wine, inviting Arthur to join him. The boy hauled himself up and Brieuse was able to see the chains on his hands and feet, the matted hair, the foul prison garment. Arthur groped his way to a chair, took the proffered cup and felt around it before drinking.

'Is the pain better?' John was sharper. 'Do you think you can defeat me by not talking?' He became almost amused. 'Your Breton friends want to see you – that would hardly do at the moment.'

Arthur pushed his chair back and staggered around the cell.

'Careful! You may hurt yourself. I let them think you were dead. An accident while trying to escape.' A hardness came into his voice. 'You could be dead – you would be if I was not merciful.'

Words were finally prised out of Arthur and they came in a low, unforgiving hiss.

'Uncle if you were merciful, who was cruel?'

'Oh Hubert,' said John, carelessly. 'Hubert would have killed you if I had not stopped him.'

He had given himself away and Arthur at last had proof of who was responsible for his mutilation. In a fit of anger, the boy reached out for a chair, found it, lifted it and brought it crashing down. John stepped back as the chair fell then dived forward to grapple with Arthur as he tried to lift the chair again.

John was stronger, quicker, sighted and he soon overpowered the prisoner, pinning him across the table so that a chain was across his neck. Arthur struggled as John tried to offer him rational argument.

'You were condemned to death and at the mercy of a king – what else could I do? Let you go to rise again? I could not trust you. You had broken your oath of homage to me.'

Arthur was still fighting and grunting to get free and John was steadily tightening his grip on the chains. There was something in the struggle and the resentment and the passion that excited John and made him try to press down harder and harder on the chain.

'You offended God!' he cried, moral outrage burning in him. 'I am God's anointed, Arthur. I have sworn fealty to God and he will give me back my lands.'

He had straddled Arthur now and his wrists were twisting the chain with manic power. Brieuse could see the boy's veins bulging and his resistance fading fast.

'It is God's will, Arthur, not mine. I was merciful, I was wrong. God wanted you to die, you had to die to get back my lands. Look at you – look at you! God has punished you. God's will be done!'

A final stab of pressure on the chain and Arthur was gone, the life strangled and bruised out of him. John mumbled on.

'God's will, and when the Bretons grow tired they will go home. Philip will go home, too, and there will be peace.'

John slowly released his hold on the chains and stood up, allowing the body to roll from the table and hit the floor with a dull thud. Brieuse was sick to his stomach as he looked at the thin, defenceless, violated corpse.

Becoming for the first time aware of the consequences of what he had done, John sought to dispose of the body. He glanced around, saw the grating through which refuse and excrement were dispatched towards the river, and dragged Arthur across to it. The grating was lifted and the body forced into the long, slippery, reeking tunnel. A distant splash seemed to be a signal for John to depart.

He snuffed out the flames around the room so that only his own lamp was burning.

'Where is Arthur? Who? Ah, the Lord fed a multitude with fish – he is food for a multitude of fishes. Lights out! Another miracle.'

In reaching for his own lamp, he knocked it over and extinguished the flame. John was now groping and banging around the cell in the way that Arthur had been doing. He felt his way to the door and out into the passage. He made slow progress towards the chapel but eventually entered it and felt safe.

'Now light up,' said the priest.

The darkness in the chapel became a blaze of light as ministers came in from all round with lamps and candles. John was caught, stricken with terror, branded with guilt. He waited for the accusation, the interrogation, the retribution – but it did not come.

'Lumen Christi . . .' chanted the ministers in their violet and white vestments.

John began to realise that he had stumbled into the chapel in the middle of a service. The ministers were taking down the sombre hangings in front of the altar to reveal a glorious display of spring flowers, set among gold and silver ornaments. John's confidence grew, then swelled, as the service continued. From the position he had taken up in the gallery, Brieuse was able to see John's face alight and smiling as he held out his arms in gratitude.

'I hate baths.'

'It is all over now, Isabelle.'

'I hate water, I hate scrubbing, I hate baths.'

He watched her get out of the tub, the bulge of her stomach distorting her figure but in no way reducing her attraction for him. He put his arms around her wet body and fondled her shoulders, her buttocks, her breasts. He ran his hands through her hair and then buried his face in it. The approach of a maid stopped any further intimacies and he was annoyed. Isabelle, amused and relieved, took her gown from the maid and ran off.

The girl came to move the tub of water but sensed that she had offended the King and slipped out quickly herself. John crossed to the tub in which his wife had been bathing and looked down into the hot, soapy water. He thought he saw something at the bottom of the tub, something that was difficult to identify at first but which became clearer and clearer in outline.

It was a cross, the shimmering cross he had seen in the chapel, the white corpse in a bath of red blood. He thrust a hand into the water but the cross had vanished away.

A page came into the room and announced William Marshal, Earl of Pembroke. The Marshal brought grave news.

'Château Gaillard is besieged.'

'Is that all?' he shrugged.

'My lord, Château Gaillard is the last castle between the French and Rouen. Conches was taken, Vaudreuil surrendered ...'

'I shall get them back,' retorted John. 'Remember Mirebeau.'

'You have lost everything you gained at Mirebeau. My lord we must make a strike against King Philip at Château Gaillard.'

'Naturally.' John did not like to be told what to do.

'You have been in Rouen two months. Your father and your brother seldom stayed two days anywhere. They used to ride with the army, visit the castles, direct the mercenaries, even—'

'Enough!'

'My lord...?'

'Do not talk of Richard!' He was roused. 'My father was a great king but Richard? He caused all this. He drained the treasury three times – for his Crusade, for his ransom, for his wars. Such taxes, such ravages – that was Richard. What kept English, Norman, Angevin and Poitevin together?'

'Under your father ...'

'Under Henry, mutual protection and prosperity. Under Richard, fear of Richard.'

'Leadership of Richard,' argued the Marshal.

'The dogs had not turned,' whined John. 'Who could lead the pack that I have got? Rabid with treachery. They would as soon bite me as Philip! Des Roches and Fitzwalter, the coward who gave up Vaudreuil ...'

'And Château Gaillard?'

'Château Gaillard?' He was suddenly calm, almost wistful. 'Richard called it his naughty castle. We spent Christmas there.' He became decisive. 'Château Gaillard must be relieved. We have time on our side. Roger de Lacy will be able to hold out for a while yet.'

'My lord, if it were to fall ...'

'Then we should all fall, Marshal. Muster the army. It is time I met Philip again ...'

Though King John had been scornful of his brother, Richard, the latter had taught him a lot about the art of warfare. John's plan to relieve Château Gaillard was worthy of Richard himself and bore his hallmark. While supplies were rowed up the Seine in seventy boats, guarded by a naval detachment, William Marshal was to lead an armed contingent along the left bank of the river to take the French camp unawares.

William Marshal assembled a force of three hundred knights, three thousand men-at-arms, and four thousand foot-soldiers. An auxiliary force of *routiers* under Lupescar made it a formidable army, and it was left in no doubt as to the importance of its mission. The relief of Château Gaillard was not an isolated engagement in a long war. Effectively, it was a fight to save the whole of Normandy.

John called his commanders together on the eve of the battle.

'Does Brieuse go with Lupescar in the boats?' he asked.

'All the great folk come with me,' said the Marshal, looking at Brieuse. 'Their armour would sink them in the river.'

'Attack the enemy at daybreak, relieve Château Gaillard and send me good news back to Rouen.'

William Marshal looked amazed, Brieuse less so, and the cynical Lupescar not at all surprised.

'Will you go back to Rouen *now*, my lord?' The Marshal could not believe it.

'The Queen is not well.' explained John blithely. 'I received a message to return at once. Do you imagine I would have missed a fight otherwise? I will be a day or two. If you should capture Philip, send him to Rouen.'

He walked off without another word. William Marshal shrugged and Lupescar grimaced. Brieuse, still haunted by what he had seen in the prison cell at Rouen, was bitter and contemptuous.

'God forbid!'

The army attacked at daybreak and inflicted great losses on the French army, driving them back across a pontoon bridge which Philip was having constructed. When the bridge broke and armoured Frenchmen fell into the Seine in hundreds, it seemed as if there might be a rout. But John's battle-plan depended on a simultaneous assault by the men in the boats and the flotilla was held up by contrary tides. The French forces rallied and their superior numbers began to tell. It was a savage encounter in which axes, swords, lances, arrows and bare hands did their work, making the Seine a graveyard for thousands.

When John's banner with its leopards was chased from the field and the fleur-de-lys of France fluttered in triumph, the garrison at Château Gaillard was doomed. The last attempt repel Philip's invasion of Normandy had failed.

While his men were being put to flight further south, John was in a room in the castle at Rouen, nervously confident as he awaited the news of victory. Isabelle, now recovered, stood at the window and gazed down at the Seine as it wended its way through the city. An involuntary scream escaped her and John was at the window in seconds.

There in the river, bleeding and broken, was the body of a young knight whom John knew well for his courage. The corpse was floating along with a great gash down its face where a French axe had tried to split the head in two.

John's heart gave a jolt and his mouth became dry with panic. He was looking at a symbol of his army's defeat and at the body of the ivory Christ as it was washed in wine.

They left for England immediately.

On the feast of St. Thomas Becket that year – December 29, 1203 – Hubert Walter, Archbishop of Canterbury, conducted a service in the ice-cold cathedral.

'Let us all rejoice in the Lord, celebrating a festal day in honour of blessed Thomas the martyr; at whose martyrdom the Angels rejoice, and praise the Son of God. Rejoice in the Lord, O ye just; praise becometh the upright. Glory be.'

Hubert, clad in red vestments and now bowed by age, turned to face the tomb of the martyr. He caught sight of a figure kneeling at the foot of the tomb.

'O God for whose church the glorious Bishop Thomas fell by the swords of the wicked; grant, we beseech thee, that all who implore his help may obtain a salutary answer to their petitions. Through our Lord . . .'

Hubert moved ponderously away and the figure at the tomb looked up. King John was kneeling where King Henry, King Louis of France, and countless thousands of pilgrims had knelt over the years. Unlike them, he had not come to honour a saint and to seek a miracle.

'Thomas, I ask for justice, Thomas. When a lord breaks faith with his liegeman, the liegeman can demand justice against the lord. I am the liegeman, Thomas, the lord is God.'

His voice was hoarse, whispered and accusatory.

'Four years ago at Fontevrault I took the oath of homage to God for all the lands that I inherited. My father, as you know, and Richard gave God knee-service, nothing more. I was going to build him a cathedral. At Rouen.'

A sense of the betrayal he had suffered welled up in him.

'At Rouen – but I lost Rouen.' He was deeply hurt. 'Thomas. Thomas. I have lost Normandy. They have all turned traitor, broken their oaths, kept their lands from Philip! I kept my oath and lost my lands to Philip.'

Despair settled on him for a moment.

'Thomas, I was tried. I lost Brittany and Poitou but I kept faith. I did God's will!'

He darted a look from left to right then spoke louder.

'Hear, O God, my prayer, despise not my supplication, be attentive to me and hear me. Hear me on behalf of thy servant, Arthur, Count of Brittany, who is sick and for whom we humbly crave the help of Thy mercy.'

He leaned in close to the tomb and his tone was conspiratorial.

'Thomas, you understand. You of all people. If father had not killed *you*, you would not be a saint. I have lost Normandy. Anjou, Thomas, and Normandy, Thomas. I ask for justice.'

All the resentment, fury, exhaustion and humiliation which had been pent up inside him now burst out in a spitting rage.

'God promised to keep my lands! I lost my lands! God

broke his promise! Thomas, I ask for justice! Justice against God!'

The words were a squeal of pain.

'Where can a man find justice against God!'

In the following year, King John lost another important and irreplaceable part of the Angevin empire and the majesty which had adorned it. Queen Eleanor, after a full life which had known deep love and searing hate, the joy of fulfilment and the sorrow of failure, breathed her last and joined a husband and son at Fontevrault. Sheer vitality had informed everything she did and her impact had been felt upon half a century of Angevin history.

Eleanor had lived so long and been such a towering figure that she had conveyed an impression of permanence. Her death seemed unreal, therefore, unexpected, undeserved. There were many who loved her and many who loathed her but all agreed that with her passing, a great value had passed out of the world.

Among those who came to pay their respects was Bertrans de Born, knight of Limousin, poor, shabby, greying but loyal and loving to the end. He kissed the lips of her effigy and his last farewell summed up the feelings in thousands of hearts.

'Adieu, Queen. woman, lover. Where thou art is life, where thou hast been is death.'

'Peace on what terms?'

Philip was in his palace taking his morning draught of whey. Seated opposite him were Hubert Walter and William Marshal, suing for peace on behalf of King John.

'The restoration of his hereditary lands and titles,' said Hubert.

'But he has been dispossessed by law,' reminded Philip. 'The true heir to the dukedoms is Arthur ... Archbishop, where is Arthur?'

Hubert exchanged a glance with the Marshal.

'Tell John that I will not talk peace until I have seen

Arthur,' continued Philip. 'For if Arthur is dead, as men say, John is a murderer and an outlaw. I would be ashamed to serve such a man.'

Another glance passed between the English ambassadors.

'William of Normandy took England in a day from such a one as John. Henry Plantagenet took England. If I, on behalf of Arthur, took England ...'

'You will not take it,' said William Marshal, firmly. 'It is not Anjou or Normandy.'

Philip was on his feet now, moving around as he revealed his ambition with chilling straightforwardness.

'The geographical and historical unit of the world is France, its centre Paris. This is the true successor to Rome. We are such another nation as the Romans and we shall conquer the world for civilisation.'

'England was a kingdom under Alfred,' argued the Marshal, defiantly. 'If we are to have nations, then England is a good garrison for the castle.'

Hubert was standing as well now, flapping his hands in exasperation.

'God forbid! Let us fight for Christ! Let us fight for ourselves if we must! But for God's sake let us *not* fight for a country. The heart of the world is God, not man.'

'I must have England or there will never be peace!'

Philip's violent declaration startled even himself. He became embarrassed and apologetic and missed the restraining influence of the Black Monk. He sat own again and lowered his head.

'Forgive me.'

The Marshal made one final attempt to secure honourable peace terms for his King.

'Lord King, make some offer to King John to ease his hurt. I have found a wounded man more dangerous than a whole one.'

'No, Marshal,' urged Hubert. 'Do not ask for charity but what is right! King Philip, give us leave to say you will restore his patrimony to him.'

Philip looked up and relished his moment.

'The world has taken two steps since we started. Marshal, you would restore a man his sword because you are both gentlemen. Archbishop, you would share a man your cloak because you are both Christians, I am afraid that Christian gentlemen are out of fashion.'

'What answer do you give King John?' asked Hubert.

'Conquer or die.'

King John stood beside a frozen River Thames and heard the message from Philip. It puzzled him.

'What does it mean? That he conquers and dies – or me?'

Before Hubert Walter could answer, he was interrupted.

'Look, my lord, it is safe!'

Peter of Colechurch, a sprightly old man, was jumping up and down on the ice. Along with a young rival, Isambert of Saintes, Peter had come to discuss the building of a new bridge across the river. Isabelle, lost in furs, was the fifth member of the party.

'What else did he say?' asked John.

'He threatened to invade England,' said Hubert, confidentially.

'The devil he did! He could probably walk across in this weather. Isambert!'

'Isambert, eager to impress, came forward wearing the emblem of his brotherhood – a cross and a bridge.

'Could we fortify this bridge and make it another wall of London?'

'This bridge?' Isambert looked down his nose. 'Regrettably non, seigneur. The design is inadequate, the execution incompetent ...'

'What is he saying?' shouted Peter. 'My bridge is the first stone bridge in London since Roman times.'

'My bridges at Sainte and La Rochelle are *bon fortifié* ...'

John let them bicker on and moved away with Hubert.

'It means a war to get my lands back, then?'

'I fear so. Frenchman against Englishman. Christian fighting against Christian.'

'Did you go south to see my mother?' He was irritated by the other's surprise. 'I have a mother, Hubert. You *could* have seen her.'

'Queen Eleanor is dead, my lord.'

John turned away as if struck. He showed no emotion and engaged Peter in conversation. Isabelle joined Hubert.

'He did not know. And he does care.'

'Four sons,' Hubert mused, 'Henry, Geoffrey, Richard, yes, they loved her – but John?'

'John most, because he needs most.' Isabelle thought about her own concerns. 'What happens now to Angoulême?'

'King Philip did not say. La Rochelle is loyal and Niort – as long as they remain, Angoulême is safe.'

Isabelle moved aside as her husband rejoined them. She stepped on to the ice and began to clear some of the snow off it with her foot. John was speaking rapidly to his Archbishop and Chancellor.

'To prepare for an invasion, every man over twelve will be mustered and sworn to defend the realm and keep the peace – against foreigners. With regard to Aquitaine – now that the Duchess is dead – I must establish my claim by an armed presence. I will make an expedition in the summer . . .'

'John! John, look!'

Isabelle had moved the snow off a section of ice and was staring at something with horror an fascination. Frozen solid in the ice was a skiff full of people, all drowned. Isabelle was shocked by the sight of the women and children who had been in the skiff. Peter took the calamity in his stride.

'Ah – so there it is. They were crossing the river and collided with the pier just before the great frost.'

Hubert offered up a silent prayer and Isambert crossed himself. John, however, could not take his eyes off the frozen bodies and the more he looked, the more macabre they became. He saw the cross in the blood-red water again and the body of the young knight floating past Rouen castle.

He saw a figure without eyes.

'Not that!' He was on his knees, beating on the ice. 'Drowned! Found! Where?'

The others were baffled as he continued to hammer on the ice with his fists and yell out. Hubert lowered himself to his knees and put a consoling arm around his shoulder.

'Lord King, it is nothing, nothing.'

John fell into a brooding silence.

'No God – nothing!'

The surrender of Château Gaillard, the loss of Rouen, the treachery of some of his Norman vassals, the intransigence of Philip himself, and the threat of invasion, combined to prompt King John into action. In the spring of 1205 he summoned his barons to meet him on Porchester Downs. He was to be disappointed.

'We will not, my lord,' explained a spokesman.

'*Will* not! *Will* not!' The now familiar signs of his rage were immediately apparent. 'You have no will in the direction of wars. You have pledged your service in return for your estates. You have assembled here to sail to La Rochelle with me to fight for the recovery of my inheritance. You can not say now that you *will* not go.'

The baron who had been elected to speak for them all was a big, bluff man and he was unafraid at John's outburst.

'My lord king, we answered your summons because it was our duty according to our oaths of fealty. We will sail with you to Normandy, but our duty does not stretch as far as Poitou.'

Muttered agreement ran through the ranks of armoured men. John was scornful.

'Yes – you have estates in Normandy. Your oaths do not stretch as far as God!'

The spokesman was still undeterred. Endless years of being asked to fight for Henry, Richard, now John, had made the barons weary. They would not fight simply because they were summoned to by a king.

'Lord King, the dukedom of Normandy descended to you

from King William and has since been part of the English crown. Poitou was your mother's and no part—'

'*I am part of my mother!*'

His anger had such a hold on him now that he flung himself to the ground, tore lumps out of the earth, and hurled them at the barons.

'Traitors! The common men of England will sail with me, the seamen and the common men! But you, my lords, my earls, my barons, my sworn liegemen – go, I order you to go, go, go!'

He was face down on the grass now and his weeping could be heard by all. There was hesitation and whispered conference and then the spokesman raised a point.

'There is the question of our rights and ancient privileges, our castles and our freedoms . . .'

He stopped and looked around. The others were moving away in groups, unimpressed and disgusted by the King's tantrums. They had quailed before a Plantagenet temper in Henry, even Richard; but John's outburst and high-handed treatment of them was not to be borne. They expressed their point of view with their feet.

When John finally sat up, he found that he was alone. Then he caught sight of two old men hurrying towards him. He sighed and got up off the ground as Hubert Walter and William Marshal came across the downs.

'My lord,' gulped Hubert, 'we wanted to avoid a confrontation.'

'Some cowards, begging to be left behind, Hubert. I sent them away. See that they pay the tax instead of service. I will go without them.'

'Oh Lord!' The Marshal was deeply hurt.

'What, Marshal?' asked John, almost amused by his reaction.

'I hoped that they might persuade you, my lord.'

'Cowards!' snorted the other.

'They were not cowards,' said the Marshal, reasonably. 'Nor were they rash fools to go sailing to a country they do not know, to fight an enemy greater than they are, and –

unless the Poitevins have changed their ways – fight friends as well.'

'I said they were not coming.'

'They *are* your army,' sighed the Marshal. 'The rest are just little folk.'

'*Brave* little folk. They will come with me.'

'My lord,' pleaded Hubert, 'you must not leave England. You have no son. If you should meet death, there is no heir to England.'

He knelt on his old legs to implore John not to go and William Marshal knelt as well. It was an absurd sight – the Archbishop of Canterbury and the Marshal of England on their knees in the middle of Porchester Downs. John redeemed the situation from its absurdity with a rage gesture of compassion. He put his hands on the two grey heads to give comfort and there were tears in his eyes.

'It is gone, all gone. Marshall, did you know that my mother died? It is all gone.'

'Not all,' murmured Hubert. 'Not all, my lord ...'

When they had left him alone and disappeared from view, John looked up to the sky with defiance. The wind was tugging his clothes and hair, and its whistle was threatening to drown his voice. But he was in no way deterred from his purpose. Standing fair and square on the soil of England – his inheritance, his nation, his kingdom – he shouted with all his might into the full force of the wind.

'Alone! I am alone! I trust no man. I trust no god.'

He reviewed the contract he had made and found it wanting.

'God – you have forfeited my faith. I renounce my homage to you. God. Henceforth, I am myself alone!'

CHAPTER TWELVE

The death of Hubert Walter robbed England of its most brilliant administrator and gave King John the opportunity to disturb the peace of Canterbury Cathedral.

'Come out! All of you!'

From the arches on either side of the nave, the monks of the chapter emerged slowly and reluctantly to face the King. He had burst into the cathedral with a violence and clamour that had reminded the older monks of the fateful day when Thomas Becket had been murdered. Armed soldiers stood all around him in the shadows.

'Are you all here?' demanded John.

'We are all here, my lord,' replied the most ancient member of the chapter.

John stepped into a pool of light near Becket's tomb and issued a stern challenge.

'Do you deny me the right to nominate the next Archbishop of Canterbury?'

Most of the heads remained hidden in their cowls and it was the oldest monk who eventually answered.

'It is the ancient right of every cathedral chapter to elect its bishop.'

John relaxed and opted for a more reasonable, persuasive approach.

'God forbid that I should trespass on your ancient right; but the Archbishop of Canterbury is by his ancient right the chief adviser to the king; and it is my ancient right to say who he should be.'

The wisdom of his years prevented the oldest monk from saying anything. He shuffled uneasily with his colleagues and tried not to notice the drawn swords that were glinting in the light of the candles.

'All my predecessors appointed their Archbishops. My

father chose Thomas, who was a saint. Richard sent Hubert to you and told you to elect him.' He became suspicious. 'Is all the chapter here?'

The uneasiness among the monks increased. Gerard d'Athies, at John's elbow, gave a signal to his soldiers and they moved in a pace or two. There was no means of escaping the anger which was now showing in the King's face.

'A short while ago, I came to see you and proposed John de Grey, a saintly man, a bishop, my secretary who knows the business of the kingdom.'

John waved a gloved hand in the direction of a man who stood discreetly in the background.

'There is my nominee – but did you elect him?' His voice took on more edge. 'Did you respect my judgement, my honour, my dignity? Or did you meet in secret and elect one of your own?'

The monks huddled into their cowls and bowed their heads.

'Some of you are missing. Who is missing? Where are they?'

He was striding amongst them, pulling back cowls and shouting into their terrified faces.

'Where is your Prior, Father Reginald? Is he here? Or is he in Rome? Calling himself Archbishop of Canterbury? Deceiving the Pope? Defrauding God. Defying the King?'

His anger reached its peak now and put a dark menace into his words.

'Do not listen to those who call me John Softsword. What I have lost across the sea makes me grasp what I have here the harder. So hard – you will say – that my father was a soft man by comparison. He made one Becket – I will make Beckets of you all!'

Martyrdom appealed to none of them. There was a long silence.

'Well?' glared John.

It was the oldest monk who finally found the courage to speak.

'Lord King, what must we do?' His voice quavered. 'Indeed we sent our Prior to Rome, but what he said and did, he must answer for it. Shall we elect John de Grey? He is elected. Shall we send a delegation to Rome to say he is elected? They will go tomorrow.'

John's anger faded and he chuckled, glancing across at his nominee. The soldiers moved back and there was a general feeling of relief among the holy men. John cut it dead with a sharp warning.

'But mind, I know the church. It speaks with two voices. Peter who says honour the king, and Paul who says honour the church. Thou art Peter!' He looked around. 'If there is a Paul amongst you, cast him out. I will have no Paul in England.'

King John pushed his way between the monks and strode back down the nave of the cathedral.

Prior Reginald arrived in Rome with the highest hopes. He had been elected to follow in the footsteps of Anselm, of Becket, of Hubert Walter. A fat, pompous, indiscreet man, Reginald told everyone why he was in Rome and he visited all the shrines while he was awaiting Papal confirmation.

He was annoyed, therefore, when the ancient monk from Canterbury turned up with his deputation. Prior Reginald had a competitor in John de Grey. The dispute was set before Innocent III. He decided against both nominees and chose instead a compromise candidate.

Neither Prior Reginald nor King John was pleased.

Summer had turned the cloistered garden at Godstow into a blaze of colour. There were roses everywhere but none so fine as the large, white, open rose which was growing out of a marble tomb in one of the cloisters. Isabelle of Angoulême, pregnant again, was sitting near the tomb and humming to herself.

Her husband came out of another cloister and crept up to her.

'Give me a kiss.'

217

'*Non.*'

'Are you not well?' He patted her stomach. 'How is my son?'

'What are you doing in there with those bishops?'

'Looking for precedents, Biblical authorities, arguments against the Pope.' He was determined. 'Anything to keep Stephen Langton out of England. I will not allow the Pope to appoint my bishops. Lord! We should be full of his relations!'

'Stephen is a nice name,' she mused. 'Shall we call him Stephen?'

'Stephen!' he snorted. 'We want a dynasty, not a disaster. No, he is Henry.'

He started to walk away but her question halted him.

'Jean, when can I go back to Angoulême?'

He came back and held her hand, answering with an intensity and seriousness that was quite unexpected.

'I swear that we will go back to Angoulême, to Poitou, to Anjou, Normandy and every piece of land Philip has taken from me. I will collect a great war-chest by any means I can. I will not be the least King!'

'*Dieus!* Your hand is cold!'

He took it away gently and went back to his cloister, where he found John de Grey, Bishop of Norwich, leafing through some books with Peter des Roches, Bishop of Winchester.

John de Grey looked up at the King and spoke without rancour about the man who was the Papal nominee for Canterbury.

'My lord, there is nothing to say against Stephen Langton. He was born in England, he is a famous scholar, and divided the Bible into chapters.'

'I wager he put Judges before Kings,' commented John.

'He is a doctor of arts and theology and a cardinal.'

'He has every qualification bar one. I will not have him.'

John de Grey made the King aware of the possible consequences.

'The Pope could impose an interdict and close the

churches in England. I fear, unless you accept Stephen Langton, you will be excommunicated.'

'I do not hold my kingdom from the Pope, nor my soul. I am beholden for them to my father.'

Peter des Roches joined in the argument.

'You are beholden to God. As every man.'

'Every man is not King,' boasted John. 'Every man is not Plantagenet. My family was conceived in sin. My father conceived everything in sin and from that came our disaster. I am King because my three brothers destroyed themselves.'

'Jean! Jean!' His wife called him.

'God left us, master Bishop, when we left France,' he said, and left the cloister again.

Isabelle had found an inscription on the tomb. John read it out.

> Hic jacet in tomba
> Rosa mundi non rosa munda.
> Non redolet sed olet
> Quae redolere solet.

'What does it mean?'

> Here lies entombed in this place,
> Rose of the world, no rose of grace.
> Rose of corruption stinking blows,
> Who once smelt sweet as any rose.

'Whose tomb is it,' she asked, fascinated by the white roses.

'Rosamund de Clifford's!' He laughed. 'Forty years ago, she was my father's mistress. When mother discovered her, they were both pregnant to within a day! I think that was what made her hate me, that indiscriminate dibbling.'

'I would hate you, too, if you do this to someone else,' she warned.

She saw a crack in the tomb out of which the rose was growing, and went to peer into it while John thought about the dead Rosamund.

'She led to their separation, Richard's inheritance, my lack-land, all our troubles.' He heard a sharp intake of breath from Isabelle. 'What have you found?'

'Something shining in a circle!'

The two bishops came out to watch as John crouched down and tried to see through the crack himself. His eyesight was keener than his wife's.

'A crown! The old badger buried her in a crown!'

He thrust his hand in through the crack and the bishops dived forward to protest.

'It is sacrilege to rob the dead!' exclaimed John de Grey.

'She owes it to me,' said John, grimly.

He groped around inside the tomb, ignoring the pricks from the briar, his face glowing with the excitement and effort. When he brought his hand out again, he was horrified. A green-gold snake was wrapped around his wrist.

'Kill it! Kill it!' he pleaded, holding his wrist away.

'My lord,' said Peter des Roches, 'there is nothing.'

John looked at the hand again and the snake had gone.

'There was ... nothing,' he mumbled.

He regained his composure at once and studied each man in turn.

'Do you say that I am mad?'

Neither dared to speak a word.

Four tall candles shed a clean light on the altar of St. Paul's Cathedral. The gold crucifix, the Corporal, Host and wine-filled Chalice stood in position.

The priest's voice echoed down the nave.

'Henceforth in England, there will be no sacraments of Holy Church performed. No holy masses for the dead, no benediction of marrage, no churching of women, no baptism of children, no blessing of Holy Communion, no remission of sin, no Christian burial.'

He took the Chalice and poured the wine on the ground. He took the Host and burned it in the flame.

'Lord have mercy upon us.

Christ have mercy upon us.
Lord have mercy upon us.'
He took the crucifix and extinguished the candles.
It was March, 1208, and England was under Papal Interdict.

In the hall of Marlborough Castle, William Marshal met an old friend.

'I have never spent so many years together in the same place,' said Brieuse. 'Margam in Glamorgan. I am married, with a son aged four. You have been in Ireland.'

Now seventy, William Marshal was starting to bend at the knees slightly and lose his hearing. He asked Brieuse to speak up, which pleased John who was approaching his visitors from an adjacent room. Before they could see him, he found a hiding place behind a door and listened to the conversation.

'Ireland is the place to be,' advised the Marshal. 'No Interdict, no King, no government.'

'England has too much of all three,' complained Brieuse. 'The common folk are restless – what else do they have but the church? No processions, no festivals, no services. Priests wander about begging. All the bishops have fled to France.'

The older man tried to find something in John's favour.

'He had a good campaign in the north.'

'He was set on punishing the northerners so he made them pay enormous sums to buy back their own properties.'

'Well, they all need money,' said the Marshal. 'They are not used to having a King in England, making a regular circuit to keep the law.'

'He does not keep the law, Marshal – he sells it.'

John's mouth tightened as he heard Brieuse speak on.

'There is not a baron in the country who is not – in some way – in his debt. And therefore in his power.'

'I give you – he is a stronger King than his brother or his father,' asserted the Marshal, sagely. 'For a reason. To re-take his heritage and wipe out the taint of losing.'

'John is a tainted King,' sneered Brieuse. 'Henry was

strong, and Richard. They had friends. John has made an enemy out of every man in the kingdom.' His tone darkened. 'And an animal for his use of woman.'

'What? What?'

John could not hear what was being said now. He peeped out of his hiding place to see Brieuse talking into the Marshal's ear.

'Dieus!' chuckled the Marshal. 'I heard the same story about his father! And about Richard – except that it was the man himself.'

Brieuse was blunt and emphatic.

'I *know* John.'

In the privacy of his hiding place, John decided that he now knew Brieuse.

When he formally welcomed the men to the castle a few minutes later, John was affability itself. He introduced his guests to Gerard d'Athies and to Peter des Roches, the only one of his bishops still in England. Wine was taken and William Marshal traded his news.

'I have received letters in Ireland. Stephen Langton is at Pontigny, the same abbey Becket stayed at in exile.'

'Does he feel a halo descending?' joked John.

'He has written a general letter to the barons, demanding that they renounce their fealty to you.'

'Traitor!' John was livid. 'Will they listen to him?'

'Not to him alone,' said the Marshal. 'Last November, the bishops of London, Ely and Richmond pronounced that you were excommunicated.'

Silence fell as the others considered the implications of what they had heard. John felt they were looking at him as if he had leprosy. He reached for his wine and spilled it in his nervousness.

'Nothing, a political move, that is all,' he blustered. 'An act of papal policy to force me to accept Stephen Langton – I will not! My soul is clear.' He turned on his guests. 'You have all done worse things than I have done.'

They said nothing but their expressions of embarrassment

and dread explained what they were thinking. John began to yell.

'Can I trust any of you? Now I know how my father felt when you betrayed him.'

'My lord King,' protested the Marshal, 'when your father died at Chinon, I was there! Where were you?'

Caught on the raw, John swung around on him.

'I will make sure that I am not betrayed again! Give me hostages for your loyalty! Send me your son.'

'I will send you my son,' said the Marshal, levelly.

'And Brieuse. Send me your son, too.'

'But he has no son,' argued the old man, trying to protect his friend.

'You heard him, Marshal! He said he had a son, aged four.'

Brieuse realised that his conversation had been overheard and he was shaken. John motioned to Gerard d'Athies.

'Go with him and take his son.'

Margam Castle was a small, grey fortress of Welsh stone. The two guards who manned its gate carried longbows. Brieuse nodded to them as he rode into the courtyard with the powerful Gerard beside him. The captain of the mercenaries glanced around the castle then told Brieuse to hurry things along.

'I have served three kings!' said Brieuse.

'Fetch the boy,' suggested the impassive Gerard.

Brieuse went into the castle and the guards watched Gerard with a mixture of dislike and suspicion. He shot them a look of derision and laughed when one of them reached for his longbow.

Then Brieuse came out of the castle with his four-year-old son, a lively boy with brown curly hair. Mathilda de Brieuse, wife and mother, came running down the steps after them.

'Wait!' she implored.

'We have no choice, Mathilda.'

'Let me at least brush his hair and tell him to be good. You will be good, William.' She tried to brush his hair. 'Keep still.'

'He must go with Captain d'Athies,' insisted Brieuse.

'Why not stay till tomorrow?' she asked. 'If the boy was dying, there would be more time to take leave.'

Gerard d'Athies was becoming impatient and reached for the boy. His mother pulled him away and considered a plan.

'The lord King might change his mind. Do you think I should go and plead with him? Or with the Queen? She has sons of her own. She will understand.'

'William will be educated with the young princes,' said Brieuse.

'Dear God – what an education!'

Brieuse saw the look on Gerard's face and was angry with his wife.

'Let him go, Mathilda. This man will report everything we say and make King John more suspicious than he is already.'

'Yes, yes, there is no cause for suspicion,' she muttered, then she kissed her son. 'You will go with this gentleman to the lord King. You will bear yourself properly and be brave.'

She began to weep and Brieuse pushed his son towards Gerard. As the mercenary went to lift the boy up on to his horse, the maternal instinct reasserted itself in Mathilda even more strongly and she rushed forward to snatch up the boy.

'I will not deliver up my son to King John. He is a murderer and killed his nephew, Arthur, who was in his keeping.'

'Woman, you are a fool!' hissed Brieuse, appalled.

'I am a fool to save my son from a murderer,' she replied. 'Oh God, look down on us with mercy!'

Gerard d'Athies drew his sword but the Welsh guards had already lifted their bows and two arrows threatened him. The mercenary grunted and sheathed his weapon.

'Protect yourselves for we shall meet again,' he warned,

then rode out through the castle gates.

Brieuse and his wife were struck by the hopelessness of their situation and the boy began to cry.

'We will go to Ireland,' decided Brieuse, in desperation. 'He will not follow us to Ireland.'

King John sat at the end of a long table with his feet up. He was richly dressed and wore several large rings. Petit, his valet, poured wine into a silver goblet which always travelled with the King. John dismissed him and smiled at Mathilda de Brieuse, who had been brought back to her own castle at Margam.

'I would have searched the world for you,' he said, 'and Ireland is no bigger than a dog's back.'

Mathilda was calm but watchful.

'Your husband has fled to King Philip of France, admitting that he is a traitor.'

'He is no traitor, my lord.'

'Then why is he in France?' He sipped the wine. 'He offered forty thousand marks ransom for you and your son. I refused.'

'If you mean to charge me,' said Mathilda with dignity, 'bring me before the court and have me tried by law.'

'This is a court, Mathilda. I will give you justice.'

'What you give, you can withhold.'

'I have never broken the law,' he asserted.

'Thou shalt not kill.'

The boldness of her accusation made him bridle. He brought his feet off the table and glowered at her.

'Where did you hear that story? From Brieuse? He knows nothing. He was not there.'

'Not where my lord?'

'At Falaise when poor Arthur died by accident.'

'If he died at Falaise,' she pressed, 'where is he buried?'

'I ... do not know ...'

'Your nephew, the Count of Brittany, the heir to England—'

'I do not know!' he bellowed. 'We were at war!'

He got up and walked the length of the room to where she was standing. Mathilda could see the blood mottling his cheeks.

'You have accused me, an anointed king, of a terrible crime and I am innocent, Arthur was a boy, my dear brother's son, in my keeping.' He touched a nerve in her. 'Your little boy is in my keeping. Have I harmed him? Have I?'

'No, my lord.' She was vulnerable now.

'Why do you say these things about me?' he challenged. 'If I had murdered Arthur, I would have no compunction about murdering your son. Would I?'

He did not need to make the threat twice. Mathilda immediately knelt before him.

'Forgive me, my lord.'

'Mathilda, Mathilda,' he whispered, 'it is not as simple as that.'

'You have taken our land and our castle. Take the ransom and let me and my son go into exile.'

'What guarantee do I have that you will not repeat the story?'

'Trust me. Or if you must, let my son go and keep me hostage.'

'I will trust you,' he agreed. 'I will release you but keep your son. You will not lie about me again.'

Mathilda was beaten but she still had spirit in her. She got up from her kneeling position and faced him with the courage of the doomed.

'Arthur was murdered at Passiontide at Rouen Castle.'

'A lie!'

'He was at Falaise. He was blinded and maimed at Falaise. Then he was brought to Rouen.'

'A traitor's lie!' he roared, backing away.

'He was in the cell below the chapel. It was Good Friday after Mass. You were drunk. You went down to his cell ...'

John was spluttering with fury now but she was undeterred.

'Arthur was blind and crippled and you strangled him

with his chains. You pushed his body through a grating into the river. That is where he is buried, my lord ...'

'It is a lie! A lie!' He pointed a finger of menace at her. 'You will go to prison for that lie! You will not eat until you eat that lie!'

It was a slow death. Mathilda de Brieuse and her son were shut away in a cell in Corfe Castle and starved. The boy, now white and skeletal, died first. It was said that his mother tried to gnaw his flesh. They were left in the cell a long time before they were buried.

Stephen Langton, Archbishop of Canterbury elect, a tall, spare man in his forties, was talking with King Philip of France, who was now showing signs of age. Stephen spoke quietly.

'Brieuse died at Corbeil. He had no will left to live. He charged King John with the murder of his wife and son at Corfe Castle, and of Prince Arthur at Rouen in 1203.'

'Nothing could be proved, Master Langton,' said Philip, wearily. 'And what else can be done? He is already ex-communicated and England has been under an interdict for six years. Only force will remove John.'

'I will not agree to an invasion of my own country,' answered Stephen. 'Because King John has seized church property, must we seize his whole kingdom in order to restore it?'

'I would not argue with so eminent a scholar as the Car-dinal of St. Chrysogonus,' admitted Philip with the faintest hint of mockery. 'But I assure you that John will not be defeated by argument alone. He has reigned for thirteen years now and I know him for what he is. The Devil's own king!'

A man of unlimited patience, Stephen Langton clung to the belief that a peaceful solution was still possible.

'I will make one more attempt to bring him to his senses.'

'How, Master Langton?'

'I will ask His Holiness to issue an ultimatum.'

'Another one?' Philip was sceptical.

'King John must decide by June, 1213, to submit to the authority of the Pope or be deposed.'

'By me, when I invade England. In the last analysis, it all comes down to one man killing another.'

'The last analysis is God,' affirmed Stephen.

'That is what I meant.'

Philip dismissed his visitor and summoned Robert Fitzwalter. A large, florid, English baron came in and bowed. The men understood each other.

'Master Langton will not do,' explained Philip, irritably. 'Why is he not another Thomas Becket, a rebellious angel?'

'I do not need Langton,' boasted Fitzwalter. 'I already have the pledges of the northern barons, Eustace de Vesci and the lords of Mowbray, Percy, Montbegon and Ros. I hold ties of kinship with the earls of Winchester, Clare and Essex. More than that – John makes new enemies each day. When I raise my standard, he will be alone.'

'Your standard, my lord?' Philip was sarcasm itself. 'Will you be king?'

Some of the arrogance was taken out of Fitzwalter and he became more tentative.

'The young Prince Henry will be King in name.'

'I see,' observed Philip, 'you crush the snake and rear the snake's egg. But can you raise an army to match his great men? Can you match John himself, who in three campaigns has already subdued the Scots, the Irish and the Welsh?'

'I came to ask for your support, my lord.'

'I am a king!' Philip was now scornful. 'I use men like you as torches to be ignited and cast aside when they are spent.'

Fitzwalter was hurt, angry, downcast. Philip spat out his next words into the other's face.

'Next summer, Pope Innocent will preach a crusade against England. My army will invade England under the cross – and the standard of my son, Prince Louis, King of England.' He had caught his man and now put on the pressure. 'Fitzwalter, kneel to me and swear me fealty.'

Fitzwalter had no option but to comply. As Philip took his hands, he whispered into the baron's ear.

'The signal for the invasion is to be the death of King John.'

The assassins were young and desperate but they knew their trade. They were concealed behind a shabby tapestry in a room off the Council Chamber. Eustace de Vesci, the northern baron, was observing the events in the Council Chamber as Fitzwalter spoke to the assassins.

'When it is done, make your escape. You know Nottingham and the town is full of men mustering to the army. You will be well-paid.' He saw a flicker of doubt on their faces. 'It is not the murder of a king, only the execution of an evil man.'

'They are coming to an end,' warned de Vesci.

'He will be the first to enter the room,' promised Fitzwalter.

The assassins were left alone to finger their knives and consider their means of escape.

King John was in good humour as he sat among his barons in council. He was flamboyantly dressed and wore his crown. His white gloves had sapphires sewn into the back of them. His face was quite flabby now and trembled as he laughed.

Fitzwalter and de Vesci entered the Council Chamber.

'You come late, my lords,' chided John. 'We were discussing the expedition to the Welsh marches. I had hoped to go to Poitou this year but the Welsh would have it otherwise. They will pay. I hold the sons of their chieftains hostages.'

'Lord King, Robert Fitzwalter and I . . .'

'You must wait, de Vesci. You are not the most important baron here. Wait in turn.'

'I can speak among my peers,' said Fitzwalter. 'My lord, Eustace was anxious because we have an urgent matter to discuss in private with you.'

'What matter?' John was suspicious at once. 'Tell it to the council.'

'It is a matter of treason, concerning a member of the council.'

Fitzwalter's words had every man in the room on his feet. There was a defiant panic in John's eyes as he glared at his barons. Fitzwalter took his arm and hissed in his ear.

'You are not safe here, my lord! Come with us!'

John allowed himself to be led by Fitzwalter and de Vesci through the crowded Council Chamber towards the fatal door. Behind him he left a great disturbance as he hurried unwittingly towards his own death. Fitzwalter had his hand upon the door.

'Save the King! Here is the traitor!'

Gerard d'Athies had rushed into the Chamber at the far end and caused even greater commotion. His mercenaries followed him, dragging a prisoner across the floor. The man was wild, hirsute, smeared in dung and ashes and quite naked. He was dumped in front of the King.

Mad Peter of Wakefield did not seem to be in the least upset or hurt by his ill-treatment and his manner was crankily amiable.

'John ... John ... you are going to lose your kingdom.'

It was at this point that the King became aware of the absence of Robert Fitzwalter and Eustace de Vesci. Fearing that their plot had been discovered, the two men ran for their lives, taking the hidden assassins with them. Quite by accident, the murder of King John had been thwarted.

They had adjourned to a cell beneath the castle to take the discussion a stage further. Mad Peter was in chains as John strutted up and down. Peter des Roches, who sat at a table, thought that they were wasting their time.

'My lord, this Peter is well-known. He follows the crowds everywhere. He predicts everything from swine fever to doomsday.'

John ignored this and confronted the prisoner.

'Do you know Fitzwalter?'

'John,' decided Mad Peter, 'you are going to lose your kingdom before next Ascension Day.'

'Oh get rid of him!' snarled John.

'Do you mean... ?' Peter des Roches was shocked.

'Have the madman whipped out of town. What do you think I mean?'

William Marshal came down into the cell as fast as his old legs would carry him. Gerard d'Athies was at his heels.

'Fitzwalter and de Vesci have left Nottingham,' said the Marshal. 'I had their lodgings searched. Fitzwalter left nothing, he is an old hand. But de Vesci ...'

He placed some letters on the table and identified them as the King looked at each in turn.

'From the King of France – calling on all men to rise against you! A proclamation of Stephen Langton! An account of an army invasion and a fleet lying off the coast of Flanders!' He paused. 'The signal was to be the report of your death.'

King John realised how close to death he had come and it brought out the beads of sweat on his face. He glanced again at the letters, struck dumb by what they contained.

'This madman likely saved your life and your kingdom,' noted the Marshal.

John was mastering his fear now and he resolved to meet force with force. Gerard was the first to be given his orders.

'March your men to Alnwick and destroy de Vesci's castle. Take hostages from all his kinsmen. Oh – and hang the Welsh hostages before you leave – let it be an example.'

Gerard d'Athies went out of the cell quickly and it was William Marshal's turn to receive orders.

'We shall take the army to Dover, Marshal. Reduce Baynard's Castle to rubble and let Fitzwalter go to the devil!' He rounded on des Roches. 'I want a fleet of ships to assemble at Portsmouth before Lent.' He glanced at the prisoner. 'What day?'

'Ascension Day.'

'Muster every baron, knight and freeman in England to

meet us at Dover at Easter.' He was addressing the Marshal again now. 'Let every man defend England!'

'Lord King, this is the time to make peace with Pope Innocent.'

William Marshal, the sword of war for England for so many years, was now advising peace with persuasive force.

'You have till June. While you are excommunicate, traitors will claim they act for the church and honest men will question whether they owe you fealty. Accept Stephen Langton. He can not be worse than Thomas was!'

King John thought hard for a long time, then crossed to Mad Peter.

'When?'

'Ascension Day,' said Peter for the third time.

John started to laugh and walked out of the cell.

A strong wind flapped the cloaks of the small party of earls and barons who waited near the seashore at Dover. Above their heads, the gulls wheeled and cried.

Advancing up the seashore towards them were two prelates, trailed by a few gaping citizens. Pandulf, the Papal Legate, was a thin, beady-eyed man, surprisingly young for his office. Stephen Langton walked beside him, thrilled to be back on English soil once again.

As the two men reached the waiting group, someone darted out and flung himself at the feet of Pandulf in an attitude of grief and humility. Pandulf was at once taken aback and embarrassed but John had learned his piece off by heart.

'We offer and freely yield to God and His holy apostles, Peter and Paul, and to the Holy Church, our mother, and to the lord Pope Innocent and his catholic successors ... the whole kingdom of England and the whole kingdom of Ireland, with all their rights and appurtenances, for the remission of our sins and of the sins of our whole family, both living and dead; so that from henceforth, we hold them from him and the Holy Church as a vassal ...'

Bells were heard throughout England that day as the interdict was at last lifted. That evening, King John remembered something.

'What day is it, des Roches?'

'Ascension Day.'

'Hang the madman.'

'But my lord . . .'

'Hang him! Hang all liars!'

The service was held at Winchester Cathedral with a pomp and ceremony that would have delighted Richard. Cold and dark as a tomb for six years, the cathedral was now bathed in light, graced by the presence of the noblest in the realm, and sanctified by a welter of pious activity.

King John was in his coronation robes and approached the service with a high seriousness. When beckoned forward by Stephen Langton, Archbishop of Canterbury, he gave and received the kiss of peace. John was led to the altar, where he knelt and looked up at the Great Screen as it soared above him.

'I swear to love and defend the church, to restore the good laws of my ancestors, to do away with bad laws . . .'

He swore the oath with patent sincerity and then added his own private comment.

'Lord, we have been parted altogether too long.'

When the service was over, he spoke with Pandulf and Stephen.

'We are ourselves again. But better than ourselves, for now we hold our royalty from the Pope and England is a papal fief. A rebellion against us is a rebellion against God.'

The thought made him quite jovial.

Robert Fitzwalter and Eustace de Vesci had been strangers to joviality for some time. As they prowled around the sacristy at St. Paul's Cathedral, they were disgruntled and pessimistic. Stephen Langton sat among the treasures, manuscripts and vestments, and reminded them how they came to return to England.

'It was only at my insistence. I am responsible for your behaviour.'

'Are you responsible for John's behaviour as well?' asked Fitzwalter. 'Or do we now have to refer everything to the Pope?'

Stephen Langton was peevish for a moment.

'I did not know that he was going to make Pope Innocent titular sovereign of England. And I did not approve.'

'It is done, nevertheless,' said de Vesci.

'Yes,' added Fitzwalter with bitterness. 'Religion and politics are now the same thing and the slightest opposition to the King is heresy.'

'There is opposition, however,' noted Stephen. 'A meeting of barons here at St. Paul's decided to oppose the expedition to Poitou and the renewal of the war with France.'

'But there will be war.' Fitzwalter had no doubts. 'And if John wins, my lord, we are all lost!'

Eustace de Vesci emphasised the problem they faced.

'The minute you speak against the expedition, Pandulf is on his hind legs, yapping about conspiracy.' He stood over the Archbishop. 'King John has found the key to tyranny! St. Peter's key to the kingdom of Heaven!'

'That is not true!' denied Stephen. 'The church will not condone a tyrant. I have already remonstrated with the King.'

'To what effect?' wondered Fitzwalter.

'To the effect that there is no punitive expedition to the north.'

'But the war in Poitou will go on.'

'It is a just war to regain his father's lands, my lord.' He looked straight at Fitzwalter. 'I would expect King Philip's man to protest against the war, not King John's.'

Robert Fitzwalter realised that he was on dangerous ground and changed his tack.

'We have endured years of tyranny and prayed that the church would lift our burden.'

'The King has sworn to be ruled by law.'

'He makes his own laws!' concluded de Vesci.

'He swore his coronation oath at Winchester again,' said Stephen.

'Yes!' Fitzwalter was unimpressed. 'He swore it at his coronation.'

Stephen Langton searched among the parchments on the table in front of him.

'There is a precedent for a stricter definition of the charter.' He found an ancient document and held it up. 'The charter of Henry I.'

Fitzwalter was openly cynical.

'Your grace, there have been oaths and charters, and kings have made them and broken them. Good kings are good, bad kings are bad.'

'We are all made up of good and bad,' argued Stephen. 'I will remind you of this King's predecessor – Henry.'

'And I will remind you of yours,' said Fitzwalter. 'Thomas Becket!'

The two visitors left Stephen Langton alone with the charter.

In the armoury of the Tower of London, the forges were glowing and the hammers busy. Henry Plantagenet, eldest son of King John, ran about fascinated by the range and quantity of the weapons that were stacked there. He found his father examining some armour.

'When can I come to France, father?'

'When I have won it, Henry!'

He set the six-year-old boy on a table and spoke with an intensity that was quite frightening for the child.

'When I have beaten Philip on the anvil of the great alliance – Boulogne, Louvain, Flanders, the Emperor. When I have seen his bleeding entrails deposited in St. Denis. O God of war – give me victory!'

Henry burst into floods of tears and his mother came running.

'What have you done to him?'

She lifted him down and comforted him. John sent the boy to play with his younger brother, Richard. Then he turned to stare into one of the forges.

Isabelle noticed the deep lines that had been gouged in his face by the years of endurance. She also noticed that he seemed to be in some pain.

'Is it your gout?'

'How like my father I really am,' he said, abstracted. 'He began with nothing and forged an empire so great that they said he was the Devil's man. I began with nothing – John Lackland – and my God! I have been through fire that would not disgrace hell.'

He turned to her, caught up in the power of his own vision.

'We shall win, Isabelle. I have built up a greater treasury than Henry ever took to war. I will have everything he had again. I will give them as he gave them.'

Isabelle was wondering if he was seriously ill.

'Henry will inherit England, Normandy, and our old land of Anjou and Aquitaine. Next year he will be crowned at Rouen. Richard – do you love Richard best? Maman loved Richard best.'

She offered a supportive hand but he ignored the gesture.

'Richard will be crowned Duke of Aquitaine and Count of Anjou. Joanna must marry the Lord of Toulouse and join Toulouse to Angoulême in the south.' He smiled. 'Yes, it is all coming back to me ...'

He moved out of the firelight and the flames died in his eyes.

'And John will have nothing,' he decided.

Then he went off angrily towards the door, leaving Isabelle both puzzled and distressed. She shook her head.

'But we have no son called Jean.'

She hurried out after her husband in some consternation.

The roar of the forges increased as the coals flared up, and the hammers continued to strike out the chorus of war.

CHAPTER THIRTEEN

A summer storm raged outside the Abbey Church at Fontevrault with an almost Plantagenet fury. The atmosphere was hot and oppressive, the rain a sizzling torrent, and the lightning a great flame that lit up the sky for miles around. Men were soaked, horses were frightened, time was short, and there was every reason to be away from the place.

The captain dismounted and hurried into the Abbey.

'Lord, I have nothing ... I can do nothing ... I am nothing.'

The voice came from somewhere near the altar. It was slurred, maudlin, full of self-pity.

'I am ready to fall to pieces ... unless Thou help me ...'

'My lord?'

Gerard d'Athies found him sitting on the steps of the altar with a flagon in his hand. He was pale, unshaven and sweating profusely. He was still wearing his chain-mail, his torn surcoat with its shabby leopards, and his helmet.

'To reach Nantes by morning, we must leave now,' insisted Gerard.

John stayed huddled in the darkness and took another drink from the flagon. A flash of lightning illumined the whole Abbey for a second and he saw the figure of Christ judging him from the altar.

'Gerard, what was the name of that bridge where Philip triumphed against our Allies?'

'The bridge of Bouvines.'

'That bridge crosses me!' said John with feeling.

'There is a French army at Chinon! We must go!'

'Every damned thing!' wailed the King. 'Since I submitted to God and the Pope, every damned thing has gone wrong for me!'

He pulled himself up and shuffled towards the tombs.

Gerard became even more urgent.

'It is too late to fight, my lord. Soon it will be too late to run.'

'What? Have all the Poitevins quit?' He sighed. 'Judas had sons.' He looked down at one of the tombs. 'How did you do it, Richard?'

'My lord ...'

'Oh Gerard – give me a moment's grace!' he begged.

The captain of the mercenaries shrugged and walked off down the nave, leaving John to gaze at the effigy of his brother.

'You are already chronicled in gold in the convenient memory of the world,' he said bitterly, 'and your disasters are remedied by mine. Richard among the angels – O Fortuna! I pray there are no holes in heaven!'

He crossed the choir unsteadily and came to Eleanor's tomb. More lightning flashed and her stone features seemed to glisten.

'And you, dear mother, how are you sleeping in delicate decomposition? Frenchmen are pissing in the Loire, turning our sweet wines sour. They are hanging troubadours with their lute-strings. Silent adieus.' He looked up and shouted. 'Hey! Hey!'

He lifted the flagon to his lips, found it empty, and hurled it away. He staggered across to his father's tomb and leaned heavily against it.

'For whom the world was not enough! What? Have you acquired hell, married the Devil's daughter, and raised a brood of Jupiter Plantagenets? Father ...' He bent down to whisper his secret. 'Father ... I have lost the empire.' John waited for a minute or more. 'Nothing. Nothing! There was a time when that would have raised him from the grave.'

'My lord ...'

It was Gerard d'Athies in the doorway at the far end of the Abbey.

'It is time!'

'It is not time,' answered John, mournfully. 'I must drag

ay faggots back to England until in God's time I am re-
eased from time. And in the meantime, I abide.'
'My lord! We must not stay!'
'Be with me ...'
It was a pathetic whimper and he started to cry like a
child.

Stephen Langton had waited for several years before he was
able to come to England as its primate. He therefore found
his hour-long wait in a room in Worcester Castle no test
of his patience at all. When John finally came in, furtive
and overweight, Stephen jumped to his feet with an affable
welcome.

'The blessing of God be on you and your family, lord
King.'

'I wonder sometimes!' replied the King with bad grace.

'I heard the lady Queen was delivered of a girl,' congratulated Stephen. 'I have a gift for her grace – a topaz
which the late Hubert bought in the Holy Land.'

John took the stone without a word, scrutinised it,
belched, punched his chest with a fist, then slipped the topaz
into his pocket. More cheerful news awaited him.

'And for you, my lord, some bottles of wine I discovered
at Canterbury.'

'Not Thomas's Haut Brion!' chuckled John no longer
somnolent. 'It is said that Thomas once used it by mistake
for Communion and the first lucky sinner drank the lot!
Where is it?'

'Your butler is bringing it.'

'During the interdict, that was one thing I missed –
dinner at Canterbury.' The door opened. 'Fetch it in, Petit.'

John poured red wine into two goblets and handed one
of them to Petit to taste. Stephen was reproachful.

'My lord, you might have trusted me.'

'Eh? Oh no – you see, my father sometimes used to send
Thomas some bottles of wine.'

Stephen shuddered at this grim reminder of the strife
between King and Archbishop, but he felt better when Petit

had nodded his approval and been dismissed. John sampled the wine himself.

'This is as old as I am and a good deal better,' he said with appreciation. 'The damps got into me, Stephen, in Poitou.'

'I regret the outcome ...'

'At least I kept the better part of Gascony and Angoulême.' He emptied his glass and refilled it. 'Now, what do you want?'

Stephen decided to grasp the nettle straight away.

'The barons who met at Bury St. Edmund's last November ask that you respect the oath you took at Winchester and restore the good laws of Henry I.'

'Stephen ...'

'They represent a great interest in London, the eastern counties, and the north,' he added, quickly, as if the information would conclude the argument.

'They represent themselves,' sneered John. 'Fitzwalter and de Vesci – I can thank you for them! – Mowbray, Bigod, Clare! Their fathers rebelled against mine. And as for the good laws of Henry I, Master Langton – Henry I hanged their great-grandfathers!'

'There *are* abuses here, my lord,' insisted Stephen.

'You are a scholar and a saintly man. You have no experience of humanity, which is why I did not want you as my Archbishop. You do not know England. You do not know men.'

'There are abuses here, my lord,' repeated Stephen, firmly. 'The imposition of fines and taxes, the sale of justice, proceeding against men without the law ...'

'You speak for a handful of self-interested traitors!'

Anger made John belch again and this time he put a hand to his stomach. He tried to put his argument more calmly.

'See my side of it. The cost of everything has risen three times since my father's day. How am I to govern, to make my circuit, to keep the law, to fortify my castles, to protect my coasts?'

'My lord ...'

'I must charge my tenants for their land. They used to pay me with military service, now they must pay with money.'

'The barons only ask that certain ancient rights and common practices be re-established and circumscribed within the confines of a charter.'

Stephen's tone was coldly legalistic and it irked John.

'Do the barons ask – or do you?'

'My concern is peace and the stability of the kingdom.' He became more blunt. 'We are talking of forty or so barons who can muster two thousand armed men.'

'And King Philip is waiting on the other side of the Channel!' His hand clutched his stomach again. 'The Devil take my stomach! I was fine before you came!'

He finished the bottle and mellowed slightly.

'Go and tell them I will amend my ways.' Stephen inclined his head. 'And stop looking so pious!' He dismissed the man. 'Hypocrite! Good wine! Charter! I will write to the Pope – my mother!'

John stood up and was troubled by the stomach pain once more. He began to walk towards the door, stopped, smiled, came back to the tray, and picked up Stephen's untouched goblet of wine. He drained it in one go and then stared with satisfaction at the silver goblet.

'Item: one hundred and thirty cups of white silver, ten cups of silver-gilt, a cup with sapphires ...'

The clerk was helping to check the contents of the royal treasure chests, which had been brought up from the vaults in the Tower of London.

'Item: a staff with rubies, a staff with sapphires and diamonds, a staff with a heliotrope, a staff with an emerald, twelve other staffs ...'

Watching the operation were Gerard d'Athies and Hubert de Burgh, former castellan of Falaise and now Justiciar. The two men chattered together but neither let his attention wander from the treasures that were cascading out of the huge chests.

King John entered with Pandulf and Peter des Roches, now the new Chancellor. John wore a surcoat emblazoned with a large red cross. He noticed a crown in the clerk's hands.

'Be careful with that – it belonged to my grandmother.'

'Item : one crown, property of the Empress Matilda . . .'

John turned to carry on his conversation as Stephen Langton came in with William Marshal. The newcomers heard what the King had to say.

'Yes, Master Pandulf, things have worsened. Our rebellious subjects met in arms at Stamford and renounced their allegiance to us. Even though we are the special son of the Holy Church and have taken the Cross.'

'The lord King decided to be a crusader last week,' observed Stephen with irony.

Pandulf sided with the King.

'A crusader's vow frees him from all worldly cares until he has discharged it. The barons must return to their allegiance.'

'They are not children to be put to sleep with a story,' said Stephen, hotly. 'The earls of Norfolk and Clare, Mandeville, de Lacy, Percy . . . a half of the great men of the kingdom !'

'Led by the traitor Fitzwalter,' noted John, 'who now calls himself Marshal of the Army of God and the Holy Church.'

'He is a heretic !' pronounced Pandulf.

'He merely opposes the King,' countered Stephen.

'That is the same thing.' John was glib. 'If it comes to war, then I am not responsible.'

'Nobody wants war, my lord,' promised Stephen.

'Then why do they call themselves an army? Why are they besieging Northampton Castle?'

'Because you will not listen to them !'

Stephen Langton's boldness even took himself by surprise. John smiled sadly and moved away to watch the clerk taking his inventory. The regalia of England was being taken out of the chest and the King was unable to take his eyes off it.

'Item: one wand of gold with a cross; a gold wand with a dove; a red belt with precious stones; a black belt with roses and bars of gold; a collar set with diamonds, rubies and....'

When each item had been checked off, John turned back to the waiting lords and addressed himself to Stephen.

'Go back to them once again and tell them that I have withheld my anger longer than they could decently expect. I will not seize them or disposses them or proceed against them, except by law or the judgement of their peers in the court, until such time as we meet and resolve the differences between us.'

Stephen, the long-suffering intermediary between King and rebel barons, was once again sent off with a royal message. Pandulf and William Marshal went with him to lend weight and authority.

When all three had departed, John called across Hubert and Gerard so that he could disclose his true feelings.

'It is important to isolate these buggers and take the middle ground. Then we shall go at them.'

He noticed that the clerk at the treasure chests was now holding his own crown and checking it off against his list.

'I will keep that,' smiled John, and took it from him.

The dissidents preferred the argument of sword and lance. John soon found himself with civil war on his hands as the ambitious, the over-taxed, the disappointed, the unjustly-treated, and the vengeful raised their banners against him. When London itself was occupied by rebel forces, he was compelled to take their demands more seriously.

The civil war did not help his sleep.

'Come to bed, Jean.'

Isabelle, not yet thirty, was still a beautiful and desirable wife.

243

'You must not stare out of that window all night.'

John, approaching fifty with heavy tread, was no longer the uxorious husband that he had been.

'Everyone is talking about a charter, Jean.'

She came up behind him and looked through the window with him at the river glittering under the moon.

'I used to watch the English river running through the water-meadows at Windsor as grey as silk ...' He turned to her. 'Mother said that to me.'

'Will it stop the trouble?' she asked, hopefully.

'What did *she* know about England? Or the others?' He was derisive. 'England was father's park, mother's prison, and Richard's money-box! None of them understood it as I do. Or loved it. As I do.' He saw her standing beside him and became brisk. 'My chancery clerks are drawing up a charter. The barons sent me a list of demands so badly written – Florence the washerwoman could have done it better. I refused to put my name to it.'

'Will this charter stop the trouble?'

He gazed at her with affection and ran a finger under her chin.

'Isabelle, you should have married old Hugh of Lusignan and hung out the washing every Friday.'

'*Mon Dieu*! I forgive you for abducting me, Jean.'

'Is that all? What about Henry, Richard, Joanna, little Isabella – do I get some credit there?'

He lay down on the bed and looked at the ceiling.

'In all the years I have been King, I have never felt remorse,' he confessed, happily.

She came to join him on the bed and saw his smile harden and his eyes close with tiredness.

'Isabelle, if there is trouble and we are separated – take care.'

'It has never worried you before.'

'I may not live,' he explained. 'Take care of Henry, the King.'

'Is it the gout, *chéri*?'

'There are more glorious conclusions than a clap of gout!'

he shouted in sheer frustration.

He was roused again now and got off the bed to return to the window.

'What can you see out there, Jean?'

'Nothing. There is nothing to see.' He swung round. 'All that my father built collapsed and fell on me – the empire, the church, the barons – yes, the taxes they oppose were all started in his reign. God knows that I am being punished for my father's sins!'

Realisation came to her slowly and she gave a muted scream.

'Oh my poor little Henry!'

Pinned upon the gold cloth of the King's pavilion was a parchment. Stephen Langton read it out aloud.

> Now wrong has warrant, law is wilfulness.
> Who has the power is worth all the rest.
> Truth is treason, faith is falseness,
> Guile is good, and guiltiness is blest.
> Men swear by God and mean by nothingness
> (Great God is held in irreverence).
> The cause of this any man can guess,
> Wise men are wanting, fools sit in governance.

He opened the flap of the pavilion and walked between armed soldiers to stand beside a long table. Seated at the table, with faces composed to meet the gravity of the occasion, were King John, Pandulf, Peter des Roches, Hubert de Burgh and William Marshal.

The charter was lying on the table. Its sixty-three clauses defined the liberties of Englishmen and set contraints upon the power of a king. John did not read the articles again. His eye fell upon the writing at the bottom of the Charter.

> Given by our hand in the meadow which
> is called Runnymede between Windsor

and Staines on the fifteenth day of
June in the seventeenth year of our reign.

He dipped the Great Seal into a pool of red wax and
affixed it to Magna Carta.

Those closest to him saw the smile on his lips.

The barons who had celebrated their victory at Runnymede
soon found it an illusory triumph. Bickering with King John
continued and in the following September the Pope annulled
the Charter altogether. England was troubled by civil war
again, Stephen Langton was troubled by his conscience,
Isabelle was troubled by another pregnancy, King John was
troubled by his stomach pains, and Robert Fitzwalter was
troubled by the prospect of defeat.

'My lord, my liege, unless you send an army to England,
we are doomed!'

King Philip of France was propped up in his throne with
silk pillows and furs. He showed little interest in Fitzwalter's lament.

'The King collected a host of mercenaries and marched
north, wasting the country, taking fines and ransoms, burning and sacking the towns that had declared against him
– so violent and devastating a march that the ignorant folk
recalled a curse and cried – "The dragon is unchained".'

There was still no response from Philip and his son,
Louis, a strapping man in his late twenties, was equally
impassive. Fitzwalter played his trump card.

'In the fervent hope that you will come speedily to
London, the barons and citizens offer their allegiance. The
greatest of us have elected Prince Louis as King of England.'

'Father?' Louis was involved now.

Philip remained detached, even contemptuous.

'Two years ago, Louis, I was to be King of England.' He
indicated Fitzwalter. 'John outplayed him then by submitting to the Pope; he outplayed him again by submitting to
the Charter. And you notice now that he has disposed of
them both, one against the other.' He coughed and sat up

slightly. 'This little man is the most accomplished and politic of them all.'

'Father, let me go to London,' asked Louis.

'You have no cause, Louis.'

'I will be King of England in the right of my wife, Blanche.'

'There are five princes with better claims than Blanche,' said Philip. 'One of them is John.'

'John resigned his crown two years ago to the Pope,' argued Fitzwalter. 'Since when England has not had a King.'

'What of John's eldest son?' Philip was still unconvinced.

'Henry will be betrothed to Prince Louis' daughter. He will inherit Gasgony and Angoulême and you will tie them to your crown.'

Louis looked at his father, anxious for his approval. Philip kept him waiting while he thought it out.

'Well, Louis, you can fly that scrap of legality from your banner.'

'I can go, father?'

Philip looked back over a lifetime's struggle with the Plantagenets and his reservations vanished.

'Let all the proud insolence of that house be dispersed, and the empire be reduced to nothing. Perish John! Perish England!'

Dover Castle was buffeted by a heavy storm but John would not desert his post at the open window that overlooked the sea.

'Sire, no ships will sail tonight,' assured Petit.

'You are wrong. My ships are waiting outside Calais for the enemy. They will sink Louis' fleet.'

'You need rest, my lord.'

Petit closed the window and gestured towards the bed but John shook his head, keeping his eyes on the sea.

'Call Hubert. Then you can go to bed. Oh, and put out some more wine.'

'Your stomach, sire,' warned Petit.

John ignored him and the servant left. Five minutes later,

Hubert de Burgh was sitting down with the King to enjoy a goblet of wine. Hubert sensed that his companion was in need of cheer.

'Your ships will ride out the storm, my lord.'

'There was a storm the night before the Conqueror sailed.'

It was an ominous thought and it seemed to plunge John into a well of self-pity. Drinking too much wine too fast, he began to identify the demons that stalked him.

'What shall I do, Hubert? Where shall I go? This is my last land. After this there is only drowning ... I have had visions of drowning. In Rouen, Hubert, I saw the river turn to blood and a corpse rising to the surface – God! – I thought it was Arthur!'

Hubert drank more wine himself. He had his own memories of Arthur with which to live.

'Then I saw people drowned in the Thames, but frozen in attitudes of life and *watching* me. And I put my hand into the slime of a tomb to grasp the crown, and it turned into a snake ...'

'Lord King,' promised Hubert, 'Louis is more likely to drown! But if he does reach land, you will defeat him. You have an army.'

'But will they fight, Hubert?'

'If you pay them.'

'I have nothing left to pay them with except the crown!' Panic made him get up and roam. 'Louis will offer them a share of the whole country.'

'Set your standard up and raise the country!' urged Hubert.

'But when I call ... who will come?'

Hubert could not be certain and John's melancholy deepened. He had finally run out of money, influence and friends.

Outside on the battlements, the watchman's voice was strong and clear.

'Sails!'

King John was bent almost double with the pain in his bowels.

*

The French landing was unopposed and it had dire consequences for John. Some of his most powerful supporters – the Earls of Surrey, York and Salisbury – paid homage to Louis, and King Alexander II ventured back over the Scottish border again. London gave Louis a rapturous welcome and he was soon hounding John out of Winchester. The English King was chased south and took refuge in Corfe Castle.

He was sick and feverish and had been lost in the castle passages for some time. When he saw a flight of steps, he ran down them and found a door at the bottom. It opened into a cell with the smell of starvation in it and he came charging out again. He went back up the stairs, and along a passage, and up more stairs again.

There was no sign of Petit or William Marshal or Pandulf or des Roches or even Florence the washerwoman, yet he knew they were in the castle somewhere. He blundered on and was aching with the strain of climbing more steps and bumping into more stone walls. A door faced him and he opened it to enter an empty room. Another door invited him and that was empty, too.

He was breathless now and a river of sweat ran down his face. Then he saw another passage with a great flight of steps reaching up to an oak door. He tried to run, but his legs would permit only a slow and punishing climb.

'God ... it was not me ... I will build a chapel for the eternal rest of Mathilda de Brieuse. And her son ...'

With an effort he reached the top step and stood panting outside the door. He was not sure whether he would find friends or enemies inside the room and so closed his eyes as he thrust open the door. When he opened them again, he saw several people all gathered in silence around a bed.

He began to recognise the people – Petit, William Marshal, Pandulf, Florence – and he lunged forward to meet them.

'The Queen, my lord,' said the Marshal.

'The child was born early,' explained Petit.

'The Queen is well,' Florence reassured him.

He pushed forward with awakened eagerness as he heard

the child's cry in the washerwoman's arms.

'John? Is it my son, John?'

'No, my lord,' said Florence. 'Eleanor ...'

The Abbey was deserted when they arrived. Candles still before the altar, vestments lay abandoned on the steps and the altar plate was still there. Savaric de Mauleon, a big, hefty man, led the way in.

'Where are we?' asked John.

'Crowland Abbey, my lord.'

'Good. I will eat the abbot's supper and sleep in the abbot's bed.' He sat in a stall and put his head in his hands. 'I am tired. How far have we ridden, Savaric?'

'Some thirty miles today.'

'And since we left Corfe a month ago?'

'Dieus! From one corner of the kingdom to another. Reading, Cambridge, Stamford, Lincoln, Grimsby ...'

'What do you think of England, Savaric?'

'I like it, my lord,' grinned Savaric. 'It is a pity to burn it. I loved Winchester and then I had to set fire to it.'

'Rather than let Louis have anything – I would eat it!' said John.

Petit came in and saw his master.

'Has the baggage train caught up with us, Petit?'

'Not yet, sire.'

'Savaric, send a man to tell them to stay on the road to Lynn and we shall join them there.'

Savaric left and John called for some water. Petit went searching in the shadows as the King talked about England.

'I would eat it rather than let Philip call it his. Stones, earth, excrement, corpses rotting in the ground! That would not be worse than losing it!'

'There is a little holy water,' said Petit, bringing a pannikin.

John tasted it and spat it out. He sent Petit off to get some wine and strolled up to the altar. Suddenly, he was reeling with the excruciating pain in his stomach.

'God, take away the pain! Give me some wine to take away the pain!'

He lurched forward and fell against the altar.

'God, I burn. God, how I burn!'

Seeing the chalice, he grabbed it in the hope that it might contain some Communion wine. It was empty and he sent it clattering to the floor.

The pain was almost unbearable now, an animal gnawing at his entrails. He looked up at the cross and yelled his revenge.

'I will exact payment for every ounce of pain I suffer ... I will burn God for making me burn!'

He knocked the cross and the plate off the altar and seized the lighted candle. Setting fire to the vestments on the floor, he swung them around his head like a madman.

'Burn God! Burn in hell!'

He dropped the burning vestments as the pain cut through him again. When Petit and Savaric rushed in, they found him rolling on the floor in agony. They were able to stamp out the flames from the vestments but they could no nothing about those which consumed the King.

A loyal address from the burghers of Lynn, welcoming you and begging you to accept fifty marks.'

He nodded his thanks and carried on eating.

'A letter from the Bishop of Winchester, informing you that the lady Queen and all the royal family have arrived safely in Worcester.'

The clerk picked up the next letter and tried to ignore the slurping sounds as the eels were washed down with cider.

'A letter from Hubert de Burgh in Dover Castle, requesting immediate assistance or permission to surrender.'

'Good Hubert,' said John, 'he has stood out for four months. I can do no more more him.'

They were in Lynn and the King had so far recovered from his attack as to be ready to eat the most enormous meal of fish, eels, peaches and cider.

He dismissed the clerk and called a local man over to give him some guidance with a map of the area. The map was spread out on the table and showed the coastline from Lynn, west to Cross Keys and south to Wisbech. The estuary of the Wellstream was clearly marked.

'I want to get to Nottingham in three days,' said John. 'Lynn to Swineshead, Swineshead to Newark, Newark to Nottingham.'

'You can, my lord, but not your baggage wagons.' The man pointed a grubby finger at the map. 'It will take them three days to go round to Long Sutton.'

'They can cross the estuary at low tide and save two days,' insisted John, starting on the peaches.

'Low tide is noon, my lord. They will not get there by noon tomorrow, that means the day after.'

'They will not need long to cross!'

John was becoming impatient with the man's slowness.

'There are four and a half miles of the sea and the Wellstream that are dry for maybe three hours,' said the man. 'And you must watch for quicksands. They will need all of that time.'

Reluctantly, John agreed to a day delay for the baggage waggons. He summoned Petit and told him to ride with the treasure, charging him with the responsibility of guarding it.

Two days later, the treasury wagon rumbled along a gravel road with Petit, Florence the washerwoman, and William in the back. They sat between the great chests of treasure which travelled everywhere with the king. All three passengers were muffled against the weather. It was a cold and misty day as they headed for the Wellstream.

Gravel gave way to hard sand as the treasury wagon led the long column off the road and on to the first part of the estuary. The mist was thicker now but the wagons rolled on smoothly. A bell could be heard ahead of them.

'I hear a bell,' said Florence.

'It is the guide,' called the old waggoner, who was sitting

up at the front of his vehicle. 'The bell guides us.'

'We shall soon be across,' assured Petit, trying to cheer his companions. 'The sea goes out for miles.'

For an hour or more the wagons continued on their way through the swirling mist, guided only by the uncertain tinkle of a bell. Old William dozed off in the back of the treasury wagon, and Petit talked to Florence. The sand was getting wetter now and there were shallow pools to splash through. Deep tracks were left by the wheels of the heavy wagons and water soon filled them.

Whips could be heard now as waggoners goaded on their horses. There was a squelching sound now as the sand became even wetter. Petit was peering out of the back of the wagon but he could see nothing. Florence became alarmed.

'There is no bell!'

They listened carefully but the bell had gone. Only the crack of whips and the squelching noise could be heard now.

'Tell him to hurry,' pleaded Florence. 'For God's sake, hurry!'

'Hurry, man!' ordered Petit.

But the wagon went no faster. With a great lurch and jolt, it stopped dead in its tracks, throwing them all over. As they picked themselves up, they heard another sound now, an insistent, menacing, relentless sound of the tide coming in.

Their wheel had been buried up to its axle in sand and the waggoner knew only one remedy.

'Lighten the wagon! Throw everything out!'

'No!' screamed Florence. 'This is the King's treasure!'

'Lighten the wagon, curse you!'

The roll of the waves was much clearer now and water was lapping around the horses' hoofs. The waggoner did not stay to argue.

'He is gone!' cried Petit.

Florence was crying but old William sprang into action, shoving one of the smaller chests towards the tailboard. Florence started to beat him and shout.

'Stop! Stop! It is the King's!'

The sound of the waves removed any scruples that Petit may have had and he started to struggle with another of the chests. Florence hit him, too, but she had second thoughts when a first playful wave slapped the side of the wagon.

The horses were neighing, the tide rising, the wheel sinking deeper and deeper into liquid sand. Florence realised that there only hope of survival was to lighten the wagon.

'The chests are too heavy!' panted William.

'Open them, Petit!' Florence felt another wave slap against the wagon and she became hysterical. 'Open them!'

The chests were open and all three of them began to throw the contents out into the salt water. They scooped up handfuls of jewels, they grabbed robes and gloves and staffs. The sea was all around them now and it drove them on with a greater frenzy as they opened another chest and hurled its contents out.

Florence paused when she found that she had the Empress Matilda's crown in her hands, but it could not be saved. Petit knocked it down and it rolled off the tailboard and into the sea. William was laying rough hands upon the regalia of England now – all the robes and jewels and belts and chains of majesty. The royal tunic of red samite went overboard, then the gold wand, then the sceptre, then the sword.

Treasures which had taken the Plantagenet kings years to amass were disposed of into angry waves in a matter of minutes. The horses were neighing and struggling, the wagon jolted by their efforts to get away. William took out his knife and clambered through to the front of the wagon. He cut the animals loose and tried to cling to the back of one of them, but it had no idea where it was going in the mist and it galloped straight into the oncoming waves.

Florence and Petit were now doomed. The sea was rocking the wagon and there was no means of escape. Around them stood the empty treasure chests of England, ransacked to save three poor lives. Petit had kept one item back –

the King's crown, the crown of England. He held it up high as water began to pour into the wagon and it was heaved over at an angle.

Florence was screaming and Petit was praying but the crown stayed aloft for a long time. It was the last thing to disappear beneath the waves. The Devil's Crown was no more.

King John sat on his horse further down the estuary and peered into the thick mist. He had waited for hours for the wagons and had been in some discomfort. The saddle-cloth and the flanks of his horse were covered in blood and excrement that seeped through his clothing. The pain was like the thrust of a lance.

He had lost two hundred men, forty horses, the treasures of the realm and his will to survive.

He was taken to Newark Castle and began to fade fast. His dying prayer was no act of homage to God but a renunciation of all that the church had taught him.

'There is no Father, there is no Son, there is no Holy Spirit, there is no kingdom of heaven, there is no kingdom on earth, no God but self, and then no self but excrement and agony ... Nothing, no, less than nothing. Darkness beyond darkness. Dread emptiness. No thing, no piece of earth or heaven, no word, no thought, no breath, no soul ... no John ...'

After a long funeral procession from Newark, guarded by men in armour, King John was buried in Worcester Cathedral in October, 1216. His five children came to pay their respects and stood around his tomb. There was a Henry, the next King of England; there was a Richard; and there were three daughters – Joanna, Isabella, and Eleanor.

But there was no John.

Fontana Books

Fontana is a leading paperback publisher of fiction and non-fiction, with authors ranging from Alistair MacLean, Agatha Christie and Desmond Bagley to Solzhenitsyn and Pasternak, from Gerald Durrell and Joy Adamson to the famous Modern Masters series.

In addition to a wide-ranging collection of internationally popular writers of fiction, Fontana also has an outstanding reputation for history, natural history, military history, psychology, psychiatry, politics, economics, religion and the social sciences.

All Fontana books are available at your bookshop or newsagent; or can be ordered direct. Just fill in the form and list the titles you want.

_____

FONTANA BOOKS, Cash Sales Department, G.P.O. Box 29, Douglas, Isle of Man, British Isles. Please send purchase price, plus 8p per book. Customers outside the U.K. send purchase price, plus 10p per book. Cheque, postal or money order. No currency.

NAME (Block letters)

_____

ADDRESS

_____

_____

_____